A Woman's Place by Carol Cox
Amelia Donovan's wild ways are unconventional, to say the least, sometimes embarrassing to her family, and never what Ranger Jake Thornton would have expected to attract him. But Amelia's heart is pure, and she only wants to be appreciated for more than her pretty face. Won't someone listen to her ideas on how to catch the cattle thieves?

Serena's Strength by DiAnn Mills
Serena Talbot seems small and frail. In fact, for the two years Ranger Chet Wilkinson has known her, he believed her to be a young teenager. Suddenly Serena has proven herself to be a woman of uncommon strength, and Chet has taken notice. But Serena's very protective father won't hear of a ranger courting his only child.

The Reluctant Fugitive by Darlene Mindrup
Caught up in a bank robbery, April Hansen finds herself the prisoner of Ranger Yellow Wolf Jackson and under suspicion for aiding a band of gangsters. How then can April feel peace in the midst of stormy weather and pending trial? And what is this undercurrent she experiences every time Wolf looks at her, a plain seamstress?

Saving Grace by Kathleen Y'Barbo
Captain Jedadiah Harte is ready to walk away from his old lifestyle as a Texas Ranger and serve only God. A stray bullet, though, has thwarted his trip to Galveston to start a ministry, and it seems to be the answer to Grace Delaney's prayers. Jed may be willing to help her keep her river supply landing running for awhile, but can he make an even greater commitment when asked?

Yellow Roses

Four Historical Novellas
Featuring Rangers and the
Women Who Love Them

Carol Cox
DiAnn Mills
Darlene Mindrup
Kathleen Y'Barbo

BARBOUR
PUBLISHING, INC.
Uhrichsville, Ohio

A Woman's Place ©2001 by Carol Cox.
Serena's Strength ©2001 by DiAnn Mills.
The Reluctant Fugitive ©2001 by Darlene Mindrup.
Saving Grace ©2001 by Kathleen Y'Barbo.

Illustrations by Mari Goering

ISBN 1-58660-113-X

Published by Barbour Publishing, Inc., P.O. Box 719, Uhrichsville, Ohio 44683 http://www.barbourbooks.com

 Member of the
Evangelical Christian
Publishers Association

Printed in the United States of America.

Yellow Roses

A Woman's Place

by Carol Cox

Dedication

To Kevin, my favorite Texan

One

Amelia Donovan bounded up the porch steps of the ranch house and stuck her head through the kitchen door. "Ma, when is Pa coming home?"

"By dark, I expect," her mother replied, rolling piecrust dough into a neat circle. She glanced up, then took a closer look at her daughter. "Amelia, what on earth have you been up to? You look like you've been rolling in the dirt."

Amelia barely spared a glance at her mud-streaked dress. "I've been down in the barn. Bessie's ready to calve, and she looks like she's going to need help." She swiped a strand of hair out of her eyes with the back of her hand, leaving a grimy trail along one cheek.

Mary Donovan shook her head. "Rob's nearly old enough to take care of things like that. And your father ought to be home anytime. He went to a meeting at Virgil Webb's."

"More talk about the rustling?" At her mother's nod, Amelia snorted and rolled her eyes. "A fat lot of good that will do. They've talked themselves hoarse, but they haven't come up with anything helpful. If there isn't less talk and more action, we'll soon be wiped out."

Mary transferred the crust to the pie plate and sighed. "They've done what they could. The ranger they sent for should arrive soon. Maybe he'll get things moving."

Amelia brightened. She couldn't wait to meet the ranger. She had plenty of ideas to share with him—ideas the ranchers only laughed off. Surely a lawman would be willing to hear her out. She turned and headed back outside.

"Where are you going, Dear?"

"Back to the barn." Bessie needed watching, and Amelia had plans to make.

Jake Thornton shifted in his saddle and squinted into the westering sun. By his estimate, nearly three hand widths spanned the space between the fiery orb and the horizon. About three hours until sunset. If he'd figured right, he should reach his destination well before then.

The information Cap Samson had given him had been scanty. Area ranchers had been losing cattle steadily for months, and no one knew to whom or why. It was up to Jake to find the answers.

As far as Jake could see, the so-called mystery wouldn't present much challenge. With a little tracking and a few well-placed questions, he should be able to come up with the solution in short order. At least it would be a change from dealing with a riot or a feud.

A rider skylined himself on the crest of a low hill. Jake reined his horse to a halt and watched cautiously, hand flexing to pull his Henry rifle from its scabbard if the need arose. The rider moved toward him without pause, then drew up a few yards away.

"You the ranger?" The speaker, an older man, tipped his sweat-stained hat farther back on his head.

Jake nodded, noting that the weather-beaten cowboy rested his hands casually on his saddle horn and kept them away from his side arm.

"Name's Bart Sloan. I ride for the T Bar Seven. The boss sent me to meet you and bring you in."

Jake eyed the man closely, then allowed himself to relax. Together they headed back the way Sloan had come. Within thirty minutes, they came within sight of a log house and scattered outbuildings. Jake glanced quizzically at his guide of few words, who nodded. Jake surveyed the place as they drew up before it.

"Looks like quite a crowd," he said, nodding toward the bunch of horses tied out front.

Sloan merely grunted, then rode off toward the barn.

Jake mounted the two steps to the porch and rapped on the front door. It swung wide, revealing a tall, broad-shouldered man who beamed and extended his hand in greeting.

"You're the ranger, I take it?" Without waiting for Jake's acknowledgment, he turned to a group seated inside and announced, "Here he is, the man of the hour."

A roomful of faces turned toward the door. Jake stood patiently while they looked him over.

"I'm Jake Thornton," he said to the group at large. "I hadn't expected the escort. . .or this meeting."

The tall man burst out in a good-natured laugh. "Samson wired us when you left, so we had a fair idea of when to expect you. To be honest, though, we never expected Sloan to catch up to you quite so quickly." At Jake's curious glance, he added, "We'd planned to meet today anyway. Having you show up while we're all together just makes it that much better."

Jake gave him a thin smile. He'd met horse traders who had that same overdone joviality. "And you are. . .?" he asked.

"Seth Hardy, owner of the Ladder Five."

Jake's brow furrowed. "I thought Sloan said this was T Bar Seven headquarters."

Hardy chuckled. "Right you are. Meet Virgil Webb, who let us use his place for this meeting." He waved a hand at a skinny, weathered man, who nodded at Jake.

Jake nodded back, wondering why Webb would let another man control a gathering in his own home. Hardy continued to point out the other men in the room, introducing Jake to Matt Vickery, Les Carter, and Ben Donovan. Each murmured a word of acknowledgment while eyeing Jake speculatively.

He gave them equal scrutiny, reading in their faces both hope and reserve. He'd seen that look before. They knew the reputation of the Rangers but weren't completely ready to relax and believe an outsider would be able to waltz in and solve a problem they hadn't been able to deal with on their own.

Time to get down to business. He needed more information than Cap Samson had been able to give. Might as well question them while he had them all there at once, instead of wasting time riding between the various ranches.

"I need some background on what's going on," he

told them. He studied their faces, trying to assess the type of men he'd be dealing with.

Matt Vickery, his shock of white hair a stark contrast to his deeply tanned face, slapped his beefy hands against his knees. "What's going on?" he roared. "We're being robbed blind, that's what. Stock's disappearing here and there, and we haven't been able to put a finger on who's doing it."

"If we had," put in Les Carter, angling his wiry body forward like a lean hunting dog on the scent, "they'd be dancing at the end of a rope by now, and we wouldn't have called on you." His nose twitched, making the resemblance to a predator even more pronounced. "If you find 'em, Ranger, you just leave 'em to us. We'll take care of the vermin, and no need to trouble a judge and jury."

Jake let his gaze slip over Carter without acknowledging his outburst. He wanted no part of vigilante justice or the men who instigated it. He focused on the fifth man, Ben Donovan, and raised an eyebrow.

Donovan smiled. "You aren't from Texas, are you?"

The question caught Jake off guard. "You're right," he said, his cheeks creasing in an involuntary smile. "I was born and raised in Virginia."

"My wife's from Virginia," Donovan responded quietly. "I thought I recognized the accent."

Virgil Webb spoke for the first time. "From Virginia, huh? How'd you come to join the Rangers?"

A hearty slap on the back interrupted his answer. "It doesn't matter how he wound up in Texas," Seth Hardy boomed. "What matters is that he's here now and ready to help us make some sense of this mess."

Jake shifted his shoulders uncomfortably. He appreciated Hardy's confidence, but he could do without his overdone friendliness. He moved away and leaned against the wall, facing the rest of the men. "How long has this been going on, and how many head have you lost?"

Virgil Webb crinkled his forehead. "Hard to tell when it first started. It isn't like you'd expect, with a big number missing all at once. That's something we'd have noticed right off.

"Whoever's doing this has been moving out small bunches—twenty-five to fifty head at a time, near as we can figure. It's beginning to add up."

Matt Vickery nodded agreement. "My riders were the ones who noticed it first. One of my best cows went missing. While they were searching for her, they found a lot of others were gone. I mentioned it to the others here, and it turned out we'd all been hit."

"And we haven't been able to find a trace of any of them!" Les Carter fairly spat out the words.

Ben Donovan leaned forward, scrubbing a work-roughened hand across his forehead. "There's always been some rustling going on; always will be. I don't begrudge a beef to a truly hungry person, but this is getting out of hand."

Jake glanced around the room. "And you've all been affected?"

All five men nodded. "Every last one of us," Hardy affirmed.

"Has anyone been hit harder than the others?"

All eyes turned to Ben Donovan. He managed a weak smile, then shrugged. "I don't want to sound like I'm complaining," he said, "but I'm nearly done in. All my cowboys caught the gold fever at once and took off for Arizona. It left me shorthanded, so I guess I was easy pickings."

Jake shook his head. "I don't understand why anyone would take small bunches at a time, instead of making one big sweep. It doesn't make sense."

"You're telling us!" Les Carter sprang to his feet and paced the narrow room. "All I want to know is who's behind this so I can get my rope ready."

"Take it easy, Les," Seth Hardy cautioned. "We're law-abiding citizens. That's why we called on the Rangers for help."

Carter snorted, and Jake eyed him with concern. This man would be one to watch. Someone who wanted nothing more than to stretch a rope on the rustlers would only do more harm than good.

"It's time I was moving along," Jake told them, standing erect and settling his dusty Stetson in place. "I want to make camp before dark, then I'll get started tomorrow at first light."

"Wait." Seth Hardy held up his hand. "We talked about it earlier, and Ben here is willing to put you up at his place."

The quiet rancher stood, turning his hat in his hands. "Don't expect anything fancy," he said diffidently. "But my spread is pretty much in the center of things. My family and I would be proud to have you."

Les Carter elbowed Matt Vickery. "And while he's there, he can get acquainted with Ben's daughter." Muffled snorts followed his sally. Ben reddened, and Jake fumed.

Being on the receiving end of a matchmaking effort was the last thing he wanted. He had come here to work, not have some dewy-eyed female hanging all over him.

He tried not to let his distaste show. He much preferred working alone, able to come and go whenever he pleased. Having to socialize didn't appeal to him in the least. "I appreciate the offer—" he began, intending to decline. Ben's shoulders hunched, bracing himself for a refusal, and Jake hesitated. It might not be a bad idea to be in a central location where he could pick up nuggets of gossip from people who stopped at the ranch.

"I appreciate it very much." He watched Ben's shoulders relax and felt glad he'd changed his mind.

Two

Ben rode most of the way home without speaking, a fact Jake appreciated. It gave him time to think, to sort through what little information he had gleaned that afternoon. He tilted his hat brim forward to block the last of the sun's rays and reviewed what he'd learned so far. Rustling, as Ben said, happened often enough. It generally fell into two categories: the single beef slaughtered to feed a hungry family or a big sweep of hundreds. Moving a number of small bunches over a period of several months didn't make sense. If the cattle hadn't shown up in a neighboring rancher's herd, where had they gone? Even small groups like that couldn't just disappear.

What kind of men would he be dealing with? All five of the ranchers he'd met seemed to be cut from the same cloth of grit and hard work, although they bore little resemblance to one another in physical appearance or attitude. Virgil Webb had agreed to their use of his home for this meeting, then let Seth Hardy take over the proceedings. Jake acknowledged Hardy's obvious ability to lead but found the man's overbearing manner irritating.

Matt Vickery's passionate desire to solve the mystery

and see the wrongdoers brought to justice seemed to echo Jake's own feelings. And Les Carter—Jake renewed his resolve to keep an eye on the man. Jake recognized a loose cannon when he saw one.

What about Ben Donovan? Jake shot a glance at the man who rode beside him. Stocky and of medium height, his host exuded a quiet confidence Jake admired, especially in light of the man's heavy losses.

Long shadows stretched before them by the time they reached the Four Slash D. Jake surveyed the house with pleasure. It didn't have the wide veranda or sweeping lawns of his boyhood home, but it exuded the same feeling of gracious welcome.

A plump, middle-aged woman bustled out to greet them.

"My wife, Mary." Ben's voice held a note of pride. "Mary, this is Jake Thornton, the ranger who's come to help us."

Jake removed his hat and nodded, returning her pleasant smile. "Ma'am."

"He's going to stay with us while he's here," Ben explained. "I'll see to the stock while you help him get situated."

Jake cringed inwardly. It hadn't occurred to him that Mrs. Donovan might not have already known about the lodging arrangements the men had made.

"Get down and come inside," she said. "Supper's nearly ready and you'll need a few minutes to get settled before we eat." Her gentle voice washed over him, bringing with it a wave of nostalgia. His mother would have offered the same warm hospitality to a complete stranger. He pulled his saddlebags and bedroll from behind the cantle and prepared to follow her inside. After a moment's hesitation, he shifted his burden to his left arm and pulled the rifle from its scabbard with his right. There had been no reports of violence so far, but a man couldn't be too careful.

Quick footsteps scraped in the dirt behind him. Jake whirled, his nerves taut, then relaxed when he saw a boy about twelve years old skidding to a stop at the corner of the house. His eyes lit up at the sight of the stranger.

"Are you the ranger who's going to help us get our cattle back?"

Jake stifled a sigh. That seemed to be the question of the day. Seeing the boy's transparent admiration, he forced a smile. "I'm going to try, Son. Name's Jake Thornton."

"I'm Rob Donovan." His admirer had a grin the size of Texas. He looked at Jake's bedroll and saddlebags, and his smile grew even broader. "Are you going to stay with us?"

His mother intervened. "Give the poor man a chance to come inside and get settled. Can't you see he's tired? He's had a long ride to get here."

Rob reddened and scuffed his feet. "Sure, Ma. I'm sorry." He looked up, all eagerness again. "How about if I take care of your horse, Mr. Thornton? I'll brush him down real good."

Jake's smile became genuine. He remembered how important it had been to act like a man and be accepted as one at that age. "I'll trust you to do a good job of that." Rob gave a brisk nod and led the bay toward the barn.

When he turned away, Jake saw the little girl who had been hidden behind him. Enormous china blue eyes stared at Jake from a heart-shaped face framed by flaxen braids.

"This is my daughter, Lucinda," Mary said.

The little girl offered a shy smile that warmed Jake's heart. If this was the daughter Carter had ribbed him about, he'd already fallen under her spell.

"Lucinda, you set the table," Mary told her, then turned to Jake with a smile. "Come on inside and I'll show you to your room."

Jake hefted his gear again and followed her into the house, noting its orderly arrangement with approval.

Mary led him down a short hall and stopped outside a closed door. "Here you are," she said, pushing the door open and waving him inside. "I hope you'll be comfortable here."

He smiled at the quilt-covered bed flanked by a carved wooden chair on one side and a washstand on the other. A small room, but serviceable, and certainly more inviting than sleeping on the ground.

"I hope I'm not putting anyone out, Ma'am." He suddenly felt the effect of every mile he had ridden the past four days and would have loved nothing more than to stretch out on that soft mattress, but he wouldn't feel right about taking someone else's room.

"Not at all." Mary's smile reassured him. "So many people come through here, we decided to keep this room available for anyone who needs to stay the night. We got the idea from the room the Shunammite woman kept for Elisha in the Bible," she added, giving him a probing look.

Jake chuckled. "Well, Ma'am, the Lord speaks to my heart, but I'm sure no prophet." He set his things on the floor at the foot of the bed and followed Mary back to the parlor after one lingering glance at the beckoning bed.

"Supper's almost ready," she told him. "We'll eat just as soon as everyone comes inside."

"You have a fine family. You've obviously done a wonderful job of raising your children."

A shadow flitted across Mary's forehead so quickly Jake thought it might have been his imagination. "This is our oldest daughter, Elsie," she said, picking up a framed photograph and handing it to him. "She's married to a store owner in Dallas. They have two children."

A young woman with Mary's gentle smile and Lucinda's blond hair stared back at him. "She's lovely," Jake said approvingly. "Even in the picture, you can tell she's a lady, just like her mother."

Mary might not live the pampered life his mother did, but she was every inch a woman of refinement. His misgivings about staying in the Donovan home evaporated. He knew exactly what to expect in a household like this.

Mary blushed at the accolade. She returned the photograph to its place. "We have one other daughter," she said over her shoulder.

"And I'm sure she's every bit the fair flower of the South her mother and sisters are," Jake responded gallantly.

Mary faltered and seemed about to speak when footsteps clattered outside and a bedraggled form burst into the room. Jake's travel-weary eyes took in the sight of what appeared to be a female form, disheveled copper hair stringing across her eyes and alongside her face. Bits of matted straw fell from her boots with every step, marking her progress across the floor. Streaks of—Jake didn't know what they were and didn't think he wanted to find out—smeared the front of her dress.

"I thought I'd lost her there for a minute, but she came through just fine," the apparition announced. "Where's Pa? I want him to see his fine new heifer." She stopped in the middle of the room, staring at Jake. "Who are you?"

Mary closed her eyes and cleared her throat. "This is Mr. Thornton, Dear. Mr. Thornton, my daughter Amelia."

Jake recovered enough to croak, "I'm pleased to meet you, Miss Donovan."

The apparition studied him a moment and seemed satisfied. "You're the ranger."

Jake only nodded, unable to find his voice again.

A smile lit Amelia's face. "Good. We have a lot to talk about." She whirled and ran upstairs.

Mary shook her head and spread her hands in mute apology. "I'll go finish supper." After her departure, Jake stood unmoving, trying to comprehend what he had just seen.

The door swung open again, and Ben came in, trailed by Rob. Ben smiled genially. "Mary got you settled in, did she?" He took a closer look at Jake. "You all right?"

Rob piped up before Jake could respond. "You just met Amelia, didn't you?"

Jake pulled himself together and tried to smile. No matter what that strange being looked like, he had to remember her position as a daughter of the house.

Ben turned a curious gaze on his son. "How'd you know that?"

"That's how all the men look when they meet her for the first time," Rob said with an experienced air. "Especially if they've met Ma or Elsie first. Kind of like a poleaxed steer."

Ben ruffled the boy's hair and grinned at Jake. "She's

not your typical female, our Amelia."

Lucinda appeared in the dining room doorway and spoke for the first time. "Amelia is a hoyden. I'm praying for her." She gave Jake the full benefit of her clear blue gaze. That angelic countenance reminded him of his sisters at her age. Without a doubt, Lucinda would grow into a proper lady, even out here in the wilds of Texas. Rob showed all the makings of a fine young man. What had gone wrong with Amelia?

Amelia hastened to her room, pulled off her soiled dress, and flung it on the floor. Hurriedly splashing water into her washbasin, she scrubbed her face and arms with gusto, then peered into the mirror. She groaned at the image staring back. She looked no different than she had a thousand times before—her face reddened by the wind and freckled from long hours in the sun, her hair loosened from its pins.

At any other time, it wouldn't have bothered her. But something had happened tonight when Jake Thornton stared at her with those deep gray eyes, something that made her want to look neat, well-groomed. . .feminine. Sorting quickly through her dresses, she chose a sprigged muslin, one she usually saved for church, and yanked it over her head. Her hair presented the next challenge. As a rule, it resembled an unkempt bird's nest, but after some concentrated attention with a brush and the use of enough pins to force it into submission, she deemed it satisfactory.

Amelia gave herself another appraising glance in the mirror. That would have to do, she decided, giving a tug to straighten the waist of her dress. As an afterthought, she dabbed some rose water behind her ears for good measure.

Three

At Mary's direction, Jake seated himself on her right. Rob, with his hair slicked down and his face scrubbed, sat next to him, and Lucinda slipped into one of the two empty chairs on the opposite side of the table. The sound of light footsteps approaching the doorway caught his attention. He turned his head and stared.

Surely this couldn't be the woman he'd just met. His gaze took in the neatly groomed hair, the immaculate dress, and the graceful walk. Nothing here resembled the grimy dervish that had swept into the parlor earlier.

Rob's whisper broke into his thoughts. "Cleans up real good, doesn't she?"

Jake hurried to help Amelia into her chair and caught the light scent of roses. How could she have effected such a transformation in that brief time?

After the blessing, Mary passed the food, with the admonition that rustling would not be a topic of dinner table conversation. That suited Jake fine. He needed a good night's sleep before his brain would be ready to tackle this puzzle.

He took healthy helpings of beef, potatoes, and beans, then readily agreed to seconds, savoring the rich home cooking. While he ate, he watched Amelia covertly. She sat erect, helping Lucinda cut her food into manageable portions.

Jake took a long sip from his water tumbler, wondering if he'd imagined the previous incident. It had been a long ride, but he'd gone longer without rest. Surely he wasn't tired enough to be having delusions.

At the end of the meal, he stood and offered his thanks to Mary. "That was the best sweet-potato pie I've ever tasted." She smiled in appreciation and began to clear the table with her daughters' help.

Rob went down to visit the new heifer, and Jake and Ben gravitated to the front porch, where a light breeze offered relief from the earlier heat of the day. "Can you tell me anything more than what we discussed at Webb's?" Jake asked.

Ben tipped his chair back on two legs and shook his head. "Can't say as I can. I've looked at this thing every way I know how, and it just doesn't add up. . .not to me, anyway. Maybe coming in fresh like this, you can see something we've all missed."

He sat in silence for a moment, passing a hand across his sun-creased forehead. "We've had a good life here, a fine life. I'd hate to see that end, but it will if things don't turn around soon. We can't hold on much longer." He rocked his chair forward again and got to his feet, staring across the land he obviously loved.

"I'm turning in now." He paused by Jake's chair long enough to clasp his shoulder in a work-hardened grip.

"Don't fret if you can't figure it out either. God's in control. Maybe He's leading me in a new direction."

Jake watched the older man close the door and listened to his weary footsteps climb the stairs. The evening silence gathered around Jake, and he breathed deeply, grateful for the opportunity to let the peace settle into his spirit.

Sifting through what he had seen and heard since his arrival, he stared out into the darkness. Ben's parting comment echoed in his mind. *Don't fret?* He snorted. *Not likely!* A lone cricket chirped, then another joined in, and another. Jake sighed contentedly. A man needed quiet to think. His eyelids drifted shut.

"Mr. Thornton?"

Jake jumped, angry at allowing himself to be surprised.

"Good. You're still up." Amelia held out a tray in such a way that Jake either had to take the glass she offered or have it slide into his lap. She took the remaining glass and settled in a rocking chair, turning it so that she faced him directly.

"I have some things I want to discuss with you," she continued, scooting the chair closer.

Jake took a sip of the cool cider to give himself a moment to think. At first sight, Amelia's appearance had seemed bizarre, but her deportment at the dinner table had eased his mind somewhat. Now he wondered if his first assessment hadn't been closer to the truth.

He shot a glance at the front window, noting only a single light flickering there. Obviously, the rest of the family had retired, yet here she sat, alone in the dark with him and practically in his lap. The scent of roses wafted toward him. Didn't the woman have any sense of propriety? Even when his sisters were younger than Lucinda, they understood the rudiments of common decency.

"Do you have any idea where to start?"

Jake bristled at her abrupt tone and the implication he might not know how to handle this investigation. "If you're asking whether I suspect something specific, the answer is no. But I intend to find out." He started to rise, but Amelia leaned forward and held his forearm in a surprisingly strong grip.

"Even when the ranchers who know every bit of this area haven't found any sign? Doesn't that strike you as odd?"

The weariness Jake had been trying to hold at bay swept over him in a mind-numbing wave. *Everything* about this case struck him as odd— the disappearance of so many cattle into thin air, his staying as a guest instead of being free to move around on his own, and now the behavior of this most disconcerting woman. He pushed himself to his feet.

Amelia stood, too, bringing them almost nose to nose. "Wait. I know you're tired. We can talk again after breakfast."

Jake took a step backward to widen the distance between them. "I won't be around for breakfast." He bit off each word, struggling to maintain some measure of courtesy. "I'm heading out before first light to get an idea of the lay of the land."

"Wonderful! I'll go with you. I know every inch of this country." Enthusiasm radiated in her voice. "I'll help you look for clues."

Jake clenched his fists, trying to keep his anger from showing in his voice. "Under no circumstances are you to accompany me. Not tomorrow, not ever. This is an official investigation, not a Sunday school picnic. I aim to do my job alone and unhindered. Do you understand?"

Even in the dim light, he could see Amelia draw herself up rigidly. "I've met your kind before, Mr. Thornton. I understand all too well." She yanked the door open, then slammed it shut behind her. Jake could hear her steps echoing up the stairs and down the hall.

He waited a moment before entering the house and stared out again into the velvet night. *I'm going to need Your help here, Lord. I've got more trouble than I know what to do with.*

He stopped short at the door to his room at the sight of his bed covers neatly turned back for him, then proceeded to unbuckle his gun belt and hang it over the back of the chair. Wearily, he shucked off his clothes and sat on the edge of the bed with his face in his hands.

He should have known better than to accept Ben Donovan's invitation. Too many distractions lay in wait for him here. Mary and her open hospitality brought back sweet memories of home, but he couldn't play the part of the polite guest and rout out evildoers at the same time. On top of that, he hadn't counted on having a couple of kids under foot, either. And then there was Amelia.

Jake blew out the lamp and slid between the cool sheets, making sure the chair with his gun belt stood within easy reach. He laced his fingers together behind his head and stared toward the darkened ceiling.

Amelia. He'd never met a woman like her and would

be heartily relieved when she no longer occupied a role, no matter how small, in his life. He tried to imagine his well-bred mother and sisters behaving in such an unfeminine way, and failed.

Amelia. The name sounded sweet and gentle, bringing to mind thoughts of moonlit nights and the heavy scent of magnolias, but for all the name implied, this girl had all the gentle attributes of a prickly pear.

Amelia burrowed her way into her nightdress and jerked the brush through her hair with harsh strokes. She stalked barefoot across the floor, careful not to wake Lucinda, and planted her elbows on the windowsill.

Tears stung her eyes, and she brushed them away with an impatient gesture. What had possessed her to expect this ranger to be different from any other man she knew? Experience had taught her that men expected women to keep house, tend to their needs, and stay conveniently out of the way. She knew the men in the area viewed her as an oddity, little more than a joke. She should have known better than to think Jake Thornton would be an exception just because he stirred something within her.

If she had learned nothing else in her twenty years, she knew how to face facts and keep on going. If Jake wouldn't accept her help or advice any more readily than the local ranchers, so be it. She would look for the truth, with or without his approval. There had to be a solution to this mystery, and if Amelia couldn't enlist his help in finding it, she'd go it alone.

Four

J ake pulled his horse to a halt in the shade of a live oak and used his bandanna to mop both his forehead and the sweatband of his hat. A swig from his canteen chased some of the dust from his throat. He wished the clouds of confusion could be washed from his mind as easily.

Scanning the vista before him, he fit his location onto a mental map of the area. Days spent riding from dawn to dusk had given him a clear picture of the terrain and the boundaries of the different ranches but no more idea of what had happened to the missing stock than when he started.

A rider appeared in the distance. Squinting, Jake thought he recognized one of Les Carter's men. He waved his hand in a broad arc, and the cowboy returned the salute. Jake had talked to every cowpuncher he had come across on the range, but none of them seemed to know anything beyond what he'd already been told: Cattle were missing, but no one knew when, how, or by whose hand.

He had been sure a little looking around would disclose an area where the missing cows were being penned up, waiting until a large enough number had been gathered to make a decent-sized drive profitable. Days of investigation, though, had revealed no such place nor any sign of one ever existing.

Sign, that's what he needed. Trailing a herd of several hundred animals across the range left an unmistakable mark on the land. The trail of a couple of dozen faded quickly. Too quickly.

Jake blinked. There in the dust before him lay a faint depression. He studied it, his excitement mounting when he recognized one track, then another, faded but unmistakable.

If only he could find the reasoning behind this, he told himself, reining his horse in the general direction of the ill-defined trail, he would be able to get into the mind of the thieves, figure out their thought process, and determine what had happened. But the purpose behind the raids and subsequent disappearances remained a mystery, and the unanswered questions were eating away at Jake's confidence.

Only that morning he'd snapped at Rob when he offered to saddle his horse. Jake grimaced, knowing he'd have to apologize to the boy when he got back to the house. He knew he'd been as touchy as a bronc with a burr under his saddle and didn't have any idea how to tell Rob his foul temper came from anger at himself over his lack of progress.

Would he be one of the few failures in the annals of Texas Ranger history? The idea galled him.

The trail petered out near an open area between broad clusters of cedars. A hillside dotted with large rocks rose on his right, and Jake felt a pang of disappointment. No place to conceal stolen cattle there. But the area on his left. . .

Closer inspection showed that those trees concealed the rim of a ravine. A prickle of anticipation ran up the back of Jake's neck. With nothing more to go on than instinct, he felt sure this place would tell him something.

He dismounted, then approached the edge, scanning the ground for any sign, no matter how small, that would prove his suspicions correct. Walking along the rim, he could see a sandy, grassy bottom. In short, a perfect place to hole up with a few cattle. As yet, he couldn't spot an entrance, but everything within him cried out that he might be near the turning point in this investigation.

Rather than wasting the remaining daylight searching for a way in, he decided to climb down inside and see what he could turn up. He approached the edge with caution, but the spot appeared to be solid. A twisted tree trunk leaned out past the edge, offering a handhold, and Jake swung himself out and onto the ledge below.

He lit on the balls of his feet, ready to flatten himself against the side and scramble back up if need be, but the rock held firm. He eyed the rocks below, searching out handholds and footholds, then lowered himself over the ledge and began a cautious descent.

Two-thirds of the way down, the rocks ended in a steep gravel slope. Jake dug in his boot heels and half walked, half slid downward, trying to maintain his balance. From above, he heard a grating sound, then the rattle of small stones that grew to an ominous rumble.

He risked a look upward in time to see a cascade of melon-sized rocks heading his way, gaining momentum with each bounce. Grabbing at any handhold he could find, he scrambled to one side, but the rock slide moved faster than he could and carried him to the bottom of the ravine.

He lay in a heap under a shallow layer of rubble, willing his limbs to move. At least, he thought, his head hadn't been covered. Eventually his fingers wiggled, then his toes. More effort brought movement from his arms and legs, and Jake sighed with relief that nothing seemed to be broken.

He wormed his way out from under the debris and brought his knees up underneath him, then groaned and fell flat again. He might not have fractured anything, but his right leg had been wrenched severely in the fall.

He rolled to his back with a grunt and studied his situation. No one knew where he'd be riding today or when to expect him back at the house. He usually wound up there by supper, but a couple of times he had slipped inside the house long after the Donovans had retired. No one would be unduly concerned if he didn't show up tonight. He had to get out of there, and he had to do it on his own.

Jake stared up at the rim, impossibly far away, then dug his left heel into the loose dirt and pushed. Sharp gravel gouged his raw palms, and he grimaced, eyes closed tight against the pain shooting from his knee and ankle.

He opened his eyes again and groaned at the realization he'd moved all of a foot. How many feet remained to the top of the gravel slope, and once he'd attained that, how could he possibly climb those rocks?

Jake gritted his teeth, dug in his left heel again, and pushed. After half an hour, he lay at the base of the rock wall, sweat soaked and panting. He felt the sting of sweat in each spot on his back that had been laid bare where the gravel had shredded his shirt. His strength spent, he knew he couldn't go any farther.

But he had to. He grasped the nearest overhang with both hands and began hoisting himself up, inch by painful inch. One rock at a time, Jake hauled himself up, scrabbling for a hold with his hands, then pushing with his good leg while trying desperately to keep the weight off his injured limb.

What seemed an eternity later, he reached the rock where he had begun his descent. Clinging to a sturdy root, he stretched out his free arm and caught the tree trunk, then dragged himself over the edge. He lay in an exhausted heap, chest heaving.

Brushing the sweat from his eyes and propping himself on one elbow, Jake spotted his horse grazing where he had left him. The sight cheered him momentarily, but he knew his ordeal was far from over. He still had to get back to the Donovans', and to do that, he had to mount his horse.

He dragged himself another ten yards to a large rock and whistled for his horse, who threw back its head and whickered. It picked its way around the brush and came close to nuzzle Jake.

Jake sat on the rock and planted the sole of his left boot on its surface, then grabbed the saddle horn with his left hand, the cantle with his right. With a mighty effort, he pulled himself upright, praying the horse would stand still. Standing proved to be only half the battle. Jake leaned across the saddle and eased his bad leg over to the other side.

Finally, he sat in the saddle, fighting off waves of nausea that threatened to unseat him. Even so, Jake felt a small sense of triumph. Now all he had to do was stay on until he got back to the house.

Amelia stood in her stirrups to gaze across the expanse before her and frowned. She spotted jackrabbits and cottontails aplenty, even the occasional coyote, but not what she'd hoped to see. No sign of her father's cows could be found on that part of the range.

She didn't see any sign of Jake, either, although she'd halfway hoped she might run across him today. If she caught him away from the ranch and other distractions, he might finally listen to her. Her hope of seeing him, she assured herself, had nothing to do with that cleft in his chin or the dark brown hair that curled just over his collar. Given his outlook on women, she wasn't about to act like a mindless ninny over the man, no matter how appealing he might be.

With a sigh, she turned back toward the house, not knowing whether she felt more irritated with Jake or herself.

Jake watched the ranch house come into view. Rob spotted him from a good hundred yards away. He started to wave, then hesitated, and Jake remembered his earlier unfriendly behavior with disgust. No wonder the boy faltered, after the way he'd treated him.

Jake tried to sit straighter, not wanting to reveal the severity of his injury, but his change in position sent a shaft of agony through his leg and set him weaving in the saddle. Through pain-dimmed eyes he saw Rob come alert and start toward him at a trot.

By the time the boy reached him, Jake had no choice but to sit passively in the saddle while Rob led his horse toward the house, hollering for help. He slouched over the saddle horn until they reached the dooryard, then spilled off the horse. Feeling Rob waver under his weight, Jake made an effort to support himself as much as possible.

The door swung open just before they reached it, spilling light into the gathering dusk. Mary's cry of alarm brought Amelia running.

"What on earth happened?" Mary asked.

"It doesn't matter now. We need to get him to his room." Amelia slipped her shoulder under his other arm.

With the two of them helping, he hobbled down the hall and let them ease him onto the edge of his bed. He closed his eyes, hearing their words swirl about him.

"It's his right leg," Rob said. "He's favored it ever since he piled off his horse."

"Let's get that boot off." Amelia's tone was as firm as her grip on his foot. With one hand planted under the heel and the other on the toe, she worked the boot back and forth to ease it off his swollen ankle.

Rob whistled. "Look at that!"

Jake slitted one eye open and stifled a groan. His ankle had already ballooned to more than twice its normal size.

Amelia knelt and probed his ankle with her fingers.

Jake grimaced from both the pain and the unseemly familiarity. "It isn't broken," she pronounced, "but you won't be going anywhere for a couple of days."

Jake opened his mouth to argue but knew she was right. He couldn't begin to pull his boot on again, much less put any weight on that foot.

"What about that knee?" Amelia continued, pointing. "It's swelling so much the fabric is stretched tight. Get me the scissors, Rob, and I'll slit open his pant leg."

"Oh, no, you don't." Jake struggled up onto his elbows, ready to fend her off physically, if need be. No well-bred lady would suggest such a thing, but this was Amelia Donovan. Amelia, who didn't have the first idea of propriety or polite behavior. Amelia, who might very well do just what she suggested. Amelia, who looked at Jake as though weighing her chances of overpowering him.

"All right," she conceded. "But you need to peel off those pants right away. Rob can help you." She stood back, and for a moment Jake thought she intended to stay and supervise the process. To his vast relief, she turned toward the door.

"Come along, Mother. We'll leave them to it." She stopped and turned back to Jake. "Don't take too long. I'll be back in a few minutes with your supper."

Jake flinched. Right now, the mere thought of food made him nauseous.

Mary halted long enough to smile and say, "You can relax now, Mr. Thornton. You're in good hands," before closing the door behind her.

Jake wished he could be sure of that. He glanced at Rob, who fiddled nervously with the scissors. "Before we start cutting, I want to apologize for growling at you this morning. It wasn't anything you did. I was just mad at myself and taking it out on you."

Rob shrugged it off, but Jake could see his smile as he bent over to slit the fabric.

Five

A melia ladled broth from the steaming kettle into a crockery bowl. She set it on a tray and placed a mug of coffee next to it. "What do you think?" she asked her mother.

"About the meal or Mr. Thornton?" Mary asked, casually adding a napkin to the tray.

Amelia huffed in disgust. "The meal, of course. As peaked as he looked, I didn't think he could handle solid food."

"I think you're right. Go easy on the solid food tonight and see if he's ready for something more substantial in the morning." Mary paused, then added, "And if you want my opinion on Mr. Thornton, I think he's a fine figure of a man."

Amelia felt the blood rise to stain her cheeks. She grabbed the tray, sending the broth sloshing perilously near the rim of the bowl, and wheeled toward the doorway. "Really, Mother!"

She intended to march straight to Jake's room, but her hands shook so badly she had to set the tray on the hall table to compose herself. What had her mother meant? Did she think Amelia had some interest in Jake Thornton? Surely not! Simpering, flirtatious ways drew only scorn from Amelia. She wouldn't lower herself to do such things, even if she did have some interest in a man. And she didn't; she was sure of that.

True, since Jake had come to stay with them, she had taken extra pains with her clothing and her hair, but that was only because he was a guest. Contrary to what everyone seemed to think, she did have some appreciation of social niceties.

Amelia patted her hair into place and pressed her hands against her cheeks, reliving for a moment her panic when she realized Jake had come home hurt. She had tended to plenty of ranch accidents before—broken bones, cuts, and worse. Jake's injury wasn't nearly that serious. Why had her heart raced and her mouth gone dry when she saw him limping toward the door?

She shook herself, brushing her skirt into smooth, neat lines. In command of herself once more, she picked up the tray, squared her shoulders, and strode down the hallway with brisk steps.

At the doorway she paused, trying not to smile at the sight of Jake lying in the bed with the sheet pulled up under his chin. His eyes were closed, but his fingers clutched the sheet in a white-knuckled grip. He stirred when she entered the room and set the tray on the washstand.

"Let's get you sitting up so you can eat," she said, plumping up his pillow with vigorous swats and propping it against the headboard. Jake scooted himself up and settled back against the pillow, wincing slightly when his head touched it.

Amelia frowned. "Did you hit your head?" she asked, running light fingers along his scalp. Her practiced touch detected a large, tender bump at the same moment Jake flinched and pulled away.

"Do you enjoy making people hurt?" he growled.

Amelia ignored him and bent to stare into his eyes. "Look at me," she commanded, when Jake would have turned away. "Mm-hm. You may just be staying in bed longer than I thought." She seated herself on the edge of the bed, the bowl in her hands.

Jake bristled and started to speak, but she dipped up a spoonful of the broth and stuck it in his mouth before he could get a word out.

"I can feed myself," he muttered as soon as he swallowed.

"Suit yourself." She scooted the chair over to the bedside and shifted the gun belt so the holster didn't poke her in the back when she sat down. "I'll keep you company while you eat."

"You'll do no such thing—" Jake began.

"And just how do you plan to stop me?" she asked pointedly. "Are you going to jump up and chase me away?"

The corner of Jake's mouth twitched upward. "You win," he conceded. "This time." He spooned up another mouthful, apparently resigned to her presence.

Amelia watched the lamplight flicker on his hair. It was thick hair, she knew, from running her fingers through its dark waves moments before. Thick and soft and. . . She pulled her thoughts up short. If she didn't watch out, she'd give her mother reason to question whether she cared for this man. She only wanted to make sure he wasn't injured more seriously than he let on before she left him alone for the night. Nothing more than that.

She watched Jake slurp coffee from the mug. "You don't like me, do you?" she asked.

Jake sputtered, sending the hot coffee across the bed in a fine spray. He slapped at the drops on the sheet and sent more coffee sloshing over his lap. Amelia calmly picked up the napkin and dipped it in the pitcher, blotting the spots on the sheet.

He swatted her hands away and pulled the sodden napkin from her. "I can do that." He ground out the words one at a time. "I may not be able to ride or even get out of bed and eject you from this room, but I am at least able to clean up my own messes."

He scrubbed at the stains, half soaking the sheet in the process. To his amazement, Amelia sat obediently in the chair without comment. He continued wiping at the sheet even after the spots disappeared, uncertain whether he'd be able to hold his tongue and temper if he looked at her again.

What had she been thinking, asking him a question like that? This woman didn't think, he corrected himself. She spoke every word that entered her head without considering the consequences. He had never met anyone with such utter disregard for convention. If she had any sense of decency, she'd leave him alone, but he knew better than to expect that.

He surveyed the white fabric. Any more scrubbing, and there would be holes where there should be sheet. Having run out of delaying tactics, he glanced up to find Amelia regarding him with solemn green eyes, awaiting an answer to her outrageous question.

Jake fumed at being put in such a position. "It isn't that I dislike you," he hedged, hoping he'd be forgiven for a slight stretch of the truth. "It's just that you. . .well, you don't behave the way a woman should." He braced himself, waiting for the explosion.

Amelia didn't move, although her eyes shone with an ominous emerald light. "And just how is a woman supposed to behave?" she asked in a quiet voice.

Heartened by her question, Jake forged ahead. In matters of proper deportment, he stood on familiar ground. "A woman's behavior should be modest at all times," he began, reciting the litany he'd heard his mother repeat to his sisters so many times. "Her appearance should be neat, and she should stay in the background while men are discussing business, not intruding into their conversation."

He glanced at Amelia and felt encouraged by her attentive expression. "In short," he continued, "a woman should remember her place, and—"

Amelia's derisive—and most definitely unladylike—snort cut him off. "So in your mind, a woman's function is to be a brainless, spineless piece of decoration, is that it?"

Jake floundered for words that refused to come. He knew he had transgressed but didn't know how to redeem himself. He'd only voiced his honest opinion, but hearing it restated by Amelia made him squirm. Her version made his words sound demeaning, but he couldn't put his finger on where the difference lay.

Resentment flared. He hurt, and exhaustion washed over him. All he wanted was to be left alone to finish his broth, then rest. Sparring with this woman hadn't entered into his plans at all.

Amelia gave him a level glance and spoke with calm dignity. "You are absolutely filthy."

Jake opened his mouth to make a heated retort but saw that she stared at his neck and arms where the sheet had fallen loose. Her words were only a statement of fact, not an assessment of his character. Jake nearly laughed at his mistake but caught himself. No telling how she'd take a note of levity at this point.

As if their altercation had never happened, Amelia rose and poured water into the basin. "What did happen to you?" she asked in a matter-of-fact tone.

The abrupt change of subject made Jake's head spin, but he tried to focus enough to answer her clearly. If he could heal the breach between them, it would be worth the effort. When she perched on the edge of the bed and began sponging the dirt from his head, he didn't object but related his story instead.

He winced when the cloth went over places that had been scraped raw, but he had to admit she had a gentle touch, far more so than he would have expected, given her abrasive behavior.

Amelia listened to the story unfold without comment then replaced the basin on the washstand and stood back to survey her handiwork. "Much better," she pronounced, eyeing him critically. She glanced at the murky water in the basin. "If all that dirt came from just your head, you probably need to wash all over."

Jake clutched the sheet under his chin again. "I'll deal with it," he said forcefully.

Amelia chuckled and sat down. Jake frowned. Why was she still there? He had finished eating, was clean from the neck up, and tired to the bone, to boot. All he wanted was to get some sleep. Why wouldn't she go away?

"Now that you've got something inside of you, maybe you'll feel like listening."

Suspicion stirred. "To what?"

"I have an idea or two about the rustling situation."

Jake opened his mouth to protest but thought better of it. Giving at least the appearance of paying attention would be the quickest way to mollify her. Knowing Amelia, she would be capable of sitting in his room all night if she took the notion. He clamped his lips shut and nodded at her to continue.

Amelia noted the reluctance on Jake's face but steeled herself to continue. Being female didn't mean she didn't have a brain in her head. She had ideas, plenty of them, but men in general were too full of their own importance to give them credence. A woman, to their way of thinking, need only be concerned with domestic issues. Jake's earlier comments made it painfully clear that he shared that opinion. The knowledge galled her, but if he showed the least bit of willingness to hear her out, it put him miles ahead of the others.

"Everyone says the thefts don't make sense," she began. "If I've heard that once, I've heard it a hundred times. But it *has* to make sense, somehow. I think we've all been looking at it the wrong way." She rose and paced the room, trying to put her thoughts in order. "The thefts haven't followed the usual pattern, but since they've continued, it must make sense to *someone*. What we have to figure out is who and why."

She looked back at Jake to gauge his reaction. His eyelids had closed, and the lines of strain around his eyes and mouth had relaxed. A gentle snore emanated from his parted lips.

Amelia stared at him a moment, hands on her hips. No telling how much he'd heard, but at least he had made the gesture, more than anyone else had done. She shook her head and reached for the tray, then paused. Released from his grip, the sheet had slipped down past Jake's shoulders. Amelia pulled it up and tucked it around him gently, then brushed a stray lock of hair back off his forehead. A faint smile crossed her lips. Gathering up the remains of Jake's supper, she bent to blow out the light, then left, pulling the door closed behind her.

Six

Voices. Footsteps. The sounds wove in and out of Jake's awareness without bringing him fully to the surface of consciousness. At first he tried to stay awake, but found the effort too great and drifted back into the welcome depths of sleep.

Heavy footsteps, followed by lighter ones, approached his bed. "How much longer is he going to let a little thing like a twisted ankle keep him down?" a harsh voice rasped.

A cool hand covered his forehead and a cooler voice responded, "His leg is nearly healed. It's the blow to his head that is taking time. Give him a few more days, and he'll be back on the job."

Jake relaxed, recognizing Amelia's voice and touch. In a day or so he'd be back on duty. Right now, it felt mighty nice just to lie still. Funny that someone with such a prickly personality would be the one who could put his mind at ease just by her presence.

Sometimes she spooned broth down his throat, and for now, Jake didn't object. Soon he'd sit up and tackle a nice, thick steak on his own, but at the moment he felt too tired to make a fuss. Other times, she would place a cool cloth on his forehead with a tender hand or let him know he had a visitor.

Rob stopped by at least once a day to assure Jake he was taking good care of his horse. Ben spent long days gathering his remaining cattle back toward the main ranch pasture where it would presumably be easier to keep a close watch on them. He left before daybreak but checked in every evening before supper. Mary spelled Amelia from time to time, occasionally with Lucinda's help, but seemed content to leave the nursing to her daughter.

Though he rarely opened his eyes, Jake knew Amelia kept the chair with his gun belt within arm's reach of the bed, a fact he deeply appreciated. He had no idea whether he could stretch his arm out far enough to reach it if the need arose, but its very nearness gave him comfort.

Strange fantasies invaded his dreams. Once he jerked upright in pitch blackness, mouth dry and chest heaving, knowing he'd had a narrow escape but not sure from whom or what. He lay back on the pillow, willing his heart to stop racing. Little by little, he relaxed and was nearly asleep again when he heard a soft step near the door. Jake smiled in the darkness, knowing Amelia was close by. He waited for her to come lay her hand on his forehead, but she didn't. Eventually he faded back into sleep.

"Ready to try some real food?" Amelia came through the doorway carrying a tray that held not Jake's usual bowl of thin soup but a fragrant, steaming dish. A dish that smelled like chicken and dumplings.

His stomach rumbled, and Amelia laughed at his embarrassment. "I have to admit you've been patient about not eating hearty," she told him, setting the tray on the washstand and bending to plump the pillow behind his back.

Jake withstood her ministrations with nary a murmur. Their proximity over the past days had brought about an easy camaraderie, something he would never have expected to experience with this woman. For all her lack of femininity, she knew a lot about making a man comfortable.

Jake's mouth watered. Once he got that chicken and dumplings inside him, he'd be ready to tackle the world. He took the bowl with alacrity.

Amelia scooted the chair so she could sit and watch him eat, an action that would have nettled him only a short time before. Now it didn't seem so bad. He marveled at the lessening of tension in their relationship. Since he had agreed to stay under the Donovans' roof for the duration of his investigation, it would be much easier for all concerned if he and Amelia could get along instead of scrapping all the time.

He forked up a chunk of dumpling and chewed slowly, eyes closed, enjoying its savory flavor. When he opened his eyes again, Amelia grinned at him. "You look like you're definitely on the mend."

Jake smiled back at her. "You're right about that. I'll be back on my horse in no time."

"Soon," Amelia agreed. "But don't rush it. You haven't put any weight on that leg in days. Give yourself a chance to get some strength back into it first."

Jake nodded, concentrating on his meal.

"Have you decided what you're going to do once you're up and around again?"

He wiped his mouth with the napkin and considered. "I didn't find a thing in that ravine," he mused aloud. "Nothing but rocks, anyway," he amended. "I believe you're right that this would all make sense if we just looked at it the right way, but I'm stumped if I can figure out what that is."

He shifted his weight, scooting himself higher on the pillow, and noted with pleasure that the movement produced no more than a mild twinge in his leg. "I should have at least been praying about what to do next."

"That's all right," Amelia assured him. "I've been praying for you."

Jake stirred uneasily. Though he knew her intentions were good, it still seemed like an intensely personal thing to do.

"Not just for your healing, either," she went on. "For direction, too. For wisdom and guidance to know where to look and to recognize the truth when you see it."

"Thank you," Jake said, unsure of how to take this. He had reluctantly come to concede that Amelia had a sharp mind, along with a comely face. The disparity between her sometime gentleness and her refusal to stay in the background like a proper lady still unnerved him. Just when he thought he saw the real Amelia, she shifted like quicksilver.

She rose and collected his tray when he had finished. "It was entirely too convenient, you know," she said, her brow furrowing.

Jake frowned in confusion. "What?"

"That rock slide." She rearranged the quilt at the foot of his bed.

"I don't understand."

"I know that ravine. I've ridden there for years whenever I wanted a quiet place where I could think." She shook her head slowly. "Those rocks aren't unstable enough to start a slide like that on their own. It seems entirely too advantageous for someone that it happened just when it did."

Jake's eyebrows lifted. "Then you think. . .?"

"Someone deliberately tried to put you out of the way."

He sat up straight and leaned forward. "Do you realize you're talking about attempted murder?"

Amelia tilted her head to one side and considered. "I don't think so. It was probably an attempt to injure you, not kill you outright. Think about it—you kill one ranger and they just keep coming. If you were dead, whoever did this would be in real trouble now. Just having you incapacitated would mean you'd be slowed down. . .but to let them do what?"

Her eyes narrowed, and she stared at the wall above Jake's head as if she could find the answer there. Then she shrugged and turned toward the door. "At least it'll give you something to think about," she called back over her shoulder.

Jake settled back against the pillow, her words echoing through his mind. *To let them do what?* What, indeed? Had he been closer to finding the truth than he'd thought? He turned the facts over in his mind, trying to look at them from different directions.

To his chagrin, his mind refused to focus on anything but Amelia. Much as he hated to admit it, her incisive comments did help him see things from a fresh perspective. He snorted in disgust at the thought of him, a Texas

Ranger, leaning on a woman to do any part of a man's work.

Amelia poked her head around the doorway. "Did you have enough, or would you like seconds?"

"If I wanted more, I would have asked for it," Jake snapped, irritation with himself sharpening his tone. Amelia's eyes widened, then she whirled and disappeared. Jake could hear her boots stomping down the hall, followed by the slam of the front door.

Amelia threw a saddle on her buckskin with a force that made the mare widen her eyes and stomp a front hoof in protest.

"Sorry," Amelia said, giving the horse's neck a soothing pat. "I'm disgusted with our fine Texas Ranger in there, but I shouldn't have taken it out on you." She drew a calming breath and finished saddling the horse with slow, easy movements.

After a final check of the cinch, she mounted and rode out of the barnyard.

Spending time with Jake had been pleasant, and not only because he had been willing to share his ideas with her. She felt a warmth in his presence, a contentment that would be all too easy to get used to. *But he's made it plain you'll never measure up to his ideal of womanhood, so you'd best put that kind of thinking right out of your mind, my girl.*

He hadn't taken her seriously, but she knew her theory was sound. If no one would listen to her, she'd go and look for proof herself.

Seven

Jake eased his weight onto his right leg and took one halting step, then another. With care and determination, he managed to hobble to one side of the room and back again. He reached the chair and sank into it gratefully, propping his leg up on the edge of the bed. He looked up in surprise when Lucinda appeared, bearing a welcome tray of roast beef and potatoes. She served him with her usual prim demeanor, wished him a good appetite, and left.

Now that, Jake told himself, was the way it should be done—his meal served courteously, then being left in peace to enjoy it. He'd nearly finished eating before he realized Lucinda hadn't told him why Amelia hadn't come.

Setting the tray aside, he leaned back in the chair and pondered this new mystery. He hadn't seen Amelia since her abrupt departure earlier. Could she have taken offense at his brusque rejoinder? He couldn't blame her if she had. His behavior had bordered on being boorish. Based on his experience with Amelia, though, he would have expected her to take him to task for his offense instead of going off to pout. Amelia didn't strike him as a woman given to sulking.

Could he have hurt her feelings? Jake turned this new idea over in his mind, trying to picture a teary-eyed Amelia sobbing brokenheartedly. He had to admit the image appealed to him. She was pretty, no question about it, but his concept of the ideal woman included more roses and fewer thorns.

A welcome breeze fluttered the curtain at the open window. From outside, Jake could hear Mary and Lucinda talking while they hung out clothes. This time of day, Rob would be checking the stock in the barn, and Ben would soon come home for the night. All present and accounted for, except Amelia.

Where could she be? Jake massaged his knee, trying to ignore his concern. He should be savoring the success of his brief walk, enjoying the peaceful sounds of a summer afternoon, devoting his efforts to figuring out where those cattle were. Instead, thoughts of an exasperating woman with green eyes teased at the edges of his mind and refused to leave him alone.

He missed hearing her voice, her opinions on everything from the thefts to his recovery, and he couldn't fathom why. She might be—no, she was—easy on the eyes, but her behavior rubbed him as raw as a scraped hide. She honestly seemed to feel she could reason as well as he could.

He heaved a frustrated sigh. Too bad her attitudes and behavior couldn't be more closely aligned with her appearance.

Amelia stepped into Jake's room to find him up and dressed and in the act of strapping on his gun belt. She stood quietly for a moment, noting the way his back muscles rippled through the taut fabric of his shirt.

"You ought to know better than to turn your back on an open doorway," she said softly and had the satisfaction of seeing him stiffen and slap instinctively at his empty holster. Amelia chuckled, seeing his glance dart to the Remington revolver lying on the bed. "Here." She reached it first and flipped it over, offering him the handgrip.

He took the revolver and settled it in the holster, his lips compressed into a thin line.

Amelia suppressed a smile at his obvious discomfiture and leaned against the doorjamb. "What are your plans?"

Jake strapped the holster to his thigh, then smoothed his hair back with both hands. "I am going to continue my investigation," he said evenly. "That's all you need to know." He picked up his hat.

Amelia folded her arms and regarded him thoughtfully. "You obviously don't want any suggestions, but here's one anyway. Why don't you check out the horse tracks on the hill by the ravine?"

The hat brim crumpled under his tightening grip. "What tracks?"

"A very interesting set leading up the hill and into the rocks. There's a nice spot there just out of sight of the rim. There are also marks on some boulders at the top that look like they were made by a metal bar. Looks like someone saw you coming, then waited until you were over the edge to send those rocks down on top of you."

"And just how did you come by this knowledge?" Jake's voice took on a steely quality.

"I did a little detecting of my own while you were out

of commission." Amelia tried to keep the triumph from showing on her face. Seeing Jake's visage darken, she doubted the success of her attempt. He balled his hands into fists, then crossed the room in swift strides to stand directly in front of her.

"Miss Donovan," he said, his tone icy, "I want to ask you a simple question." His gray eyes bore the color of a Texas sky before a lightning storm, and Amelia felt a quiver of alarm begin in her stomach, then spread through her extremities. "As you may or may not know, the first duty of a Southern gentleman is the protection of women and children. Would you please explain to me," he demanded, his voice growing louder with every syllable, "just how a man is supposed to do that if a woman refuses to keep her proper place?"

Amelia's alarm receded before the tide of her own anger. "Am I to understand that you have no respect for a heroine like Joan of Arc? And look at the women of the Bible—strong women like Deborah, a judge of Israel, and Jael, who slew the enemy king with her own hand. Would you consider them beneath your standard of womanhood, as well?"

Jake slapped his twisted hat against his thigh and raked his fingers through his hair. "We're dealing with an unknown quantity here, someone who is quite willing to injure me, perhaps fatally. What makes you think they wouldn't be equally willing to harm you as well?" He drew a deep, shuddering breath and shook his head. "You haven't lived long enough to realize that something like this could turn deadly at a moment's notice. It's not a game."

The words hung between them in the heavy silence.

Amelia had lost patience with the male viewpoint many a time, but she couldn't ever remember being as angry as she felt at this moment. Fury, like hot acid, swept through her veins.

She straightened her shoulders and lifted her chin. "I may have lived only twenty years," she said, grinding the words out between clenched teeth. "But I have experienced a great deal in that relatively brief time."

She leaned forward, forcing Jake to take a step back. "When I was thirteen, my father went off to fight the last two years of the Civil War. He'd held off, thinking the conflict wouldn't last long but decided he couldn't count himself a man any longer if he didn't stand for what he believed.

"Rob was five years old, and Lucinda had just turned one. They needed my mother's constant attention. Elsie had gotten married and gone to live in Dallas. That left me responsible to see that everything ran smoothly. In those two years, though I was hardly more than a child myself, I weathered northers and tornadoes, doctored cows and delivered calves, and tended people with everything from snakebite to dysentery."

Her voice quavered with the intensity of her feelings and she fought for control. If he thought he'd reduced her to tears, he would have won. She cleared her throat and continued.

"I didn't have a lot of experience when I started, but I learned, Jake. I learned. And this ranch survived. If it hadn't been for me, a *woman*, we wouldn't be here today. I will not stand by and see a bunch of no-account rustlers destroy what I worked so hard to save. What gives you the right to tell me what a woman should and should not do? How dare you imply I'm not every bit as capable as you are?" She broke off at last, her chest heaving.

Jake stared at her through narrowed eyes. Without saying a word, he brushed past her and stomped out of the room. A moment later Amelia heard the front door slam.

Good riddance, she fumed, trying to ignore the ache created by his open disapproval.

Eight

Jake inhaled the familiar scents of horse, hay, and leather with delight. Even in the short walk from house to barn, he rejoiced at being outdoors again, feeling the sun on his face. It gave a man room to breathe. He needed some space right now, after his row with Amelia.

Her stinging words rang through his mind again. Jake snorted. Joan of Arc and biblical heroines! Trust Amelia to dredge up examples like that to reinforce her position. Looking back from the safe distance of centuries, they might be women to admire, but they wouldn't be the kind he'd want to be around from day to day. Not the kind he'd want to marry.

His head snapped up. Where had thoughts of marriage come from? Enough of such foolishness; he had work to do.

Jake brushed and saddled his horse in the relative coolness of the barn, shifting his weight from one leg to the other every so often. Other than a bit of stiffness, he seemed no worse off than he had been before the accident.

He gave a final tug on the cinch strap and looked up

to see Rob standing in the doorway. At the sight of Jake, the boy broke into a broad grin. "You gettin' ready to ride out?" He hooked his thumbs in his pockets, affecting an air of nonchalance. "Can I go along?"

Jake opened his mouth to say no, then took a closer look at the shy hope on the boy's face and reconsidered. After his surly treatment the day of the accident, Rob had rushed to Jake's aid as soon as he knew he needed help, even before Jake apologized. He deserved some appreciation.

"How quick can you saddle up?" Jake grinned at Rob's rush to comply. He'd let the boy ride with him for a bit, then find some excuse to send him home. Jake didn't think he'd be riding into danger, but it wouldn't do to put Rob at any risk. Besides, taking it slow at first would give him a chance to get his thoughts in order.

They set out at an easy canter, Jake savoring the creak of the saddle leather and his horse's smooth rhythm. Rob said little, seeming content just to spend time in his presence.

Jake pulled the bay back to a trot, then a walk, and the warm humidity wrapped around him, clinging to his skin the way thoughts of Amelia clung to his mind. In all his days, he didn't think he'd seen a woman as boiling mad as she had been.

Rob finally broke the silence. "We going anyplace in particular?"

Jake surveyed their position. They were little more than half a mile away from the ravine. He hadn't consciously set out in this direction, but as long as they were there, they might as well head over that way. No telling what Amelia had seen, but it wouldn't hurt to check it out. Jake rolled his eyes. Who was he kidding? If Amelia said she had seen tracks and other sign, he knew he'd find them there, just as she described.

He reined his horse to the east and Rob followed without comment until they crossed a set of tracks heading the same direction. "Looks like Amelia's been out here," he said.

Jake followed her trail to where it intersected, then paralleled, another, noting with approval the way she had kept her horse to one side so as not to muddle the sign. The tracks led up through the rocks to a position screened from view by a stand of cedars.

Even without dismounting, Jake could tell where a horse had stood tethered for a time while its rider knelt behind the sheltering tree trunks. The place made a perfect lookout, with the spot where Jake had climbed over the rim clearly in view.

Footprints led from the lookout point toward the rim. Jake motioned to Rob, and they retraced their steps, heading toward the scene of the rock slide.

When they neared the site, he dismounted. Rob followed suit and held both the horses at a short distance, keen as his sister not to disturb any signs.

Jake's pulse quickened at the recollection of the last time he'd been there. He'd been in no condition to pay attention to anything but his own survival the evening he'd pulled himself up over the edge. If he had been more alert, he would have seen the same thing that caught Amelia's notice—clear marks where a metal bar had left telltale scrapes on the rock.

Anger locked him in a grip so tight his vision blurred. His mind raced. Someone had spotted him riding this direction and gambled on him stopping there. That same someone had laid in wait for him, then loosened the boulders enough to start the slide that sent him plummeting to the ravine floor.

As quickly as it came, the blinding anger fled, leaving in its wake a cold resolve. They'd caught him off guard once, but it wouldn't happen again. If he ever got his hands on the person who did this. . .

He turned toward the horses. At last he had a starting point. He would scout out the ambusher's back trail, find some clue to his identity. A dry, whirring buzz froze him in his steps. Without moving his head, he scanned the brush. A rattlesnake lay coiled not four feet from him, its tail vibrating an ominous warning.

A quick intake of breath told him Rob had seen the snake too. He sent a brief glance Rob's way. Good. The boy and the horses were out of danger; he had only himself to worry about.

"Rob," he called in a low undertone, "do you think you could chuck a rock over on the other side of him? I need something to distract him."

"I can do it." Rob's voice held a confident note in spite of its quaver. From the corner of his eye, Jake could see the boy bend to scoop up a missile.

"All right, then. When I count three. One. . .two. . . three!"

Rob's arm flashed and the rock hit the ground just beyond the snake at the same time Jake whipped the revolver from his holster, relieved to feel it slip into his hand easily, as though he weren't out of practice at all. The snake struck in the direction of the new threat at the moment Jake pulled the trigger.

Click. The hammer snapped down harmlessly.

Time seemed to stand still, as though in a dream. He fanned the hammer twice more. Nothing happened.

Jake saw the snake coil again. He felt the weight of the useless six-shooter in his outstretched hand, knew the snake's next strike would be directed at him, and knew he'd never move fast enough to prevent it.

On the periphery of his vision, he saw Rob grab another rock, a larger one this time, and hurl it at the snake with all his might. Jake watched the stone fly unerringly toward its target, crushing the snake's head into the ground.

Not until Rob reached his side and stared up into his face with worried eyes could Jake will himself to move. He threw his left arm around the boy's shoulders and pulled him to his side in a quick, tight hug. "That's another one I owe you," he told him with a lopsided grin.

Jake then turned his attention to the gun. It had been a part of him for so long that he knew by its weight it was fully loaded. What could have caused the misfires?

He thumbed the hammer back and stared, his stomach knotting.

The firing pin had been filed off.

❦

Amelia stared into her mirror. Did she really present a totally unfeminine appearance? She pulled a few strands loose from her newly fashioned chignon, allowing them to fall in tendrils along her cheeks, then considered the effect. It did lend new softness to the determined lines of her face, she decided. . .but her spirit remained the same.

She swallowed hard. It wouldn't work. Much as Jake stirred her, much as she would like to see the light of acceptance in his eyes, she couldn't—wouldn't—change herself just to win his approval.

Who could have done it? Jake pondered the question all the way back to the Four Slash D. *When* could it have been done? Since he rode in from Austin, the gun had never left his side. Even when he was confined to his bed, the chair with the gun belt had never been out of his reach.

To his chagrin, Jake remembered the times he had drifted in and out of consciousness. Did that mean the deed had been done while he lay there helpless? The thought unnerved him.

He shook his head. He couldn't think of any other time it could have happened. And that meant it had to have been done by someone he knew and possibly trusted.

All right, who could have been involved? The list of suspects seemed unlikely. Lucinda? Rob? Ben? It would be like accusing a member of his own family.

Amelia? A memory floated unbidden into his mind. . . Amelia handing him the gun earlier, handling it with easy familiarity.

Amelia? Surely not. The intensity of his desire to deny that possibility staggered him. But who had greater opportunity?

Another memory returned—awakening with a start in pitch blackness, hearing a noise he thought at first had been made by Amelia. Silence instead of the expected soothing hand on his forehead. The silence of someone caught tampering with his gun?

Suspicion became certainty. On that night, someone familiar with the house had crept into his room and set him up for another "accident." Whoever did this must have had free access to the household, which argued for one of the family. Even as he turned over the possibility, his mind rejected the idea, but the thought persisted and refused to go away.

❖

"What difference does it make who came to see you while you were laid up?" Amelia pitched another forkful of hay to Bessie, considering Jake's peremptory question. Her eyes narrowed, then widened with realization. "What's happened now?"

"Just tell me who was here." Jake knew his grim expression invited no argument.

Amelia leaned the pitchfork against the wall and took a seat on the grain box, studying him. "All the family, of course. But you know that." Her brow knitted in concentration. "Virgil Webb came to see Pa and found out you'd been hurt. He looked in on you before he left."

"Who else?" The words came out sharper than he intended. Amelia blinked in surprise at his tone, but she made no comment.

"Les Carter heard about it from Virgil. He rode straight over to see when you planned to quit lollygagging and get back to work." Her lips twitched at the remembrance.

Carter. That would have been the grating voice he remembered. He wouldn't put much past the fiery rancher. But what would be the point of his endangering the ranger who had come to put a stop to the rustling? Perhaps so he could exact his own idea of justice?

"Anyone else?"

Amelia spread her hands. "People stop by all the time. But no, there was no one else who came specifically to see you." She rose and planted her hands on her hips. "Would you mind telling me what this is all about?"

Before Jake could speak, Rob rushed into the barn's dim interior. "Did you figure out who messed with Jake's gun?"

"Messed with. . ." Amelia sank back onto the grain box. "What are you talking about?"

Rob's glance flitted uncertainly from Amelia to Jake. "Didn't he tell you?" Confusion replaced the excitement in his voice. "The firing pin's been filed down on his gun. If I hadn't been there to kill that snake, no telling what might have happened."

"Snake?" Amelia's voice grew fainter, and she swayed ever so slightly.

Jake knelt next to the box and put an arm around her shoulder to steady her. "And here I thought you could handle anything." A low chuckle rumbled deep in his throat.

"I'm fine," she snapped, irritation lacing her voice. "I just. . .don't like snakes." But she made no move to pull away from his support.

The warmth of her arm sent tingles of pleasure through Jake's fingertips, almost as pleasurable as the realization that Amelia had difficulty dealing with at least one thing. If not for the seriousness of the matter at hand, he would have enjoyed prolonging the moment indefinitely, but he reluctantly acknowledged his duty.

"I admit it could have been bad." He kept his voice at a low, soothing level, reveling in this new sensation of acting as Amelia's protector. "Making my gun useless was an obvious attempt to set me up again. If God hadn't put Rob there at the right time, it might have succeeded. What I need to do now is figure out who could have done it. If Carter and Webb were the only ones beside your family who were in my room, that narrows it down."

Amelia's arm muscles bunched under his hand. She stiffened and drew herself upright, shrugging away from the contact. "I know neither of them did it because I was right there all the time they were in your room. I wanted to make sure they didn't get some fool notion about trying to wake you." She lifted her chin. "I suppose that means you've 'narrowed it down' to my family. . .or even me. Is that right?"

Caught off guard, Jake hesitated a moment too long.

"So now I'm a suspect, am I?" The words echoed through the barn loudly enough to make Jake flinch. "Do you honestly think I spent all that time taking care of you to turn right around and put you in danger?"

Jake recognized the truth of her argument and a knot of shame twisted his stomach. His ranger's mind considered, then rejected, the possibility that her outburst constituted nothing more than a clever smoke screen.

"And what about Rob?" The words erupted in an angry shout. "What if he had been hurt? Do you think I'm capable of engineering that, too?"

Jake glanced around nervously. If she got any louder,

she'd draw the rest of the family. He had to stop her, but how? Trying to halt Amelia in full spate was like trying to hold back a flash flood with a teacup. Only one idea presented itself.

He grabbed her by the shoulders, pulled her tight against him, and kissed her soundly. She stiffened and tried to pull away, uttering a muffled protest. Jake tightened his grip and felt her body tense even more, then relax.

Jake released his hold and slowly stepped back, feeling like he'd just been through another rock slide. He wouldn't have blamed Amelia if she hauled off and slapped him, and he halfway expected her to do just that.

Instead, she stood without moving, staring at him with astonished eyes set in a face suddenly gone pale. Over her shoulder, Jake got a glimpse of Rob's dumbfounded expression.

He needed to apologize, to explain. No gentleman would have done what he just did. He opened his mouth, but no words came forth. Unable to face those questioning eyes any longer, Jake pivoted on his heel and left the barn.

Amelia stood motionless even after the hoofbeats of Jake's horse faded into the distance. The memory of his crushing embrace assailed her senses. She could still feel the grasp of his hands on her shoulders, the pressure of his mouth on hers. She raised an unsteady hand and pressed it lightly against her lips.

"What in the world got into him?" Rob's question shattered the fragile moment.

Amelia whirled toward him. "Say one word about

this, Rob Donovan, and so help me. . ."

"Aw, come on, Sis. It wasn't any big deal."

"Wasn't any. . ." Choking back the tears that threatened to clog her throat, she lifted the hem of her skirt and bolted from the barn.

Nine

P ushing the bay to a hard run, Jake leaned forward in the saddle, calling himself every kind of fool. What kind of idiot preached to a woman about proper behavior, then behaved in such an appalling way?

An idiot like him, apparently. He'd done nothing to move this case forward and everything to botch it. All he had wanted when he joined the Rangers was to test his mettle and serve justice, and what had he managed to accomplish? Getting himself ambushed and becoming entangled with a girl as frustrating as she was intriguing. His enlistment in the Rangers would be up in a couple of months. Maybe when that time rolled around, he'd go see Cap Samson, tell him he didn't think he was Ranger caliber after all. Maybe he wouldn't have to wait that long. After the way he'd handled this fiasco, Cap might tell him the same thing as soon as he got back to Austin.

Lord, I know Your word says all things work together for good for those who love You. You know I love You, but I don't see the good in this. Help me to understand and know what to do.

With an effort, Jake pushed thoughts of Amelia and

his ineptitude to the back of his mind and concentrated on his surroundings. He had nearly reached the ravine. On the way home, Rob had told him of a brush-covered entrance near one end. He hadn't been willing to explore it earlier with a faulty gun and a kid on his hands, but now the time for action had come.

Following Rob's landmarks made it easy to find the hidden opening. Jake checked around the entrance for tracks, but it appeared no one had been there in recent days. Making sure the spare gun he had retrieved from his saddlebags sat loose in the holster, he pushed past the brush and urged his horse inside.

Beyond the narrow entry, the floor broadened out. Jake picked his way through clumps of scrub brush, grimacing when he passed the scene of his earlier descent. Farther along, he rounded a corner and pulled his horse to a halt.

Before him, the sandy floor turned into a richer loam, a surface hard enough to retain the unmistakable sign of cattle. Jake pressed on, fully expecting to find a hidden pasture capable of holding a good-sized herd, but in only a short distance, the ravine came to a dead end.

His initial elation faded to be replaced by bewilderment. He felt sure this hideaway had held the stolen cows, but it wouldn't contain more than the small bunches the ranchers said had gone missing at any one time.

Jake dismounted, scanning the rocky walls to see if another hidden passageway existed and kicking at clumps of grass when he found none. Now what? He had made progress, but the question still remained: What happened to those cows?

He pulled off his hat and mopped the sweat from his forehead, trying to determine his next move. What if his earlier visit had spooked the rustlers, forcing them to move their base of operations? Now that he'd seen a glimpse of the way they operated, he knew what to look for.

He took a long swallow from his canteen and remounted. If he remembered correctly, he'd seen an area with terrain similar to this one in another part of the range. It just might be worth taking a look.

Low hills rolled in gentle folds across the land, while the cedars and brush grew thicker. Jake rode out of a thicket of trees and studied the range before him. Ahead, an odd texture of the ground drew his attention. He rode forward, eager to investigate, yet keeping watch in all directions. He had no intention of being the victim of yet another "accident."

The closer he got, the faster his pulse raced. The churned earth ahead of him confirmed his suspicions. He studied the fresh tracks with a resurgence of confidence. At least thirty cattle had been through here, and not long before.

Jake turned his horse to follow the trail, every sense alert. The tracks led through scattered cedars, then over a low rise. Jake pulled his horse to a stop before reaching the top, then dismounted and approached the crest in a low crouch. Keeping low and using the trees for cover so as not to skyline himself, he worked his way to the top of the ridge and scanned the scene before him.

A slow smile crossed his face. Roughly three dozen cattle milled in the pocket below, with two men riding herd. A small fire burned off to one side. Not far from the fire, a cow lay on her side, a cowboy kneeling on her neck to hold her down. Another man lifted a rod from the flames and applied it to the cow's left flank. The animal twisted and bellowed, then sprang to her feet as soon as she was released.

Jake eased his way back to retrieve his horse, then started down the slope. The possibility existed that he had come across honest cowboys doing a legitimate day's work, but his ranger's instinct told him otherwise.

He hadn't gone more than fifty yards when one of the cowboys spotted him and shouted a warning. The rest looked in Jake's direction, then the two on the ground leaped on their mounts and followed their companions, already in full flight.

Jake spurred his horse and gave chase, exulting in the knowledge that the breakthrough had come at last. In only moments, the questions that had plagued him about this case would be answered.

Surprise had given him a few seconds' advantage, and he made the most of it, urging his horse forward to narrow the distance. As the group rounded a stand of cedars, one of his quarry turned in his saddle and snapped off a shot. Jake heard the bullet zip past his ear and fired back. The riders scattered like quail, two separating to go off singly, while the other two remained together. Jake followed the pair.

He lost track of them for a few moments when he had to slow to allow the bay to pick his way through dense brush but continued undeterred, sure he would have them back in view in a moment. He picked up the trail again and rode through the cedars, following his quarry in a broad circle and wondering what they were up to.

His answer came quickly. The rustlers' tracks led back to the trail he'd followed earlier, losing themselves in the churned earth.

Unwilling to believe the chase had ended almost before it began, Jake rode back along the trail a way, alternating between studying the ground and scanning the horizon. Nothing. He slammed his fist against his saddle horn. How could they have disappeared so quickly?

Baffled, he returned to the pocket where the cattle still grazed, oblivious to the events playing out around them. Jake kicked out the fire and picked up the metal rod that lay on the ground nearby. Examining the picket pin thoughtfully, he rolled it inside his slicker and tied it in place behind his saddle. Remounting, he cut two cows from the herd and started hazing them back toward the Donovans'.

Dusk had begun to settle by the time Jake pushed the two cows into the corral and closed the gate behind them. Ben stepped out of the barn and nodded.

"Thought that was you," he said. "What have you got there?"

"Take a look." In the waning light, Jake showed him the freshly branded cows.

Ben pursed his lips in a soundless whistle. "Then it's not someone just altering a brand to add these to their own herd."

Jake shook his head. "That's a road brand. Whoever

they were, they planned to move them out and sell them. Now check the other side."

Ben's lips thinned at the sight of the Four Slash D brand on the cows' right hips.

"You know what that means?" Jake asked him.

"It means I'm not trying to sneak off with my own cows, I reckon," Ben quipped.

Jake winced, hoping Ben had no idea how closely he had followed that very line of thinking. He filled the rancher in on the holding area in the ravine and his discovery of the branding session, adding, "It means it's someone local. Even given the extent of the range, there's too much going on around here to chalk this up to outsiders."

Ben rubbed his head. "The question is, who would do such a thing? I hate to think it's any of my neighbors, but. . ." He trailed off, chewing his lower lip.

Hoofbeats clattered in the near darkness. A group of riders appeared in the barnyard and pulled up near the two men. Jake counted nine in the group and strained to identify their leader.

Seth Hardy's unmistakable voice rang out. "We've got a line on them at last, Thornton. Two of my men spotted fifty head being driven toward Fort Worth."

Jake's excitement returned. "Did they catch up with them?"

"They counted at least eight riders. One came back for reinforcements and left the other trailing the herd from a distance. We picked up Vickery and Carter and some of their men on the way here. Webb's place is too far the other direction for anyone to reach him in time, but this ought to give us a fair-sized posse."

Jake hesitated, wondering whether he wanted any of them along.

"We're heading out after them." Les Carter's hard voice was easy to identify. "Are you coming with us or not?"

Jake heard the angry mutters from the rest of the men and knew there would be no stopping them. And Carter, with his thirst for vengeance, bore close watching. He didn't see that he had much choice.

"Mount up," he told Ben, then went to check the cinch on his own weary horse.

"Can I go, Pa?" Rob's eager voice came from the porch. Jake glanced up to where the rest of the family stood in the light spilling from the open doorway.

"We couldn't help but hear the commotion," Mary said apologetically, placing her hands on Rob's shoulders.

"No, Son, you stay." Ben's voice sounded gentle but brooked no argument. "I need you to take care of your ma and sisters."

Jake barely heard Rob's protest over the excited shouts of the men as the posse headed out.

Ten

"L et's hope this puts an end to it," Mary murmured, following the departing group with her gaze. "Rob, bring in a load of firewood, please. Girls, come inside and get ready for supper."

Amelia lingered on the porch. Resting both arms on the rail, she sent up a prayer for the protection of the posse and the capture of the rustlers. After all the months of worry, could it all be over this very night? Maybe they wouldn't lose the ranch, after all, she mused, daring to let a spark of hope flicker.

Mary and Lucinda were already seated when she took her place at the table. Rob shouldered his way through the door, his chin tucked down to steady the armload of wood. Through the open door, Amelia heard a frantic bawling from the barn. Her glance met Rob's.

"It's Bessie!" she cried. "Something must be after her calf."

Rob dumped the load of wood on the floor and rushed outside. Amelia followed, lifting the double-barreled shotgun from its rack on the wall on her way. She hadn't spent all that effort on bringing the calf safely into the world to risk losing her to varmints now.

She hurried after Rob, who had nearly crossed the distance to the barn. A glow flickered just inside the wide doors, and a feeling of dread settled in Amelia's stomach.

"The barn's on fire!" Rob's yelp confirmed her fears. She put on a spurt of speed, straining to see how far the flames had spread. Silhouetted against the faint glow, she saw two shadowy figures emerge, running toward the corral.

"Wet a feed sack and try to beat it out," she called to Rob. "It doesn't look like it's made much headway yet."

With a quick glance to be sure he had heard, she redoubled her efforts and sprinted after the fleeing men.

"Hold it right there!" she shouted.

The two figures hesitated only slightly, then picked up their pace.

Amelia planted her feet wide apart and raised the shotgun to her shoulder. She couldn't see well enough in the darkness to take careful aim, but with the shotgun, she didn't need to. She cocked both hammers with a loud click.

"Maybe you think you can outrun a woman," she yelled, "but you're not going to get away from double-aught buckshot." The two shadows froze.

"Now drop your guns and head toward the house."

A brief pause, then a cautious voice said, "Yes, Ma'am." Two guns thudded in the dirt. Amelia marched her captives to the front door.

Inside, she prodded the two past her astonished mother and steered them to the pantry. "Lock them in, please, Ma." Once she'd made sure the door was secured, she ran back outside to help Rob.

The posse straggled back hours later, dejection written on each face. "I can't understand it," Seth Hardy said. "Even in the dark, he shouldn't have lost them. But surely there'll be a next time."

Jake bit back a harsh reply. Success had been almost within his grasp, only to be snatched away at the last moment. . .again. He couldn't blame Hardy for the night's wasted effort, but he sure wanted to blame someone.

Ben rode up beside him. "Something's wrong," he said in a low tone. "Every window in the house is lit up." He spurred his horse toward home.

Jake followed, alarm pushing his weariness aside. An acrid odor assailed his nostrils. Smoke? He urged the bay forward, catching up to Ben.

The front door flew open when they clattered into the dooryard, and the whole Donovan family rushed out onto the porch.

Ben and Jake jumped off their horses and ran toward them. "What's going on?" Ben demanded.

"What happened?" Jake echoed, noting with relief that no one appeared to be hurt.

Mary stepped forward. "You can be very proud of your children, Ben."

Amelia and Rob approached their father, grinning. Jake's nose wrinkled. The smell of smoke emanated from both of them.

"They tried to burn the barn down, Pa." Rob's voice carried a note of triumph. "But we stopped them, me and Amelia."

Ben uttered a startled cry and turned to the barn.

Seeing it still stood, he swiveled back to his son. "Are you all right?"

Jake took a more official interest. "How many were there? Did you recognize them? How much head start do they have?"

Amelia smiled. "There were two of them, and no, we didn't recognize them. As for a head start," she went on smugly, "they didn't get any. We have them locked up in the pantry."

"*What?*" Jake's bellow echoed through the night. He had the satisfaction of seeing her shrink back, a startled look on her face. He turned away and hailed the approaching men.

"It sounds like the excitement was here tonight," he told them. "Two men tried to burn Ben's barn. Let's see if we can find some answers."

Amelia watched the men, led by Ben and Jake, press inside the ranch house. She followed slowly, still fighting the sting of Jake's anger. She'd been so sure he would be elated to find the would-be arsonists captured and waiting for him. But, no. He couldn't accept the fact that the feat had been accomplished by a woman.

Jake and Ben stood by the pantry door, waving the puzzled ranchers back. Amelia moved closer, stepping past Seth Hardy, who stood on the edge of the crowd, as if to get a better view.

Jake cocked his pistol and leveled it at the door. "This is Jake Thornton, Texas Ranger. When the door opens, I want you men to come out with your hands up." He nodded at Ben, who turned the latch.

Amelia glanced behind her and saw the front door stood wide open. What if the men saw it and made a dash for freedom? She pushed her way between Hardy and the wall, kicking aside the chunks of wood Rob had dropped. She noted with approval that Lucinda stood well away from the crowd, out of danger.

She swung the door shut, making sure it was latched, then stood with her back pressed against it. Jake Thornton or no Jake Thornton, no one would escape through that door while Amelia Donovan was around.

Ben released the lock on the pantry door and stepped back. Two men, hands held high, stumbled into the room, squinting against the light. They paled upon beholding Jake's gun and the roomful of grim faces.

"You can see you're not going anywhere," Jake said. "We want some answers, boys, and we want them now."

"We'll tell you what you want to know," the younger of the two blurted. "Just don't shoot."

Jake's expression didn't soften. "This is all tied in with the missing cattle, isn't it?"

The two exchanged startled glances. The younger one swallowed. "You're right. We were part of that. You've caught us dead to rights. But it hasn't been all on our own hook. We're not going down by ourselves."

"I'm not asking you to." Jake's voice rang loud in the quiet room. "I know someone else is in charge. Give me a name."

Their glances darted furtively from face to face. "All right," choked out the older man. "He goes by Hardy. Seth Hardy."

Eleven

For a moment, the entire room seemed to hold its breath. Then every head turned, every eye focusing on Hardy. For once, the bluster had left him. His mouth twisted in a ghastly attempt at a smile, and he forced out a croaking laugh.

"Come on, boys, you aren't going to take the word of a couple of thugs, are you?"

No one said a word.

Hardy laughed again, unconvincingly, and took a step back, his eyes shifting from side to side like a cornered weasel.

Les Carter's face contorted in rage. "Come here, you lying coyote. I've got a rope with your name on it." He stepped toward Hardy.

With a lightning movement, Hardy drew his gun, then lunged to the side and grabbed Lucinda around the waist, holding the little girl up before him.

Amelia's heart froze. The man had nothing to lose; what wouldn't he dare do to her sister? She cast a pleading look at Jake.

Hardy tightened his grip on the struggling child.

"Back off, all of you! If I don't get out of here in one piece, neither does she."

Jake stood before Hardy, gun drawn. From her position behind Hardy, Amelia could see the grim resolve on his face but knew he couldn't risk a shot for fear of hitting Lucinda.

"Stupid." Hardy spat the word at the two men still under Ben's watchful eye. "How hard is it to set fire to a barn? All I asked for was a simple diversion, but you had to go and get yourselves caught." He took a step backward.

Amelia braced herself against the door, willing her legs to stop shaking. Surely they wouldn't let him make off with Lucinda. Over Hardy's shoulder, Jake's gaze met hers for a fleeting instant. Without changing expression, he gave her a barely perceptible nod, then resumed eye contact with Hardy.

She frowned. Had she imagined the nod? It seemed out of character, given the current situation, plus his earlier anger toward her. Had he meant to convey something to her?

"What will you do if you get out of here?" Jake moved forward a step. Amelia's heart raced. Didn't he realize Lucinda's danger?

"You can head out that door," Jake continued, "but what good will it do you? It'll only take one person to stop you, Hardy. Just one person." He emphasized the last two words, inching forward again. "One person with the guts to stop you."

For the briefest moment, Jake flicked his gaze from Hardy to Amelia, then back again. Understanding dawned, and hope flooded through her.

"What do you mean, 'one person?' " Carter's voice cut in. "Let's rush him. He can't stand up to all of us at once."

"Keep back," Jake commanded. "Let me handle this."

Amelia's glance lit on the wood billets near her feet. Slowly, so as not to attract attention, she stooped to pick up a good-sized chunk and gripped it in both hands.

Jake eased forward, forcing Hardy back step by step. Lucinda whimpered; Hardy cut her off with a rough shake.

He backed closer, almost within Amelia's reach. She waited, arms poised, the coarse wood biting into her fingers.

"I'm riding out now," Hardy snarled. "If I'm not followed, I'll leave the girl beside the trail at daybreak. You can look for her then."

The moment had arrived. Amelia braced herself, then swung the makeshift club with all her might.

Hardy toppled like a lightning-struck tree. Lucinda tumbled to the floor, then scrambled up and ran to her mother, who clutched her in a tight hug.

The room swam before Amelia, then righted itself. "Is he dead?" she whispered.

Jake knelt by the fallen man, then rose, shaking his head. "You only knocked him out." He turned to the men behind him. "Help me get these three trussed up. They can spend the night in the barn under guard. I'll take them to Fort Worth in the morning."

Amelia sagged against the door, but elation overshadowed her weakness. Jake had asked for her help! She hugged the knowledge to herself while she watched him tie the unconscious Hardy's hands and feet and supervise his removal to the barn.

Jake had his prisoners securely bound in their saddles before the first streaks of gold lightened the sky. Two of Vickery's riders would help guard the three on the way to Fort Worth. He left them to keep watch while he took his leave.

He exchanged a wordless handshake with Ben and received a hug of gratitude from Mary. "Thank you for your hospitality," he told her. "You made me feel right at home."

Rob emulated his father's handshake and gave Jake a manly nod.

Jake knelt before Lucinda. "Are you all right?" he asked. When she bobbed her head, he added, "You were a very brave girl."

"Amelia was brave, too," she said. "I'm glad she didn't act like a lady this time."

Jake swallowed and straightened, bracing himself to face the last member of the family. Amelia stood apart from the others, her hair glinting copper in the sun's early rays. She stared at him with wide eyes, her lips slightly parted and her cheeks flushed.

Amelia stood quietly, her pulse fluttering in her throat. During a sleepless night, she had relived countless times the wonder of Jake's asking for her help. At last he had accepted her, and things would never again be the same between them. In a moment, he would close the distance between them and tell her so himself.

She watched him say good-bye to her parents, then Rob and Lucinda. Finally, he turned toward her and their gazes locked. He took one step toward her, then pivoted on his heel and strode away to mount his horse. Amelia watched in disbelief as he set the group of riders into motion and left without a backward glance.

Long after her family had returned to the house, she stared after the horsemen, watching them diminish to specks on the horizon—watching Jake Thornton ride out of her life.

Twelve

Clouds scudded overhead, casting broad shadows and providing a welcome respite from the late summer's heat. Amelia pressed the tines of her digging fork into the rich garden soil and pushed down on the handle, bringing up a jumble of potatoes. Pulling them free of the roots, she knocked off the worst of the dirt and tossed them into a tow sack, wishing she could remove the ache from her heart so easily.

In the two weeks since Hardy's capture, word had come through Vickery's riders that the prisoners had been delivered safely. Nothing, though, had been said about Jake; no message had come from him. Not that she'd expected anything, but her heart had been harder to convince of that than her head.

Rob looked up from hoeing the rows of winter squash and stretched his back muscles. "There's a rider coming," he announced, staring into the distance.

Visitors to the Four Slash D were hardly an unusual occurrence. Amelia spared a quick glance in the direction he pointed, then returned to her digging.

"Look at that horse," Rob crowed, his young face

alight with excitement. "I think it's Jake!"

She squinted toward the oncoming rider, shading her eyes with her hand. Her stomach knotted. Rob was right. A surge of hope welled up inside her, only to be squelched immediately. She remembered too well what had happened the last time she dared allow herself to hope.

"What do you think he's doing here, Sis?"

She clutched the digging fork so tightly the handle dug into her palms. Whatever Jake's reason for coming, she knew it didn't concern her. He had made it abundantly clear he wanted nothing more to do with her.

Dropping her fork next to the tow sack, she headed for the barn. She would let Jake talk to the rest of the family in peace. It would be easier for them both if they didn't have to face each other.

Within the barn's cool shadows, she pulled her saddle down and took her time rubbing oil into the leather with a small piece of cloth, trying not to notice when Jake mounted the porch steps, telling herself her breath didn't quicken at the sight of his broad shoulders and confident stride.

With the saddle back on its rack, she wandered over to Bessie's calf. The heifer scampered to greet her and nuzzled her hand. Amelia knelt by the little animal and stroked her glossy brown coat.

A shadow fell across the doorway. Amelia looked up to see Jake, flanked by Rob and Lucinda. Feeling awkward, she scrambled to her feet, brushing wisps of straw from her skirt. "What brings you out this way?" she said, hating the way her voice wobbled and knowing her attempt at a smile fell flat.

Jake shifted his weight from one foot to the other, curling the brim of his hat in his hands. "I wanted to let your family know what came out at the trial."

"Ah." She waited for him to continue, then spoke again to fill the strained silence. "So you got it all pieced together? You know what happened?" She focused her gaze on his shoulder, not willing to lose herself in those stormy gray eyes.

He nodded. "I just finished explaining it to your father. He said you'd like to hear it firsthand, too."

Amelia managed a small smile. "So tell me." She leaned against the center post and waited.

"You have to give Hardy credit for clever thinking," Jake began. "He knew he could expect two or three trail drives through this area every week from April to September. His riders stayed on the lookout to see when the drives would be getting close. Once he knew, it was easy to steal a small bunch of cattle, slap on a road brand, and have some of his men trail them up to meet with the drive."

Wrapped up in his story, he stepped closer. Despite her intentions to remain aloof, Amelia felt a shiver run through her like the tingle in the air before a lightning storm.

Not seeming to notice, Jake went on. "Since they dealt with different people each time, the trail bosses had no reason to doubt their story that they'd bought the cattle themselves. They were only too pleased to buy from them to sell at a profit at the stockyards."

Amelia shook her head. "No wonder we couldn't find any trace. They were off the range almost as soon as they went missing."

Jake nodded agreement. "If things had gone his way, the losses wouldn't have been discovered until fall roundup. But when Vickery's men caught on and word spread to the rest of the ranchers, Hardy knew his time was growing short. Once they decided to call in the Rangers, he had no choice but to go along, or he'd cast suspicion on himself. With a ranger around he knew it was only a matter of time before his money machine ran down."

"That's why they ambushed you at the ravine." Amelia smacked her fist into her palm. "I knew it!"

"Exactly." Jake grinned, seeming at ease for the first time. "Just as you thought, it was designed to slow me down long enough for them to make one last major sweep. With the money he got from that, he planned to relocate and start the ruse all over again under a new name."

"So there's no way of getting our cattle back," Amelia said, her shoulders slumping in defeat.

"Not those cattle, but the judge did order Hardy's herd and property to be split among the four ranches according to their losses." He gave her an encouraging smile that made her stomach do flip-flops. "You won't lose the ranch."

"That's good news."

Jake's gaze traveled around the barn. "That heifer's coming along fine," he noted with a nod at Bessie's calf.

"She's really growing, isn't she? She was worth all that work." Amelia glanced at Jake's hands, and one corner of her mouth tilted upward. "If you don't quit twisting that hat, it's only going to be fit for a scarecrow." She dared to meet his gaze directly for the first time since he entered the barn. The gray depths of his eyes tugged at her soul.

Jake spared a glance at the hat and tossed it onto the grain box. He stepped closer to Amelia, closing the gap between them. She drew a quick breath.

A giggle from the doorway caused Jake to whirl around, suddenly reminded of Rob's and Lucinda's presence. He ran his hand over his hair and licked his lips.

"Do you two think you could find something else to do for awhile? I'd like to talk to your sister"—he half turned to Amelia—"if she doesn't mind."

"Come on, Lucinda," Rob ordered. "We'd better hurry out of here. You wouldn't believe what happened the last time they were in the barn together." The two ran off, Lucinda trying to stifle another round of mirth.

Jake turned to Amelia again, and she braced herself for whatever would come next.

"I owe you an apology," he said, flicking a glance at her then looking down at his feet.

Her lips parted. Nothing in her experience with Jake had prepared her for this.

He looked back at her, and their glances locked. "When Hardy grabbed Lucinda, no one else was in a position to bring him down. In your place, my mother or sisters or any well-brought-up woman I know would have done the "ladylike" thing and either screamed or fainted. You risked your own safety to save your sister and did a magnificent job. You were the bravest woman I've ever seen."

Amelia could only stare. "Then why. . .?"

"Why did I ride away without saying a word?" His lips twisted in a wry smile. "I'm the one who asked you to do it, remember? After all my talk about a woman's rightful place, who did I turn to when I needed help? A woman."

He stepped nearer again, standing so close that Amelia could feel his warmth. "A very special woman." With one finger, he scooped a strand of hair off her forehead and tucked it behind her ear.

"I've done a lot of thinking—and a lot of praying—these past two weeks," he continued, cupping her cheek in his hand. "Seems like God had to hit *me* over the head to get me to see that what I need isn't a woman who knows nothing more than domestic details but someone who can put up with the idea of me being in danger without going to pieces. And," he smiled, "someone who can help when I'm fresh out of ideas."

"I need *you*, Amelia. Just the way you are." He pressed his lips against her forehead, then leaned back and studied her intently. "We made quite a team dealing with Hardy, didn't we? Would you consider making that a permanent partnership?"

Amelia's hands crept up his arms to rest on his shoulders. "I've not been blessed with a docile personality," she said, then smiled. "But you know that, don't you? I'll always say just what I think; there's no getting around that."

Jake pulled her into a warm embrace. "I've learned to value your forthrightness." He chuckled.

She looked up at him, marveling at his tenderness, his acceptance. "Does this mean you've revised your ideas about a woman's place?" she whispered.

"All I know," Jake answered, lowering his mouth to hers, "is that *this* woman's place is by my side and in my heart."

CAROL COX

A native of Arizona, Carol's time is devoted to being a pastor's wife, home-school mom to her teen, active mom to her preschooler, church pianist, youth worker, and 4-H leader. She loves anything that she can do with her family: reading, traveling, historical studies, and outdoor excursions. She is also open to new pursuits on her own including gardening, crafts, and the local historical society. She has had two historical novels published in Barbour Publishing's **Heartsong Presents** line: *Journey Toward Home* and *The Measure of a Man,* and novellas in *Spring's Memory, Resolutions, Forever Friends,* and *Gift of Love.* Her goals for writing inspirational romances are to encourage Christian readers with entertaining and uplifting stories and to pique the interests of non-Christians who might read her novels.

Serena's Strength

by DiAnn Mills

Dedication

To Troy and Barbi Tagliarino.
Good friends are special gifts from God.

One

San Antonio, Texas, 1841

S erena Talbot lifted her gaze to the open road and waded a wooden spoon through thick venison stew, now bubbling over an open fire. From a distance, she heard the deep throaty laughter of her pa.

"Serena, your pa's riding in," her ma called from the cabin. "Looks like Mr. Wilkinson is with him too. They're gonna want a cool drink of water."

"Yes, Ma'am. I'll draw a bucket now."

Standing, she wiped the perspiration from her reddened face with her soiled apron. Texas heat in midsummer proved unbearable, but at least the cooking could be done outside.

Serena caught sight of the two men and waved. Snatching up the water bucket and ladle, she headed toward the well.

Ranger Chet Wilkinson. She'd just been thinking about him. In fact, he occupied quite a bit of her thoughts lately. His smile, well, it seemed to take her breath away.

Good thing Pa didn't know her fancies. He'd be lecturing her about the wild ways of Texas Rangers.

If Ma married a ranger, then why couldn't she dream about one? But Pa knew the dangers of his rugged life and the hardships it placed on families. He didn't want his daughter to suffer through the anguish of loving a man who risked his life each time he rode out.

"Hey, Little One," her pa said, "you cookin' up something good? We smelled it five miles back."

Serena grinned at the rugged, broad-shouldered man. "You want to guess?"

"Nope, it's venison stew, and I could eat it all myself." He rode his red dun mare alongside the well and rested on his saddle horn. "I think I could drink up that whole bucket of water too."

"I'll bring it to the barn as soon as I draw it up," she said and turned her attention to Chet. "Evenin', Mr. Wilkinson. We're pleased you're joining us for supper."

Chet's lopsided smile sent her pulse racing faster than Pa's prize mare. Even in the late afternoon with shadows of evening stealing across the sky, she could see his pine green eyes peering out from under his weathered hat. Or maybe she simply envisioned them. Sometimes at night, when sleep evaded her, she wondered if those green pools ever searched her out as she did them.

"I'd be much obliged, Miss Serena. I'm mighty hungry. Your pa hasn't stopped riding since sunup." A tousle of sun-colored hair fell across his forehead. Hard to believe his slight frame and boyish face followed the rough road of a Texas Ranger.

"We have plenty cooked up, and Ma's just made biscuits

with fresh-churned butter."

"I'll be hurrying along then," Chet said with a nod. "Won't take long to tend to the horses and wash up."

He's too pretty for a Texas Ranger, she thought. *After riding with Pa for over two years, he ought to be looking hard.*

Her pa reined his horse in the direction of the barn, and Chet followed. "Hurry on with the water, Little One," Pa called over his shoulder.

A moment later, she untied the rope around the bucket and dropped the ladle inside. The deep springs below their land—not far from the San Antonio River—hosted the clearest, coolest water around. At least that's what Pa always said.

"Serena, ask your pa if anyone else is expected for supper," her ma said, stepping back inside the cabin.

"Yes, Ma'am. I'll ask him now."

Serena noticed her ma had smoothed back her pecan-colored hair and changed her apron. Ma always fussed with her looks when Pa came home. Serena hoped some-day to find a special love like her parents'. They'd been together since Pa rescued Ma from a renegade band of Comanches when she'd just turned sixteen years old.

She glanced down at her worn green dress. At least she'd brushed through her hair before Pa and Chet rode up.

Toting the heavy bucket, Serena slowly made her way to the barn. She'd given up on adding a little meat to her bones. Ma called her frail; Pa called her skinny. In any event, she still looked twelve years old instead of nearly eighteen. She had height, but no outward appearances of a woman's figure.

By the time Serena made it to the open barn door, her

shoulder and arm throbbed. No one would ever hear of it, though. She felt determined to do her share of the work.

With a sigh, she stepped into the barn, and her ears perked at the sound of men's voices.

"We ridin' out again in the morning, Cap'n?" Chet asked.

"The following morning," her pa replied. He seldom talked much, seemed to be always thinking on something.

She heard the *whish-whish* of the grooming brushes gliding across the horses' sleek coats. Just as she decided to make herself known, Chet's voice caused her to linger a moment longer.

"You know, that little girl of yours is going to be a beautiful woman one day. Why, she's right pretty," Chet said.

A little girl, Serena fumed. Pa's nickname coming from Chet's lips didn't sound at all endearing.

"Well, I'd just as soon keep her around for a long spell. I ain't in no hurry to have her married off." Pa paused. "Least ways to no ranger. . .even one who carries a Bible in his saddlebag."

Pa, I'm a grown woman, she fumed. Chet had a reputation for being a Bible-prayin' preacher man, another reason why he favored her attention. A man who loved the Lord and the Rangers ranked at the top of her list.

"Yes, Sir. I just meant for as young as Miss Serena is, she's bound to be a pretty woman. But when I get ready to settle down, I want a round woman, real tall, too. Good and strong."

Silence. Serena sighed, realizing Pa had no intentions

of telling Chet the truth about her age. Frustrated, she kicked the side of the barn to announce her arrival.

Shortly thereafter, while inside the cabin and helping Ma finish supper, the matter still picked at her—like a whole patch of chiggers.

"What's wrong?" her ma asked, studying Serena with pale blue eyes. "You've been frettin' over something since you came back from the barn."

"Oh, nothing," Serena replied, pulling out tin mugs for the coffee.

Her ma set a jar of apple butter on the rough-sawn table. "Serena, you can't keep anything from me."

She gazed up into her ma's flawless face. No hint of lines around her eyes or streaks of gray in her light brown hair. She looked young, too, but not as skinny as Serena. "Mr. Wilkinson thinks I'm a little girl."

Her ma glanced up, surprise clearly lacing her face. "And it bothers you?"

Serena lifted her chin. "I'm a grown woman."

Her ma's laughter rang about the kitchen. "That you are, and don't you have a birthday coming up soon?" She gave Serena a hug, forcing a laugh from her.

"Another month, and I'll be eighteen. Ma, most girls, I mean women, my age are married with children of their own by now. Besides, any single men around here are afraid of Pa."

Ma crossed her arms over her chest. "Your pa does have a way of intimidating a body—especially if he thinks a man has his sights on you. Do you have someone in mind?" Her ma studied her curiously. "I haven't heard you mention anyone."

Serena took a deep breath, but the door creaked open and Pa and Chet walked in. "I'll go get the stew," she offered and slipped out the door between the two men.

When they all sat down to supper, Pa invited Chet to ask the blessing. Serena bowed her head and closed her eyes, eagerly anticipating Chet's deep voice. No matter how hurt she felt, he did have a way of making prayers sound meaningful.

"Thank You, Lord, for helping the cap'n and me get here safe. Thank You for this fine family and their hospitality. Mrs. Wilkinson and Serena have cooked up some good food, and we thank You for this and all of Your many blessings. In Jesus' name, amen."

All during supper, Chet's reference to Serena as a little girl bothered her. In fact, he'd succeeded in making her downright mad. As she ate, she conjured up a good plan to let him learn the truth.

"Would you like more coffee?" Serena asked her pa.

He handed her his mug, and she rose from the table to fill it. "Pa, you know my birthday is coming up soon."

"Yes, Little One," he replied, leaning back against his chair. "And I plan to be right here with you when it happens."

"Thank you. I was hoping you wouldn't be gone. Do you mind if I ask Moira to join us for supper then? She is my dearest friend."

"Fine with me as long as it's all right with your ma."

Her ma nodded approvingly.

"Birthdays were always special to me when I was growing up," Chet said, reaching for the jar of apple butter.

"And this one is more than special to me," Serena said,

swallowing the irritation of Chet's earlier remarks and tasting the sweetness of revenge—or rather nursing her pride.

"How old you gonna be?" he asked, spooning a healthy dollop between the layers of a biscuit. "Oh, let me guess. I have a fifteen-year-old sister, so give me a moment to think on it." He peered at her with a mischievous look in his eyes.

"You might be surprised," Pa said between mouthfuls of stew.

Ma glanced curiously at Serena, then picked up the basket of biscuits. "Have another, Chet. Might help your accuracy. Although I've been told never to question a woman's age."

Serena cringed and her pulse quickened. Ma knew she pined over him. Hopefully, she wouldn't tell Pa.

Chet thanked her ma and gathered up two biscuits, adding a generous slab of butter to each. He popped one into his mouth and chewed slowly as if considering her reply.

"Hmm. Since this one means a lot to you, I'm guessing. . .say thirteen."

Pa coughed and reached for his coffee. "Ah, Ranger Boy, you might want to rethink your answer."

He grinned, the same earth-shattering smile that always melted her heart. "Tell me, Miss Serena, how old will you be?"

She allowed herself the privilege of hesitation before staring into his handsome face. "Eighteen."

Chet's mouth flew agape, and he dropped his knife. "Why, why excuse me. I thought. . ."

"Surprised?" Serena asked sweetly.

His face looked as if he'd worked all day in the sun without his hat.

From the corner of her eye, she saw Pa's wry smile. *Good, Pa isn't mad at me.*

"Would you like to come to my birthday, Mr. Wilkinson? You'd probably like Moira. She's a bit bigger than me, but the same age. Funny thing about Moira, she works hard as a man—strong, too."

This time, Chet choked. He sputtered and reached for his empty tin of coffee.

"Oh, my, let me get you some water," Serena said and scooted to the water bucket.

For the first time she regretted embarrassing Chet. He looked miserable, and his face had reddened even more with the choking episode. There wasn't as much joy in seeing him squirm as she originally thought. Perhaps she should ease out of the topic and let him regain his composure. For a moment she considered apologizing, but she didn't want to own up to overhearing Chet and Pa.

"Pa, I know what I'd like," she said, handing Chet the water and avoiding his reddened stare.

Her pa raised a brow. "The palomino mare of Dugan Niall's?"

"You mean it?" Her voice quivered in anticipation.

A smile widened his dark bearded face. "Did you have something else in mind?"

She slid onto the bench beside her ma, feeling her delight nearly burst. "I was going to ask for your old rifle, but. . .no, Mr. Niall's horse is the finest gift anyone could ever want. Oh, Pa, thank you."

He pushed his plate back and rested his elbows on

the table. "What do you say, Little One? Want to go pick up that palomino in the morning?"

Serena did not hesitate. "Yes, Sir, and I'll fix you the best breakfast before we go."

He eyed Chet. "Why don't you come with us?"

He'd slowly begun to recover. "Dugan does have a good-looking stallion for sale. Yes, Cap'n, I'd like to ride along."

Pa pushed his chair back from the table, its legs scraping the floor. "Now, Serena, you owe Chet here an apology. No need to explain why. He's our guest."

Two

C het felt hotter than if he'd been branded across his face with the letter *S* for stupid. The truth burned clear to the pit of his stomach—and worse yet, he deserved it. All of his big talk in the barn about James's pretty "little girl" blared across his mind. No wonder Serena wanted to get even; she'd heard every word. Eighteen years old. Bewildered, he looked up into her angelic face. He'd landed in a heap of trouble with one skinny girl, rather woman.

Oh, Lord, I need a muzzle over my mouth.

Serena rose beside her ma from the bench and folded her hands at her waist. She brushed thick, black hair from her face. He inwardly grumbled why she didn't wear it up. Maybe then he'd have guessed her right age.

Eyes the color of nearly-ripe blueberries gazed coldly into his. He saw a tint of anger, a mirror of pride masked behind softened features and pink cheeks. Yes, she did look young. . .and furious.

Lifting her chin and wearing a sweet rosebud smile, Serena addressed him. "Mr. Wilkinson, I'm sorry for humiliating you. I don't have an excuse except I heard you talking to Pa when I brought in the water. Will you forgive me?" She tilted her head like his little sister used to do when she needed understanding. "I know I didn't behave like a Christian woman."

The word *woman* poured thick as honey from her lips, and the sound of it sent little prickles up and down his arms.

He gulped and took a swallow of water. "Miss Serena, I most assuredly forgive you, but I believe the fault is mine. You can be sure I will address you in the future according to your. . .your rightful age." He stuttered through the last of his speech as the proper words escaped him—something that seldom happened.

"Thank you, Mr. Wilkinson. I appreciate your tolerance of my bad manners. Will you still be joining Pa and me in the morning?"

He swallowed hard and attempted to gather his wits. "Yes, Ma'am. I'd be honored."

Serena glanced at her pa, and he nodded his approval. She sat down to finish her meal, but Chet noticed she picked at her food. Odd, he didn't feel so hungry anymore either. He sneaked a peek at James's daughter. Yeah, she looked way too skinny for him, but she did have a right pretty face.

Serena gave up trying to sleep. Chet's words echoed through her mind like a herd of horses stampeding across the dry plains. He hadn't noticed her as anything more than James Talbot's little girl. Even worse, when he got ready to settle down, he wanted a big, strong woman. Humph, strength didn't necessarily mean size. Hadn't Pa taught her those things? Strength meant courage in the face of danger or when she needed to stand for her beliefs. It meant trusting God to see her through bad times and thinking things through with her head and heart—not her muscles. Just because she didn't have much meat on her bones didn't mean she lacked gumption. It would serve Ranger Chet just fine to saddle himself with some huge woman who'd run from her own shadow.

Oh, Lord, could You make Chet see I'm strong enough to be a ranger's wife? Amen. And Lord, You probably need to change Pa's mind about me marrying up with a ranger.

Tossing on the straw pallet in her tiny room, she heard Chet snoring in the kitchen.

Good for him; glad he can sleep.

She cast aside his dismissal of her and tried to convince herself he didn't matter. But he did. Fighting the urge to cry, she focused on the following morning and Dugan Niall's palomino.

Staring up at the darkness, she couldn't help but feel excitement about the mare. What a wonderful birthday present. She'd never dreamed of such a fine horse. Pa and the other rangers took special pride in their mounts. A good horse often meant the difference between living and dying. Although she treasured the love from Pa for his generous gift, it didn't stop the ache in her heart for Chet.

Serena finally found a few hours' sleep before she woke to fix breakfast. Staring out the small window of her room, she saw a glaze of pink and gold ushering in the dawn. She quickly dressed, then remembered Chet was sleeping in the same room where she'd be cooking.

She told herself she had nothing to be wary about. He had insulted her, not the other way around, and, besides, he didn't know her feelings about him. Still, they were both bound to feel uncomfortable around each other, and Serena realized she needed to make things right.

Stealing into the kitchen, Serena tied an apron twice around her waist. Someday she would pile enough weight on her bones to secure it in back like a normal woman. She studied Chet sleeping on the floor and struggled with wanting to kick him or allow him to rest peacefully.

Pulling her gaze from the blanket-clad figure, she mentally calculated what she needed for breakfast. Due to the quickly rising temperatures, she welcomed the task of frying bacon, baking biscuits, and boiling coffee outside over an open fire. They might eat there, too, which would be a refreshing way to start the day. On second thought, Pa shared enough meals under an open sky. He'd prefer sitting around the table inside. After all, she'd promised him a good breakfast.

The idea of eggs floating in a pool of bacon grease would be an added treat, and the chickens had been laying good. Ma told her she could use all of the eggs she wanted.

Grinning with satisfaction, Serena collected matches, the coffee pot, and the empty water bucket before moving outside to gather dry wood. Not long afterwards, a fire crackled and spit. She loved the smell of wood burning and the sight of sunrise faintly splitting the darkness. A rooster perched on the well top and crowed. He peered about as if to make sure every living creature had heard him. Serena laughed as the birds seemed to sing a little louder in answer to the rooster's call.

A trip into the cabin produced a skillet filled with thick slices of bacon and peeled potatoes ready for her to slice into a second skillet. She'd already mixed up the biscuit dough and silently kneaded it before cutting the huge rounds.

"Can I help you, Miss Serena?" Chet whispered from his position on the floor.

"No, thank you, I'm fine," she replied in the same soft tone and immediately felt her heart race with the low sound of his voice. "Sorry to wake you."

"I've been awake. Hard to sleep in when you're used to rising before dawn."

She said nothing else but took the bacon-filled skillet outside, knowing she'd be back inside the cabin at least two more times to bring out the other skillet and biscuits. While at the fire, Serena checked the coffeepot and inhaled the aroma of freshly-ground coffee.

"Here, I brought these for you," came a voice from behind her.

Startled, she whirled around to see Chet carrying the other items she needed. "How nice of you," she said and smoothed her apron before taking the skillet and the pan of biscuit dough.

He stood barefooted with his suspenders resting haphazardly on his shoulders, and he'd buttoned his yellowed white shirt wrong with something bulging at his heart. His sun-colored hair lay every which way but flat against his head, more like a boy than a grown man. A second later, his dimpled smile gripped her senses.

It ought to be a sin for a man to affect a woman so.

Embarrassed and grateful for the dim light, she pulled

a paring knife from her apron pocket to slice the potatoes.

"Sure I can't help?"

"You can eat later," she said, "and maybe have a little coffee now."

Chet produced a tin mug from inside his shirt. "I hoped you had it ready. Can I sit and talk a spell?"

"Of course." While he settled down into the dew-covered grass and leaned back on his hands, she prepared her words. "Mr. Wilkinson—"

"Chet. My friends call me by my given name."

She took a ragged breath. "All right, Chet. I did a bad thing to you last night, and I am truly sorry."

"Naw, it's me who wronged you." He shook his head. "Funny how a man can earn a reputation as a Texas Ranger or a preachin' ranger or a big talker and still make a fool of himself in front of a woman. Leastways, I never meant to hurt your feelings."

"I know."

"So can we go back to being friends?"

How could she refuse? Masking her sinking spirits with a flair for teasing, she eyed him suspiciously. "Aren't you afraid I might poison your coffee?"

"Would you do that to me?"

She lifted the pot from the fire, and he held out his mug. "A skinny little girl like me has to fight back any way she can."

He grinned and it eased her ruffled feelings.

She slid the coffeepot back onto the burning embers. "You know what Pa used to tell me?" she asked, poking at the fire with a thick stick and sending sparks into the slowly lifting blanket of night.

"Hard to tell with the cap'n."

"He told me if Indians attacked the cabin while he was gone, that I could hide myself behind a fence post."

Chet laughed heartily. At least she could lighten his morning with a little humor.

"Be back in a minute. Got to get my eggs." Serena headed toward the cabin.

"I can tote 'em out here for you," he called after her.

"No, Sir. I don't want them broke before I fry them."

He chuckled, and she felt better since supper the night before. A lot of truth in freeing a body from sin.

Inside, Serena found Ma bustling about the kitchen, placing plates and cups on the table. She stopped and watched Serena. "Honey, you don't need to be fixing breakfast all by yourself."

"I told Pa I wanted to last night."

"I know, but I slept a mite longer than I intended."

"Good," Serena said. "You don't rest well when Pa's gone." She picked up the egg basket along with a platter to pile on the meat and eggs.

"Serena?" Her questioning voice sounded soft and tender.

She glanced up into Ma's face in reply.

"Why didn't you tell me you had feelings for Chet?" she asked, placing a hand on Serena's shoulder.

Avoiding Ma's eyes, she shrugged. "Seemed like a secret thing, and I needed to keep it to myself."

"But we've always been able to talk."

For a moment, Serena felt like releasing all of her pent-up emotions in her mother's arms. "I didn't mean to hold anything from you. It just seemed too personal to tell anyone—not Moira or even you."

"Can we talk after he and your pa leave?"

Serena felt unsure of her answer. Talking about it wouldn't change a thing. "Are you going to tell Pa?"

"Not unless he asks, and he's said nary a word." She offered a smile, and Serena returned the gesture. "Certain things only a woman can know."

Only a woman can know. She spoke the right words. "All right, Ma. We can talk." Serena turned and opened the door. She gasped. In the pale daylight, a huge, wild boar stood between Chet and the cabin.

Instantly, she set the basket of eggs and the platter on the rough-sawn table and reached for Pa's rifle leaning against the fireplace. Pulling it up to her shoulder, she rushed outside.

"James, come quick," her ma said. "Serena, wait on your pa."

Chet waved his hands above his head. "Serena, don't come any closer. It'll tear you apart."

Ignoring first her ma's warnings and now Chet's, she knew exactly what to do. Suddenly, the boar took an unexpected turn in her direction and barreled forward.

Three

The boar raced straight toward her. Serena faintly heard her mother's cries and another shout from Chet, but she had her focus dead center between the animal's eyes. She squeezed the trigger. Rifle fire echoed and the boar fell six feet in front of her in a puddle of blood.

Instantly, Chet stood by her side, clearly amazed. "You got him right square between the eyes." His face had paled, and he looked a bit angry.

Serena blinked. "I know. That's where I aimed."

He poked the boar with his boot. "Who taught you to shoot like this?"

"I did," James boomed from the doorway of the cabin. "Good shot, Serena. You didn't flinch once."

Serena beamed. "Thanks, Pa. I tried to remember everything you taught me, but it took me by surprise when it barged forward."

"Couldn't have handled it better myself."

She adored her father's praise. "You hungry? I just about have breakfast ready."

"Nigh starved," her pa replied. A grin spread across

his full face, as he wrapped his arms around Ma's waist.

Serena glanced at her ma, trembling beneath Pa's firm hold. Her grim expression left no question as to the fear she'd felt.

"She's fine," Pa said, obviously realizing Ma's apprehension. "She can handle a rifle better than most men."

Ma nodded and sniffed, blinking back tears. "There's a few things about our daughter, James Talbot, that I wish she hadn't gotten from you."

Chet cleared his throat. "Ma'am, I can understand your fright, but I'm glad she has her pa's eye and smooth pull on the trigger. Thank you, Miss Serena. I've been in a lot of dangerous places, but taking on a boar didn't rank among them. Praise God for your shootin'."

His words broke the tension flaring around them, and Ma laughed and cried at the same time.

"I'll get this overgrown pig out of the way so we can eat," Pa said. He released her ma and walked toward the dead animal, passing along a wink to Serena.

She handed his rifle to him, and he squeezed her hand. Fighting the urge to take a quick glimpse at Chet, she moved toward her ma, still quivering in the doorway. They held each other without uttering a word. Ma had been right; certain things only a woman could know, and Serena had just earned a note of admiration from Chet.

Once breakfast and chores were completed, Serena rode with Pa and Chet to Dugan Niall's. She felt completely immersed in the hill country around them—the cedars dressed in blue-green leaves and gnarly post oaks with an occasional mesquite tree. She admired patches of orange trumpet-shaped wildflowers, purple wide-leafed petals, and a host of yellow beauties. She listened to the singing insects and calling mockingbirds as they offered their lulling songs, but Serena knew the dangers of the land—more powerful than any wild animal.

Three races of proud people claimed Texas: the Mexicans, despite the war for independence; the Apache and Comanche Indians; and the proud Texans. She'd long ago decided whoever fought the hardest would have the vast land. Pa told her once if he'd been Mexican, he'd be fighting for them, and if he'd been born an Indian, he'd be warring alongside the red man. Lucky for Texas, James Talbot was a white man and believed in the Rangers.

"God did a pretty good job out here," Chet said, squinting as he stared up at a robin's-egg-colored sky. "No wonder the land's restless; everyone wants a piece of it."

"No matter the cost," Pa said. "He made Texas for those willing to die for it—or defend it like we do."

"Some folks claim we rangers are of the devil," Chet said, "but they sure call us angels when there's trouble."

Pa chuckled. " 'Cause we aren't afraid of anything—leastways, nothing we show. The only thing I hate is leaving my family so much. Guess I'm lucky Rachel knew my commitment to the Texas Rangers when we met. Sometimes it's right hard to push thoughts of her and Serena away when we're in the thick of things." He lowered his gaze at Chet. "You listen to me, now. God's done me a fair amount of blessings, but this is a life for a single man. Your head can't be clouded with anything but the job at hand."

Serena listened intently. Pa seldom talked so freely, and she knew every word meant something important.

The only thing was she didn't like what he had to say. Oh, he spoke the truth about wits and clear-headed thinking keeping the rangers alive and winning, but the yearning in her heart for Chet couldn't subside so easily. If Chet ever decided to look her way, he'd have to deal with Pa. Some said the devil could be more obliging than James Talbot when he was riled.

Lord, if me and Chet are supposed to be together, then let it happen. I'm already a Texas Ranger's daughter, and I can be a good ranger's wife. With Your help he could be right proud of me.

Dugan Niall met them as they rode up. He grinned from ear to ear. Most likely he anticipated the sale of his palomino and a stallion to Chet. Moira accompanied him along with a dozen other rusty-headed siblings.

"Aye, James, Chet, and Serena. Ya do me pleasure by stoppin' by. Is it the palomino you came for?" Dugan's Irish brogue sounded musical, and his wild, fiery-red hair and beard were a colorful match to his character.

"We sure are," her pa replied, lifting his hat and wiping the perspiration from his brow. "I want to give the mare to Serena before her birthday." He waved at the Niall clan. "Mornin' all you rooster tails."

They loved Pa's teasing and greeted him all at once.

Dugan's eyes twinkled, and he laughed till his round belly jiggled beneath his suspenders. "And you, Chet, do ya still have an eye for me stallion?"

"I'm just looking today, but I'm looking hard."

Dugan's mirth roared above the treetops. "First let's have some coffee. Me wife has just made a fresh pot."

Serena and Moira stayed outside, knowing the men

would be talking awhile. The two walked to the corral, where a half dozen fine horses grazed.

"Why's Mr. Wilkinson with you?" Moira asked, her brown eyes dancing.

"He and Pa are riding out in the morning," Serena replied, hoping her friend thought Chet's presence meant nothing to her.

"He's a mighty handsome man," Moira continued, her gaze lingering on the cabin door then back to the horses. "I'd give anything to have hair as yellow as his."

Serena frowned. "Your pa would skin you alive if he knew you were contemplating a ranger."

"Yours too. But they're right. Rangers live too hard a life for us. Besides. . ." She clasped her hands behind the back of her green print dress and teetered on her heels.

"Besides what?" Serena asked, feeling a giggle rise in her throat.

"Aaron Kent's been calling."

Clasping her hand to her mouth, Serena tried to stifle her enthusiasm. "Since when? How long has this been going on?" Aaron Kent had been widowed about a year, and he had two small young 'uns to raise.

"Three times now—and I'm not saying another word."

Serena couldn't help but laugh at her friend's serious face—the same round face as her pa's, beautiful skin and huge brown eyes. "Oh, you have never been able to keep secrets from me. And Aaron Kent is a good man, Moira, and easy to look at."

Moira blushed from her neck to her eyes. "He wants to talk to Pa."

The two girls hugged and, with no one in earshot,

began to plan Moira's wedding.

An hour later, Dugan and Chet settled on a price for a chestnut stallion to be picked up after the ranger's next pay, and Serena rode her palomino home. Pa paid a fine price for the mare, and the horse acted frisky enough to please Serena.

She patted the mare on its neck. "Pa, I know I said this before, but I really appreciate this horse. I'll take good care of her."

His dark blue eyes peered into hers. "I know you will. That's why she's yours."

Serena treasured the proud look in her pa's eyes. As a little girl, she'd lived for his special look and smile meant only for her. Now, she wished Chet would show some kind of affection. Certainly, she wouldn't have to save him from a wild boar again to get him to notice her.

Chet shifted uncomfortably in the saddle. James's little girl had gotten under his skin. First she surprised him with her age, next she shot a charging boar between the eyes without a flinch, and now she handled Dugan's newly broke mare like she'd been born in the saddle. Why hadn't he noticed these things before? It rightly embarrassed him. He needed to have shown a little more foresight or at least paid more attention to the Talbot household.

A Texas Ranger prided himself in his good judgment and intelligence. Many times he'd heard a good ranger needed to ride like a Mexican, trail like an Indian, shoot like a Tennessean, and fight like a devil. Nothing was ever said about sense with a woman. Good thing only the Lord knew his thoughts.

Ever since he learned about Serena's age, being around her made him feel rather peculiar, and today he found himself admiring her spunk. Of course, being the only child of James Talbot meant she knew how to handle herself like a man. He should have figured that out when he noticed she refused to use a sidesaddle. Scary thought when Chet had already angered her the night before.

He glanced her way, not really meaning to, and she smiled back at him. Her innocent look made his toes numb, and a chill raced up his spine. He'd never reacted like this to anything in his whole life. . .until now.

How many times had he thanked God for giving him a steady hand and a clear head? He prayed every time a bullet or arrow whizzed by without so much as piercing his clothes. Those qualities, vital to a ranger's way of life, kept him alive and able to defend his beloved Republic. In addition, he owed his life here and in eternity to the Lord. Jesus rode with him everywhere he went, guiding and giving him courage to complete the task of defending the people of Texas.

Chet prayed and studied God's Word every day of his life. He'd learned life didn't always happen like he figured, but he couldn't dwell on it. A man had to wait until the smoke cleared and see how God worked. He'd learned to expect the impossible and not flinch when trouble came knocking. But nothing had prepared him for these new findings about Miss Serena Talbot. The little lady kept amazing him everywhere he turned.

God must be chastising him for his prideful talk when he hurt Serena's feelings. Well, he'd never do it again. This strange feeling unnerved him.

"Pa, where are you headed tomorrow?" Serena asked, breaking the silence.

"Rio Grande," he said with no emotion creasing his rugged, lined face.

"How long are you going to be gone?" She knew Mexico and Texas were in heavy dispute over the border. The Republic claimed the Rio Grande, but Mexico insisted on the Nueces River.

"Couple of weeks, Little One. I plan to be back for your birthday."

Serena sighed. "It's not my birthday bothering me."

"I know." He sounded tired.

"I'm not complaining, Pa. I just love you."

Chet felt as though he shouldn't be hearing James and Serena's conversation. Rather too personal for his liking.

"Oh, if God would only let peace come to Texas," she said with a sigh. "Can you imagine Indians, Mexicans, and Texans all getting along like friendly neighbors? I mean, I know the Tonkawas, Choctaws, and Delaware sometimes scout for you."

Her pa nodded with a grim smile. "We've had some real good Mexicans help us out too."

"But I'm dreaming and talking like a child. As long as men walk the face of the earth, there will be war," she said. "And I do respect your commitment to Texas."

Her pa cleared his throat. "It doesn't matter who's threatening the lives of folks, they have to be stopped. If the Rangers don't step in, the innocent will die."

"I understand, Pa, I really do." Serena said nothing for a few minutes, then asked, "Do you believe we'll one day be a state?"

Her pa shook his head. "Hard to say. A lot of folks would like to think so."

"What would happen to the Rangers then?" she asked.

He chuckled. "Chet, you answer that one."

Serena turned in the saddle, her deep blue eyes penetrating his soul—trusting and seeking an answer.

Suddenly, Chet couldn't remember his own name.

Four

James slowed his horse to keep pace with Chet. The older man peered into his face. "Didn't you hear me?" he asked.

Again, Chet felt color burn his skin. "Ah, I reckon my mind went to wandering." Why did the cap'n have that angry glint in his eye?

James chewed on his lower lip, a sign indicating he contemplated a serious matter. "Serena wondered what might happen to the Rangers if Texas became a state."

Chet swallowed. He sure didn't like the hard look on James's face. He must have riled him, except the cap'n didn't get provoked too easily. "Hard to say," Chet began, determined to give the popular subject his best. "Statehood might be fine enough, but I don't think we'd get along with the army—have a hard enough time with the Republic's army. Too many rituals and regulations for me. I don't see any purpose in wearing uniforms or keeping my boots and buttons polished. And I couldn't ever take orders from a man I hadn't ridden with. Texas Rangers earn their rank by showing they have guts and use their heads. I can't respect a man simply 'cause he wears a fancy uniform."

Serena turned in the saddle to address him. The late morning sunlight fairly glistened in her dark hair, giving it a copper cast. "So do you think Texas could get along without the Rangers?"

"Texas will always need rangers," he said, sitting straighter in the saddle. "I guarantee you the US Army or our Republic's army would not consider any fighting without first sending us to clear the way."

She smiled, and he noticed her sparkling white teeth. "Thank you, Chet. I agree with you. Nobody can keep us safe like the Rangers." She reverted her gaze back to the path ahead, leaving him feeling plumb foolish. And he had no idea why.

"You and me need to talk," the cap'n said under his breath. He spurred his horse forward to ride alongside his daughter, leaving Chet short of bewildered.

Serena wondered what she'd said to embarrass him. He looked akin to a ripe tomato. Then she had a thought. He must be sweet on Moira and seeing her must have gotten him flustered. Serena supposed it didn't help matters any with her bold statement about him probably liking Moira. Her dear friend filled his requirements and looked comely too.

Pa had picked up on Chet's discomfort. Of course, Pa had a way of knowing what people were thinking long before they said a word.

A knot settled in Serena's throat. If Chet had eyes for Moira, Serena might as well forget anything ever blossoming between them. Her sweet friend would make a good wife. But. . .Moira said Aaron Kent had come calling, and she'd rambled on and on about him. Surely she'd rather have Aaron than Chet. At least the widower didn't live a dangerous life. Good thing she hadn't shared her dreams with Moira, especially with Chet possibly interested in the pretty redhead.

Lord, help me not to be selfish and jealous. I know I've given this to You, but it doesn't help this ache in my heart.

Maybe she did need to talk to Ma about Chet. Like Ma had said, some things only a woman understood.

By the time the three made it back to the cabin, Ma had a noonday meal almost ready for them. She'd pulled one of the hams from the smokehouse and cooked it with a bunch of fresh green beans. Ears of buttered corn boiled on the fire with a pan of corn bread baking beside the pot. Ma always cooked hearty meals when Pa came home.

Outside the barn, Ma admired Serena's palomino. She patted the mare's neck and let it nuzzle against her. "Beautiful horse. No wonder your pa had to have it for you. Have you a name for her yet?"

Truthfully, Serena had been thinking on it. "I like the name Fawn. The palomino's color puts me in mind of a baby deer."

"Sounds real fitting," her ma replied, giving the mare another pat, "and I don't recollect hearing a horse called by that name before."

"Would you like to go riding tomorrow evening?" Serena asked.

"Yes, I believe I would. Might be nice after your pa's gone."

Pa leaned up close to Ma and kissed her on the cheek. Tears welled in her pale blue eyes, a sadness seen much too often. Serena felt compassion wash over her. For a brief moment she asked herself if she really wanted the same heartache and separation in her life.

"Let me finish in the house," Serena said, gathering up her skirt. "I've had Pa to myself all morning, and now it's your turn."

Pa took Fawn's reins, and she left her parents to a few stolen moments alone. Chet tied his horse to a post and wordlessly followed Serena inside.

"Shall I tie an apron on you?" she teased. Odd, he looked uneasy. "Something ailing you, Chet?"

"No, nothing." He looked like a bull calf at a quilting bee.

"Why don't you sit down while I finish here?" She went about her business, trying to shake herself of his disturbing presence. What had happened to the free-talking ranger she'd known and grown to care about for the past two years?

Once Chet eased down onto a chair at the table and removed his hat, she ladled him a tall mug of water. He murmured his thanks and watched while she placed butter, dewberry preserves, and sliced tomatoes on the table. All the while, his piercing gaze increased her nervousness. While filling a huge bowl with the ham and green beans, she dropped a big wooden spoon on the floor. Snatching it up, she slammed the spoon on the table a little harder than she intended.

Exasperated, she began, "Chet Wilkinson, we've known each other for quite a spell, and you have never acted this way before. So, why don't you just tell me what's wrong? Are you sick? Did you and Pa have words? Are you still mad about last night or me shootin' the boar this morning?"

Chet raked his fingers through yellow hair. "You could pester a man to death with your questions."

"Oh," she said, raising a brow. "You certainly have gotten mean spirited all of a sudden. I was only trying to help."

He narrowed his pine green eyes and lifted the tin mug to his lips. In a huff, Serena covered the bowl of vegetables and ham with a clean towel and pulled out the plates and utensils. Realizing the corn must be ready on the cook fire, she grabbed another towel and bowl, then stormed outside.

What made her think Chet Wilkinson could possibly be the man God intended for her? The man had suddenly become intolerable and sullen. She didn't need a moody man, leastways one who couldn't answer a little question without getting sour as day-old milk.

She didn't need him, and neither did Moira. . .or any sensible woman. And he claimed to be a God-fearing man. He needed to spend more time in his Bible and less time on himself.

"Miss Serena."

She startled and dropped the towel, narrowly missing the fire. "That's the second time today you've scared me," she said, ready to take on the devil if necessary. Her gaze flew to his eyes, and she clearly met the contrite ranger. He held his dusty hat, toying with the brim and standing as though he'd been riding for a month without a stop. The pleading look in his eyes softened her. . .a little.

"I apologize for snapping at you. Don't know what

got into me, and. . .I didn't mean to ruffle your feelings," he said, then expelled a heavy breath.

Serena bit back a curt remark. Maybe he had the Rangers' next job on his mind—or the one they'd just come from. Pa rarely talked about the perils and circumstances about his work, and sometimes he was short when he fretted over a matter.

God instructed her to forgive.

"It's all right. You have your own feelings, and it's none of my business anyway." She bent to lift the kettle from the fire.

"I'm not used to women," he continued and bent to help her.

Serena smiled. That word sounded better all the time.

"Haven't seen my little sister or Ma in quite a spell. Guess I'm not used to y'all's ways."

She nodded. "I think we got along better when you considered me a little girl."

His eyes brightened, and he took the kettle of corn from her. "Oh, but then I learned the truth and got into trouble."

Serena laughed and the two walked toward the cabin. "I'm glad you're coming for my birthday."

"I think I'd like it. . .very much. Will I get in the way of your friend?"

"Moira?" Serena's heart suddenly plummeted.

"I didn't remember her name, but you might prefer having her all to yourself."

Her insides relaxed. "No, the more the better. In fact, Ma mentioned having all the Nialls come for supper. They're a wonderful family who care about each other and love the Lord. Mrs. Niall visits a lot when Pa's gone—makes Ma laugh and tells her stories about Ireland."

"I reckon being the wife of a ranger is real hard," he said. "Not too many women could handle it."

"Depends," Serena replied slowly, as a bushel of answers raced across her mind. "If a woman loves a man, she can't be happy unless she's a part of his life."

He opened the cabin door. She turned to thank him, but his gaze peered into hers and sent an unsettling chill up her spine.

"Imagine you would know." He hesitated, wetting his lips. "I mean, since your pa's a ranger and all. You'd know what kind of woman it took to marry up with one." His face reddened again, and she felt her own grow warm.

"I suppose," she said, placing a jar of honey on the table. "I don't know any other way."

He cleared his throat. "Would you be interested in taking a walk this afternoon and leaving your ma and pa to some time alone? Your ma looked real upset when we left them out there."

"I'd take kindly to your offer," she said. "The river's a nice cool spot."

"And I haven't been wading for fun in quite a spell."

Silence permeated the room. *Oh, Lord, are You making progress?*

Standing in the small room, arranging the rest of the meal about the table, Serena felt Chet's gaze studying her. Oh, for a woman's figure. She didn't relish the thought of Chet staring at a fence post. Her nose stuck out farther than her bosom.

She decided to sit across the table from him. With

everything ready but the corn bread, they'd eat as soon as Ma and Pa came in from the barn. In the meantime, she had the handsome ranger all to herself.

Searching for a topic that steered away from her fragile emotions, she remembered he and Pa would be leaving in the morning.

"I'll be praying for you and Pa's trip to the Rio Grande," she said, wishing her voice sounded stronger, more encouraging.

"Appreciate it," he said and laid his hat on the floor beside him. "We need all the prayers we can get."

Silence filled the corners of the cabin, and Serena wished she had something to do.

"Blueberries," Chet said, breaking the quiet surrounding them.

She lifted a questioning brow. Did he have a hankering for berry pie?

"Your eyes," he said, picking at a loose thread on the sleeve of his shirt, "are the color of ripe blueberries."

Before Serena could respond, the sounds of Ma and Pa laughing met her ears. Her parents entered. Ma's hair had slipped from her tightly wound bun, and her cheeks were rosy.

Pa's wide smile quickly changed to a frown when he saw Chet and Serena seated at the table. "After we eat," he said to Chet, "you and me are gonna have a long talk."

Five

C het had been hungry before James made his announcement, but his appetite soon disappeared. Second time today the cap'n announced a need for them to talk, which meant he planned to do the chewin', and Chet would do the listenin'.

Now he sat across from the cap'n, who cut his gaze at him sharper than a bowie knife. He was in a fine pucker about something. He'd been around James Talbot long enough to recognize a bad mood.

Serena already made him feel peculiar, and with her sitting so close beside him, droplets of sweat rolled down his cheeks. Fortunately, Mrs. Wilkinson still acted normal, and she smiled comforting-like while passing him the corn bread. Every bite of food hung in his throat, worse than his own cooking. The meal seemed to take forever.

Awhile later, James cleared his throat, rattling Chet's nerves. The cap'n stood and downed his coffee.

"Good food, Rachel," he said with an appreciative nod. "Chet, you coming?"

"Yes, Sir," he replied, sliding off the other end of the

bench he shared with Serena. "Thank you, Ma'am, for a fine meal."

Rachel smiled. "You're welcome, but you didn't eat much."

Chet noted a glimpse of compassion in her eyes. She must know what had upset the cap'n. He stole a look at Serena. She looked as confused as he felt.

Outside, he fell into step beside the cap'n. "Don't recollect what I did to anger you, but I reckon you're about to tell me."

"I am." His tone reminded Chet of the many dismal times on the trail when they'd be riding into a dangerous situation against the odds.

They strode away from the cabin and toward a huge post oak shading a corner of the pasture. Chet had enough of waiting, but the Bible had a lot to say on patience. So he leaned against the tree, first kicking up a mound of fire ants and then daring to peer into James's blue eyes, almost as intense as Serena's.

"We're leaving in the morning," the cap'n said, standing square in front of him without a trace of friendliness. He looped his thumbs in the waist of his pants.

"Yes, Sir."

"And I want you to forget everything about Serena."

Chet raised a brow. "Serena? What are you talking about?"

"Don't be acting like you've lost your senses."

Suddenly Chet felt anger race through him. "Well, maybe you ought to explain yourself, 'cause I have no idea what you're talking about."

James's jaw tightened. "You've been looking at her all

day like some moon-sick calf. And I've already told you that no ranger is going after my daughter."

Chet couldn't believe his ears. "You're seeing things. I'm not interested in Serena. I've only been making polite conversation."

James shook his head in disbelief. "For one ranger—a lick smarter than the rest—you sure are acting stupid."

Then it hit Chet. The uneasiness around Serena, the way he liked to see her smile, and those eyes. Maybe the cap'n did know something he didn't. He glanced at the cabin and back to James.

"I had no idea," Chet said, shifting from one foot to the other.

"Well, take notice," James said, jamming his finger into Chet's chest. "Don't be putting any fancy ideas in her head or dreaming up any of your own." He peered out over the horses grazing in the pasture. "I'm fixin' to promote you to lieutenant. You're a good ranger and you have the respect of the other men. Being a single man is the easiest way to do the best job."

Chet expelled a heavy sigh. "I understand about Serena, and I appreciate the promotion."

"Good. We've settled this little matter, and now we can head back and get us some more corn bread and honey."

Wonderful, Chet thought. *Something else to stick in my throat.*

Back inside the cabin, Chet couldn't bring himself to look at Serena. What had happened to him since he learned Cap'n James Talbot's skinny little girl had grown into a woman? She still looked the same, didn't she? He'd noticed her pretty face before, but he'd never really talked to her until today. Or experienced such unnerving thoughts about a woman.

He swallowed hard. Flashes of last night and today darted across his mind. He admired Serena, and she'd surprised him a time or two, but he thought he kept those notions to himself. Obviously not. He hoped she hadn't sensed the same thing.

"Chet here just got a promotion," the cap'n said after a few moments. He'd piled his plate high with corn bread, added a hill of butter, and poured honey over it. "He's now Lieutenant Chet Wilkinson."

"Has a good ring to it," Serena said, flashing him a smile.

"A lieutenant has to deal with a lot of responsibility," Rachel said, refilling his coffee mug. "But I'm sure you've earned the title."

The cap'n offered a wry smile. "You earned it last August at the Battle of Plum Creek when we fought Buffalo Hump over his prisoners and loot taken at Linnville. You demonstrated real grit, and I haven't forgotten it."

Chet remembered how the Tonkawa Indian scouts had assisted the Rangers in tracking down the Comanche warriors who had attacked and destroyed an entire Texas town. "They would have made off with it all, if Buffalo Hump hadn't been so concerned about saving his loot, especially the nearly three thousand head of horses."

James is right, Chet thought. *My life is too risky to ask a woman to share it with me.* Suddenly Chet startled. When had he begun thinking about Serena as a wife? He felt himself grow increasingly uncomfortable. No doubt he looked as red as a ripe tomato.

"I'm committed to the Rangers," Chet said, knowing the cap'n expected him to share his beliefs. "God first and Texas second."

"As it should be," Serena replied, folding her hands on the table in front of her. "Your folks will be glad to hear the news. I know I'd be proud if we were kin."

The cap'n cleared his throat, and Chet felt an invisible bullet pierce his heart. *Lord, help me. I think I've fallen in love with Serena Talbot. How does a man prepare himself for something like this? I haven't been looking, and she isn't the woman I thought You wanted for me. Worse yet, I'm bound by my pledge to the Texas Rangers and her pa to do nothing about it.*

Serena hummed her way through the chore of clearing the table from the noon meal. Pa and Chet were outside, probably talking about what awaited them along the Rio Grande.

"The palomino sure has made you happy," her mother said, gathering up the dishes to wash them outside.

"Oh, yes. Fawn is a beautiful horse." Serena remembered again Chet's likening her eyes to ripe blueberries. "Some other things besides my birthday gift have me feeling good."

Ma stood in the doorway with her hands full. She paused and set the load back on the table. "Chet noticing you?"

Serena couldn't help smiling. It seemed to start from her heart and burst through to her face. "I believe so. He asked me to take a walk this afternoon so you and Pa can have some time alone. Maybe I'll know more before he and Pa leave in the morning."

"Your pa knows."

Serena felt her stomach twist. "He does? Did he say so?"

"Yes, and he's not pleased."

She sighed and peered into her mother's eyes. "With me or Chet?"

"Both."

"So I imagine Pa will talk to him about it on the way to the Rio Grande."

Her mother shook her head. "He already has—right after we ate."

"So that's why Chet didn't say much," Serena said, thinking out loud. She blinked back a single tear and focused her attention on covering the honey jar.

"You know how your pa feels about you taking up with a Ranger." Ma's words sounded gentle, not chiding or finding fault.

Serena nodded, avoiding her mother's gaze. "Yes, Ma'am, I know. But I think I should be able to choose how I spend my life."

"I felt the same way too. I was younger than you when I fell in love with your pa—your age when I had a baby in tow."

"Have you ever regretted marrying Pa?" Serena asked, wringing her hands and turning to face her ma.

Her ma smiled through her own tears. "Never. I love him more now than ever. I fret and I miss him, but he's the man God gave me. Loving a ranger is hard, but I wouldn't have it any other way."

"And what if I have the same feelings for Chet?"

Ma tucked a loose curl behind Serena's ear and slowly nodded. "I understand, but we both have to respect your pa's wishes."

Serena considered the matter, not ready to relinquish her heart so easily. "I've already given the matter to God. If Chet and I are to be together, He will change Pa's heart and mind."

"And I'll ask God to give you the peace and courage to accept whatever He deems proper," her ma said. With a quick hug, she gathered up the dirty dishes and stepped outside.

Serena caught a glimpse of Pa and Chet walking across the pasture toward their horses. The two men looked as different as day and night—Pa with his nearly black hair, like hers, and Chet with his sun-colored, wayward locks. Even beneath his hat, Chet's hair tended to stick out every which way. But they were a lot alike, sharing characteristics neither would most likely own up to. Both had a stubborn streak, a unique way of thinking things through, a strong sense of values, and a love for the Lord.

She sensed Pa would deny a walk to the river, unless he really wanted to spend time with Ma. Odd, Chet hadn't even mentioned being interested in her, and already the thought had been dismissed. Pa must have picked up on something she didn't know about, but then her pa had a way of reading a person's mind. He simply knew things before anyone else did.

A smile surfaced through her low spirits. *Blueberry eyes.* She wondered how long it took Chet to think up such a sweet description. Serena hoped a long spell. She'd like to know he'd been pondering over her during the long nights on the trail. Impossible. He'd just found out about her age last evening.

A wave of sadness blew over her, much like the foreboding wind sweeping through the trees before a thunderstorm. Serena knew she could do nothing about Pa's bidding, but only pray and trust God to work things out for good.

After Serena finished cleaning inside the cabin, she joined Ma outside to finish washing and wiping the dishes. Squaring her shoulders and pushing away her pride, she resolved her ma wouldn't see the ache in her heart. Maybe she could fool Pa too.

"Everything will work out for the best," her ma said. She dried her hands on her apron and wrapped her arm around Serena's shoulders.

"I know," she replied more confidently than she felt.

"If it makes you feel any better, when your pa came calling, my pa ordered him to never set foot on his property again."

"What did you do?" Serena asked, curiosity gaining the best of her.

"Well, James isn't going to like me telling you this. . . but I reckon I will. He showed up at my door and told my pa he wasn't leaving until he got permission to marry me. My pa threatened him with a shotgun. No daughter of his was going to marry a wild Indian fighter, but your pa got off his horse and stood there until Pa gave his consent."

"How long did it take?"

Her ma laughed. "Close to seventeen hours. My pa

said later he figured an hour for every year."

Laughing with her ma, Serena finally sobered and asked, "Would Pa be that stubborn about Chet?"

Ma gazed into her eyes. "Since your pa decided beforehand to stand there a week if he had to, I'd say he'd be even worse now." She kissed Serena's cheek. "Better stick to praying."

Six

Before Serena and her ma could speak any further, Chet and her pa ambled toward them. One reminded her of a mountain cat, the other a bear. Pa laughed about something and Chet joined in. Maybe things between them weren't so bad after all, unless Chet had agreed to her pa's demands.

"Rachel," Pa said, "Chet has volunteered to keep Serena company for a spell so you and I can have a little time together. He first suggested a walk along the river, then decided fishing sounded better. What do you think?"

Ma beamed and flashed Chet an approving glance. "I think the new lieutenant has a wonderful idea."

"I like it too," Serena said, trying to hide her eagerness. Could it be her pa had changed his mind?

Pa frowned, narrowing his dark blue gaze. "Well, I expect plenty of fish for supper."

An inward sigh coursed through her. She guessed nothing had changed. "Oh, course," Serena said. "I'll fry them up tonight."

"And I'll clean them," Chet added.

Ma rose from the ground and handed Pa the pan of

clean dishes. A flush of pink tinted her cheeks. She whisked off her apron and smiled with a special smile meant only for him. "We're finished here, and it looks like supper is taken care of."

A broad grin slowly spread across Pa's face. "Are you still of the mind to see those mustangs I spotted a few weeks ago?" he asked, heading toward the cabin with Ma right beside him.

She slid her arm around his waist and leaned against his shoulder. Serena didn't hear what she said. Perhaps the words were only for Pa's ears.

Serena glanced at Chet and found him staring at her. The glint in his eyes didn't look like anything she had seen from him before. It made her feel downright fretful.

"I reckon we'd better gather up what we need," he said, kicking at the dust. "Suppose it's all in the barn?"

"Yes, on the wall opposite where the bridles hang." She clenched her fists to control her nervousness. "Which one of us gets to dig for worms?"

Chet chuckled. "Oh, I suppose if you bring a couple of canteens of water, I'll get the bait."

She relaxed slightly. "You have a deal. Do you want me to pack any food? You didn't eat much."

Chet studied a spider crossing over the toe of his boot. "Most likely so, especially since your pa is expecting us to catch a mess of fish. He must have a powerful taste for them."

"And we wouldn't want to disappoint him."

"Or rile him."

All the while she busied herself with food and water

for later in the afternoon, she wondered if Chet might mention Pa's ultimatum about her. Of course, nothing had ever been said to her anyway. . .except the comment about her eyes. The color of ripe blueberries. She simply couldn't get his words out of her head, simply because Chet hadn't said anything else to give her hope.

Chet stomped the shovel into the ground with such force he feared breaking it. Snatching up a couple of worms, he pitched the wiggling creatures into a wooden bucket. His thoughts spun with James's instructions about Serena. He understood the reason why the cap'n didn't want him seeing Serena, and given the same circumstances, he'd most likely feel the same way.

But something had happened to him, and now a whisper of her voice sent a funny tingle up his spine. He liked the way she wore her thick, dark hair down, the healthy glow of her skin, and the sprinkling of freckles across her nose. Most of all he liked those huge eyes. He could drown and go to paradise in them—nearly had this morning. He did wish she had a mite more meat on her bones, to make her a little stronger. A woman needed strength in this Texas wild to hold up with the hard work.

Chet sunk the shovel into the ground again. The cap'n would skin him alive if he knew his thoughts about Serena.

Oh, Lord, You've pulled me out of more scrapes than I care to mention, but this one is the worst. I don't know whether to ask You to take away my feelings for Serena or show me a way to convince her pa.

Within the hour, Serena and Chet wandered nearly

two miles up the riverbank to the fishing hole. Tall oaks and cypress trees kept them cool while the quietness of nature soothed Chet's racing mind. Now and then a crow called or the distant drum of a woodpecker broke his musings. A snake with familiar coloring slithered across his path.

"Watch out, a copperhead just raced in front of me."

She laughed lightly. "As long as he doesn't head back this direction, I'm fine."

Her laughter reminded him of a Mexican guitar on a still night, when the only sounds were singing insects and the crackling fire. Easy and soothing.

"We're almost there," she said and pointed to the river. "See that fallen tree where you can walk across to the other side? It's right on past where the river widens."

In a short while, they dipped their lines into the gently rolling water and sat down on a grassy knoll beside a cypress tree.

"Isn't this a pretty spot?" she asked, barely above a whisper.

He cradled his head in his hands and leaned back on the green earth, crossing his ankles and balancing his pole between his boots. "I like the peacefulness. Makes me wonder if heaven could be like this."

"I hope so. I mean, I can't imagine any place more lovely."

"Tennessee's pretty and green like this."

"Your family lives there?"

He nodded. "Ma, Pa, and six sisters."

She laughed. "I can't imagine you in a house full of girls. I suppose all those sisters made life interesting."

"Don't know if *interesting* is the word I'd use to describe it. But I did my share of pestering them."

She gazed out over the smooth river. "Do you miss them?"

"Oh, sometimes. We had good times, and my pa is a preacher."

"So he led you to the Lord?"

Chet chuckled and stared up at the sky. "Not exactly. When I was fourteen, I got chased up a tree by a bear. I figured that was as good a time as any to call on the Lord. Been calling on Him ever since."

"Well, I'm sure your family is proud of you."

He shrugged. "Suppose so—never thought on it much."

"Oh, I'm sure they are. Did you happen to bring your Bible?"

Her question surprised him. "No, I'm sorry. Left it in my saddlebag."

She plucked a purple wildflower and let it rest on the skirt of her deep green dress. "I've been thinking some of the Psalms would sound good now."

"Yeah, they would." He hesitated. "Serena, do you believe God has a plan for us? I mean all of us."

A bit of pink touched her cheeks. "Oh yes, and I also think we can make big mistakes by not listening to Him."

"Do you think rangerin' glorifies God? With the killing, it makes me wonder if I'm living like I should."

Tilting her head slightly, she appeared to ponder the matter. "We both know God hates killing. But if a man does nothing while his family and friends are murdered, then who's the real murderer?"

"Yeah, you feel the same way I do. I'd sure like to see

this country safe for folks to live peaceful-like. Seems like it won't happen in my lifetime, though. The Republic is having a hard time getting established, and peace with the Indians and Mexico is afar off. Makes a man tired thinking about it."

"You're just the man to help tame Texas, and I'm praying for you," she said and offered him a smile so sweet he wanted to pull her into his arms and protect her forever.

"Thanks. You know, sometimes I think I'd like to be a preacher, but. . ." He laughed aloud. "I'm afraid I'd rough up anyone fallin' asleep during a sermon."

Serena continued to smile. "Well, folks would be more apt to pay attention."

"Imagine so." He pulled himself up from the grass on his elbow and rubbed the back of his neck. "I like you, Serena."

"And I like you."

"I mean, a lot."

"And I like you a lot, too."

They went back to fishing then, neither saying a word while Chet felt perfectly content sitting beside her. An hour passed and they hadn't caught a fish, not even one small enough to toss back in.

Serena deliberated upon her pa's words. He wanted a whole string of fish, and right now they had nothing. The thought worried her. She was his only child, and her pa could be stubborn about some things. He seemed to forget she'd be eighteen years old soon.

"Chet, we haven't caught a thing," she said.

A furrow creased his brow, and he expelled a heavy breath. "The cap'n is expecting fish for supper."

"I know. He'll be disappointed."

"No, he'll be wrathful," Chet said.

"Pa wouldn't get mad because the fish weren't biting."

"He's more concerned about things other than what we pull out of this river."

Serena's heart pounded hard against her chest. "Your job along the Rio Grande?"

"No."

Silence seemed to deafen her. She couldn't think of anything to say or ask. So he lay back down on the grass, and they sat for another half hour waiting for the fish to bite.

"Are you hungry?" Serena asked when she heard his stomach growl.

"Yeah." He glanced up at the sky. "A little food would be nice."

She stood and walked over to the leather pouch containing leftovers from earlier. Refusing to dwell on Pa's anger when he would find out they hadn't caught any fish, she pulled out biscuits and corn bread left from breakfast and chunks of smoked ham and laid them on a cloth. The canteens held plenty of water.

"Here we are," she said, doing her best to sound cheerful. Spreading the cloth between them, she urged him to eat, but she had no appetite, no fish for Pa, and no endearing words from Chet.

"Aren't you hungry?" he asked, after downing a thick biscuit with a layer of ham tucked inside.

"No, go ahead. Can I ask you something?"

"Sure."

"Will you still be here for my birthday, like you said

last night?" She held her breath, almost afraid of his reply.

Chet wiped his mouth with the back of his hand and took a swallow of water. "Serena," he said softly.

She peered into his face, and if somebody had asked her, she wouldn't have known her own name.

"We both know why the cap'n is expecting a whole mess of fish."

She took a deep breath and nodded. A noisy blue jay chased a squirrel up a tree, reminding her of Pa chasing Chet.

"So what are we gonna do about it?" he asked.

The gurgling sound of the river hitting the rocks masked her fluttering heart. She wet her lips and tried to form her words. "I don't know."

"I've been praying for what's right—not saying a word to you and abiding by your pa or speaking my mind."

Her heart pounded so hard, she could barely breathe. "Since you spoke up, what have you decided?"

"Aw," and he tossed a pebble into the water, skimming it in wide circles. "Both."

Stunned, Serena gazed into his eyes, then hastily glanced away. "Then say your piece."

He leaned on his side again, still balancing the fishing pole with his boots. "I need to tell you how I feel. Not sure why, except I'm about to explode like a hundred shotgun blasts." Taking a deep breath, he continued. "I believe I've fallen in love with you, Serena, and your pa would have my hide for saying it."

She felt herself trembling. How many nights had she lain awake dreaming of Chet telling her those words? Did she dare reply? "I. . .I feel the same," she managed.

He snapped off a blade of grass. "Might be easier if you didn't. I didn't mean to stir up any more trouble than I already have."

She fidgeted with the petals of her wildflower. "So you believe there's nothing we can do?"

The tension between them could have been split with an axe.

"Well, I certainly hadn't planned on this, and life with me wouldn't be easy. I reckon I could give up rangering. It might ease things with your pa."

Serena shook her head. "You belong with the Rangers. It's your life, like breathing. I wouldn't ever ask you to give it up. There's bound to be another way."

He chuckled and squinted up at her with the blade of grass sticking out his mouth. "Sure wish God would tell me what to do."

"Me too."

"Funny how I've known you all this time and never thought about you as more than a friend. . . ."

"James Talbot's little girl."

He grinned. "And now I can't seem to get you off my mind."

About then his pole jerked, and he grabbed it. Sure enough, Chet had a fish. "By golly, look at the size of that bass," he said, pulling in the line.

"And there's bound to be more." She studied her line. It wiggled and bobbed up and down. "Chet, I've got one too."

A moment later, she pulled in a huge bass, bigger than his.

Suddenly they both started to laugh. How utterly

ridiculous to become so excited about two fish, yet they were. They both quickly baited their lines and tossed them out again. Before she could consider what was happening, Chet swooped her up into his arms and whirled her around.

That started the trouble. The moment his hands touched her waist, she felt her arms chill and her toes grow numb. Chet must have sensed her feelings, for his gaze softened and he lowered her to the ground. His fingers reached to brush across her cheek, then trace her lips. He lifted her chin, and she felt her pulse race faster than she believed possible. Staring into his pine green eyes, she believed her dreams had come true.

"Serena, I have to kiss you this once. I may never have a chance again."

When he bent to lightly touch his lips to hers, she encircled his neck and allowed him to draw her closer. His kiss deepened, and she gladly melted into his arms.

"Oh, Serena," he whispered, "I shouldn't have done this, but I can't help myself." He drew his fingers through her hair.

"What is going on here?"

Serena and Chet instantly stiffened. James Talbot stood before them, pistol in hand.

Seven

Serena instantly tore herself away from Chet's embrace. With a gasp, she felt a tinge dizzy and her knees weakened. Pa stared at her as though she'd done something terrible. And he looked at Chet as though he'd done something worse.

Ma dismounted from her bay mare and touched Pa's shoulder. "Easy, James. We talked about this," she said, but the scowl on his face could have carved out a mountain.

"Pa," Serena said, lifting her chin. "Nothing's going on here. We. . ."

Chet touched her arm. "This is my fault. I'll handle it."

"Like you handled my daughter today?" her pa asked evenly. He handed Ma the reins to his horse while his finger rested a hair's span from the trigger.

"I'd like to explain, Cap'n, if you'd give me a chance."

Chet's words relayed confidence, but a sideways glance at him told Serena he felt anything but self-assured. Serena refused to move, believing her silence might hold Pa back from ending the dilemma about her and Chet once and for all.

"I have eyes," Pa said, slowly nodding his head to

emphasize each word. "Didn't I tell you what wouldn't happen between you and Serena?"

"You did the talkin' and I listened," Chet said. "I understand how you feel about your daughter, but you don't understand how we feel about each other."

The surroundings grew oddly quiet. A few insects braved the tension, and a mockingbird seemed to mock them. The air grew hot and humid.

"Maybe you need to calm a bit, James," Ma said, breaking the silence. "Serena's old enough to know her mind."

Thanks, Ma. Lord help us. We've got ourselves in a fine fix.

"Not when it comes to Texas Rangers," Pa said. His voice sounded cold and steady. "Rachel, you and Serena head back to the cabin. Chet and I have business right here."

"Please, Pa. You're sending me away like a child."

"Serena." His voice rose.

She stopped herself, knowing better than to defy her pa when he had his mind set. She glanced at Chet, and he motioned for her to step toward Ma.

"Cap'n, forbidding me and Serena to see each other isn't going to help the situation at all."

"I'll be the judge of that, since I'm her pa."

"By filling me full of holes once the women are gone?"

"I might."

"James, you and Chet have no business fussin' with each other right now. Won't solve a thing," Rachel said, slipping her arms around Serena's waist. "You two have been friends for quite a spell, and this is not the way to end it."

"You're right," her pa said, not once glancing at Ma or Serena. His fingers still rested entirely too close to the trigger. "So I'm a fixin' to send him on ahead to meet the other boys. You two head back to the cabin, and I'll give the *lieutenant* his orders. He might need special instructions, since he appears to be hard of hearing."

Serena saw an angry spark in Chet's eyes. How could the two men she loved be at such odds with each other?

"Cap'n, this won't work," Chet said, crossing his arms defiantly and standing square. "You can send me on ahead, but you can't stop me from having feelings for Serena."

"Feel what you want—but you ain't touching my daughter again."

"You make it sound like I've done a bad thing here."

Ma urged Serena to take Pa's horse. Grasping the reins, she climbed on the saddle, braving one last look at Chet. His composed expression gave her the chills. No wonder he was one of Pa's best rangers. She wouldn't want to face either one of them knee-deep in trouble.

Brokenhearted, she pulled Pa's horse behind the mare. How could he not understand a man and a woman in love? As they passed the men, Chet made a comment, but Pa bellowed about God intending for a man to respect another man's words.

The horses clipped along at a trot, single file along the path she and Chet had walked hours before. Behind her the muffled sounds of the arguing men churned her insides, and before her lay nothing but loneliness without Chet—before it had even begun.

When Ma slowed her mare to ride side by side with Serena, she could no longer contain her sorrow. "Ma, how could Pa be so mean?" she asked, her eyes brimming with tears.

She sighed and slowed her horse to a halt. "Oh. . .he simply sees too much of himself in Chet," her ma replied. She gazed at her through pale blue eyes and smiled sadly. "I hate this for you because I remember all those same feelings."

"But you two made it just fine."

"Yes, we have. Your pa loves you, Serena, but he doesn't want you spending night after night alone and worrying over the man you love."

Serena stiffened, her heart beating furiously in righteous indignation. "Ma, I'm a full-grown woman. I know my heart and mind, and it's with Chet."

"Then you best be praying God does a mighty work in your pa 'cause his mind is dead set against any ranger courtin' his daughter." She sighed and glanced up into the treetops. "I ought to know, I spent the better part of the past few hours trying to convince him."

Gratitude entwined with love washed over Serena. "Oh, Ma, I'm so sorry. You didn't have to use your time with Pa discussing Chet and me. He and I will figure this out."

Her mother raised a brow and peered into Serena's face. "That's what I'm afraid of."

"Ma, you know I mean we're expecting God to work out this problem with Pa."

"And He doesn't need your help."

Chet expelled a heavy sigh as he reined his horse away from the Talbot cabin. The orangey-red shadows of evening clung to him, reminding him a portion of his life was fading into a memory. He'd found love and lost it in two short days. He'd known Serena better than two years and liked her as a little girl—and loved her as a woman.

The cap'n had sure enough wanted to blow a hole through him. Never had he seen him so mad, and nothing Chet said could move him. Not once had the cap'n moved his hand away from his gun.

"I'm not out to hurt her," he'd told the cap'n.

"Don't you think being away from her all the time is gonna hurt her? It ain't just hard, ya fool. The pain in a woman's eyes stays with you all the time."

He realized then how much James loved Serena. Maybe Chet needed to do some thinking on it. Maybe the cap'n made sense after all. He didn't want to be selfish or come between a man and his daughter. Swallowing his pride, he had walked back to the barn, packed up his gear, and left, not once seeing Serena inside the cabin.

Now he rode alone to meet up with eighteen rangers who served under Cap'n Talbot. They'd be anxious to head for the Rio Grande as soon as they could. God have mercy on anyone who got in James's way on this job, be it the enemy or a ranger.

Lord, I don't want this to be hard on Serena. She looked powerfully unhappy riding away with her ma. Her sweet face seems to be branded on my mind and heart. What choice do I have but to turn it all over to You and let You work on my heart and her pa's? So I'm trusting You with my love for Serena and whatever is best for her.

He felt better. A sense of peace settled upon him like a cool breeze on a hot day. No need to fret over the matter because God had already handled it. Chet would simply do his job, think about Serena when night folded in around him, and wait for the good Lord's answer.

For a moment, he wondered if God had any idea how intolerable James Talbot could be when upset.

Days later, after a bloody battle with a gang of Comanches, Mexicans, and white raiders, scattering some *bandidos* by the wayside and others racing deep into Mexico, the cap'n approached him.

"You're a good ranger, Chet, and I've always been able to depend on you."

Surprised, since James hadn't spoken more than two words to him in three weeks, Chet stuck out his hand. As the two men grasped calloused hands, he stared into the cap'n's eyes and saw respect, nothing more.

"I hate this difference between us," Chet said. "Wish we could talk it out."

The cap'n expelled a heavy breath and released the handshake, as though contemplating Chet's words. "Someday you might have a wife and family. Until then you won't understand what I have to do to protect mine. There's no changing my mind. You know my Serena is a frail thing. She couldn't handle this life."

Chet said nothing. God had already spoken to him about the cap'n's daughter. In his heart, he knew God had a plan for him and Serena. He felt certain they would end up together.

Serena pulled a brush through her dark tresses, as always, her mind on Chet. Today marked her eighteenth birthday, and he'd promised to be there, but Pa had come in late last night alone. She'd been foolish to think Pa would allow Chet to visit.

Her pa had refused to talk about Chet before he left the last time, and their good-bye had been strained. She remembered her and Ma's words.

"Why does Pa have to be so mule headed?" she'd asked, digging her fingers into her palms as she and Ma watched Pa ride just beyond earshot.

"You'd be the best one to answer that," Ma said, smiling and waving although she could no longer see him. "Since you're both just alike in many respects. You, James, and Chet. . .stubborn and lovable."

The reply stung and brought a well of tears to her eyes. She turned away and headed back inside the cabin. The truth always hurt more than she cared to admit.

She even confessed to Moira about the whole thing with Chet. Her dear friend listened and held Serena while she cried. Neither of them could think of a solution but to seek God for the answers.

They didn't hear from Pa for nearly four weeks, and when he'd ridden in last night, Serena felt uncomfortable. Oh, she hugged him and welcomed him home, but uneasiness rested between them.

She wanted to tell him about the palomino and how the horse responded so well to her commands, but the words wouldn't come.

She wanted to tell him how she'd worried he might have been hurt, but her heart ached to hear about Chet.

She wanted to cry on his big strong shoulders and tell him how miserable she felt since their parting, but she wanted Chet's arms around her too.

Serena knew she needed to talk to Pa and had prayed about it more than once, but the words refused to come. As the beginnings of light filtered through her tiny window on this, her birthday, Serena felt miserable. She wanted her relationship back with Pa and Chet. Had God forgotten her?

Rising and dressing in her favorite sky-blue dress, she attempted to concentrate on the Niall family coming later on in the afternoon. Yesterday she and Ma had cooked most of the day for the birthday dinner. It would be a wonderful celebration, and Serena vowed to cover her broken heart with a smile. No one would see how she truly felt about Chet Wilkinson, and she knew he dare not be there today. Pa had probably threatened to shoot him on sight.

As was her custom when Pa first arrived home, Serena went about making breakfast while her parents slept. But her determination did not stop a few tears trickling into the coffeepot.

All too soon she heard the murmuring of voices from the other room. Determined and inhaling deeply, she pasted on a smile.

"Mornin', Little One," Pa said, standing barefoot in the kitchen.

He sounded cheerful and it nearly broke her heart with the differences between them. "Mornin', Pa. I've got coffee brewing outside."

"Sounds good. Happy birthday."

"Thank you, Pa." She smiled into his eyes, the same color as hers. "I'll fetch you some." She snatched up a mug and started for the door.

"I'll get it," he said, his eyes searching hers. "I'd like to take a look at your horse."

"She's a fine mare." Serena felt like her words were memorized from some book. She hurt all over.

"Would you go with me to take a look?"

She fought the urge to cry and tried to suppress every semblance of her emotions. "Sure, Pa, but breakfast is almost ready, and I don't want it to burn."

"We won't be gone but a minute."

They stepped through the door and saw Chet sitting atop his horse, leaning on the saddle horn.

"Cap'n, I told Serena I'd be here for her birthday."

Eight

H ave you no more brains than a stunned mule, Wilkinson?" Pa asked, his fists clenched as he stepped toward Chet. "We settled this weeks ago. You're not to see Serena, not now or ever."

Chet's gaze didn't waver. He straightened and pushed back his weather-beaten hat. "I told her I'd be here, and I aim to keep my word." He paused. "Although I discovered another matter over the past few days that should interest you."

Pa's eyes narrowed. "What might it be before I run you off?"

"You've been followed, and it might be a bit serious."

Pa leaned against the door, disbelief pouring from him like a swollen water hole.

"Do you want to take a look at the tracks or blow a hole through me?"

Serena held her breath. Chet spoke calm, quiet-like, causing her to shiver. He had yet to glance her way, but then again, she didn't expect him to.

Pa licked his lips. "You'd best not be lyin' about this."

"I don't have a reason to."

"All right, show me. Serena, get my rifle and boots."

She felt riveted to the wooden step beneath her feet, but a second look from Pa spurred her after his things. A moment later she emerged from the cabin to see Chet had dismounted and tied his horse to the hitching post. Still, he avoided her.

"Let's see those tracks and hear you out before you get going," Pa said, reaching for the firearm and his boots. He glanced back at her and scratched his stubbly cheek. "You wait inside."

"Pa. . ."

"Tend to breakfast, Little One. This ain't easy for me either." His gaze softened before he turned and ambled toward Chet.

Resigning herself to obey, she allowed one glimpse of Chet's face. She met his smile and saw the love she'd dreamed about every night since she could remember. Her spirit soared, and without a word, she whirled and walked inside.

Ma stood in the cabin, still dressed in her nightgown, sleep etched on her face. "Chet's here?" she asked, combing her fingers through tousled brown hair.

"Yes, Ma'am. He and Pa are talking outside. Not all of it about me. Chet said someone trailed Pa here last night and—"

A rifle shot split the air. Serena's gaze flew to her ma's. Color drained from her face, and Serena felt her heart seemingly leap from her chest. They scrambled through the door. Fear for Pa and Chet ran deeper than anything awaiting them.

Not forty feet from the cabin, Pa lay on the ground,

one hand clutching his side and the other wrapped around his rifle. Blood oozed through his fingers, forming a crimson pool beside him.

"James, no!" Ma's screams pierced the air.

Serena lost any thoughts of danger, and despite her ma's and both men's protests, hurried to his aid with her ma close behind. She and Serena bent behind his head and each grabbed under an arm to pull him from the blood-caked earth toward the cabin.

With one hand on his rifle, Chet peered in the direction of the barn and helped drag Pa on to safety. Another shot clipped Pa's leg.

"We got you, Talbot," a man's voice called in a heavy Mexican accent, "right where we want you."

Raucous laughter rang from the barn, enough to tell Serena more than one man lay in wait. Terror ripped through her body. For a moment it paralyzed her thoughts, except for a need to help get her pa inside. She caught his dulled gaze before he closed his eyes with the pain obviously wrenching through his body.

Chet snatched up a pistol then his gun belt and powder horn from his saddle. He fired again just before another shot zinged over his head. Stepping inside the cabin after Serena and her ma, he slammed the door shut.

Ma gathered up clean rags and pressed them against Pa's side. "It's gone clean through," she said, her features rigid and her hands trembling. "Good, I guess. . .no bullet to remove."

Serena lifted her pa's rifle from his arms and laid it on the table. "His leg's not bad, Ma. I'll wrap it."

"Cursed *bandidos*," Pa managed, biting his lower lip.

"We should have chased them into Mexico and ended it."

"They'll wish they'd stayed there by the time I'm finished with them," Chet said, staring out the window. "I counted three of them, Cap'n."

Ma used her apron to wipe the sweat trickling down Pa's face. She took a clean piece of muslin from Serena and dabbed at the blood running down his leg. "Who are they?" Ma asked.

"What's left of a murdering bunch we chased across the Rio," Chet replied, searching the area between them and the barn.

"We got two bloodthirsty Texans," the unseen man called out, his boasting echoing around them. "You both come out and the women go free."

"Do they think we're stupid?" Serena asked, picking up Pa's rifle and toying with it in her hands. *God, help us. I'm scared, real scared.* Bloodstains on the wooden floor tore at her senses.

"Give me my rifle," her pa said, his words raspy and labored. He lifted his arm, but his strength failed him.

"No," she replied, feeling a strange mixture of anger and courage. "You aren't in any shape to help Chet. Besides, I'm a ranger's daughter, and I know how to use this." She turned her attention to Chet and hoisted the rifle into her arms. "Pa knows I've beat him a time or two at target practice."

"Sere—" But Pa couldn't finish. He'd passed out.

"All right," Chet began, still keeping watch through the window. "We can handle this. Mrs. Wilkinson, I need you to keep the guns loaded for Serena and me. Looks like three apiece." He glanced about him. "Do you know how to measure the powder and load them?"

"Yes," Ma managed, not once taking her sights from Pa's face. "I. . .I can keep them loaded."

"Serena, take the window in the other room." He motioned to Ma and Pa's bedroom. She grabbed a pistol. The two guns were heavy, but at least she knew how to use them.

"What do you think they will try to do?" she asked.

"Shoot at us until they get tired, then most likely set fire to the cabin."

Her gaze swung in his direction. "So what do we do?"

"Prayer would help." The look he gave her pointed to the seriousness of their position.

Another rifle shot pierced the air and lodged in the side of the door. Thankfully, Pa had insisted on a heavy piece of wood.

From her position, Serena saw Chet haul a chair across the floor to the window and balance one of the rifles on it and through the window. Snatching off his hat, he propped it atop the trigger.

"I'm going out the back," he said, grasping a loaded rifle and a pistol. "Keep 'em busy."

She nodded while a hundred warnings darted in and out of her mind. She tried to pray, but all she could muster was a plea for deliverance.

Serena's mind raced. *Lord, I've never shot a man before. It's killing, but if I don't, they'll kill us for sure.* Meeting her ma's gaze, she saw fathomless sorrow. Regret. Fear. Both of them had jobs to do. *Help us,* she prayed repeatedly. *Pa looks terrible, and he's losing blood. Ma's as scared as I am. Lord, keep us safe. I can't do this without You.*

"Go, Serena," Chet instructed, touching her arm. "Time's wasting, and we don't know what they will do next." He followed her into the bedroom and pulled back the tiny flowered curtains she'd help Ma sew. "You have a clear shot of anyone coming out the barn. Don't be afraid to hit them."

She swallowed hard. An attacking boar looked a whole lot different than a man. Serena and Chet bent beneath the window, so close she could feel his warm breath against her face. Another time, another circumstance, she'd have welcomed his nearness.

"Serena," he whispered, "we only have a few moments, but something needs to be said."

She tore her concentration from the barn and into the beloved face of her ranger. Biting her lip to keep the tears from overcoming her, Serena waited for him to speak.

His finger traced her lips. "So many things I'd like to say, but I can't. Pray without ceasing—like the Bible tells us to do. I love you. No matter what happens, remember that."

"I love you too," she murmured. "God will deliver us. I know He didn't bring us together to die today."

He cupped her chin in his hand as if memorizing every feature about her. His ineffable glance spoke volumes. "Do not let them take you or your ma," Chet said with deadly gravity. "I have an extra pistol." He pulled the gun from his side. "If they get inside. . .use it on you and your ma. Don't let them take you. . . . Promise?"

She hesitated. Taking her own life and Ma's went against God's commands. How could this man of God ask her to do such a terrible thing?

"I've seen what they do to women," he added, as though reading her frenzied thoughts.

And she clearly understood his meaning. "I'll do my best."

"You have a special strength, Serena, one God doesn't give everybody. You are going to need it."

He touched her lips with his and offered a faint smile. Without another word, he left her alone to ponder what manner of sin she dare commit—murder those men in the barn or take her and Ma's life. Confusion and fear raged through her, leaving her stunned and cold. *Your will, Lord. Whatever You want of me, I'll do.*

She watched the empty barnyard, blinking back the stinging tears. Chet loved her, and if she died this morning with him, the thought would help her take Jesus' hand into eternity.

The rooster took his station on top of the well, calling in a new day. Then it grew quiet, not like other mornings. Pa had always said the waiting proved to be the hardest. He'd spoken the truth.

"We smoke 'em out," a voice called, breaking the stillness, "kill rangers and have women for ourselves."

Nine

Serena aimed the rifle and fired into the dark shadows of the barn in reply to the Mexican's threats. She laid the firearm aside and snatched up a loaded pistol. Glancing at the one left by Chet, she shuddered. *For Ma and me.* She refused to let it happen.

Within moments, her ma had carefully measured the gun powder and slipped a bullet into the rifle. Laying it on the floor beside Serena, she stared at Pa, still unconscious.

"How is he?" she asked, studying what she believed to be the figure of a man lingering close to the barn door.

"He's doing fine for right now. When this is done, you and Chet can help me get him into bed." She sounded more optimistic than Serena knew Ma truly felt.

"Good. Soon Chet will have them sprawled out there in the dirt."

"Serena, I've never heard you talk this way," her ma said, shock edging her words, "but. . .in all the nineteen years your pa and I've been married, we've never had danger at our door, either."

Serena refused to let her emotions overrule good

judgment. "All I know is we have to stop those men out there." She stole a glance at her ma. Nothing else needed to be said, for reality cut deep.

Ma nodded and paled again. "Praise God, your pa taught you how to shoot. I wish I'd taken the time to learn. Then I could do my share now."

Serena steadied the pistol. "Simply keeping these guns loaded is help. And please pray I won't lose my nerve when the time comes, 'cause I'm scared."

Ma brushed an errant strand of hair from Serena's face and tucked it behind her ear. "I will. . .I am, but you'll do just fine. I'm sure of it."

"Thank you." Serena waited for a wave of emotion to pass. "I love you, Ma. We've had lots of good times together, haven't we?"

Ma nodded, sorrow etching her smooth features, and her hand touched Serena's arm. "And we'll have years more. Someday your babies will crawl on my lap, and I will tell them what a beautiful, brave mother they have."

"And how I spent my eighteenth birthday? This isn't how I pictured today." She nodded toward the cook fire. "And would you look at breakfast? The eggs and bacon have burned." She wanted to make light of their precarious situation, but instead tears stung her eyes, and she hastily wiped them away.

"I'm proud of you," Ma said, ever so gently. "We'll make it through this thing. . .and work out you and Chet's problem too."

Before Serena could reply, movement from the side of the nearest corner of the barn caught her attention. At first she thought the figure to be Chet, but the man wore a sombrero.

She stared at the far corner, where a second man, dressed like a Mexican but more closely resembling an Apache, studied the cabin. Chet had said three men followed Pa. Then she saw a third lurking inside the barn, near the entrance.

Dear Lord, I'm so scared, but I can't let them get to the cabin.

She realized then what they planned. She figured while the two men rushed and covered the man in the barn, he would head for the cook fire and a burning log. In the dry heat, he'd toss the log through a window. A simple plan for three ruthless men who thought they dealt with one badly injured ranger and another single man. A lot they knew about the women inside. If only she knew what Chet wanted her to do. But what God wanted of her ranked even higher. The Indian raised his rifle.

"They're coming," she said, wanting to shout. Her heart pounded more fiercely than before, and she clenched her fists in an effort to dispel her shaking hands. Every breath became a prayer.

"We have God on our side," Ma said, "and He does not forsake His own."

Serena refused to think of Goliad and the Alamo. The brave men who died at the hands of the Mexicans believed God had been on their side too.

"Yes, of course we do," she replied.

Raising the rifle, she took careful aim at the man wearing the sombrero, hoping Chet had his sights on the other. The Mexican stepped into the sunlight. He made a dreadful mistake.

He raised his pistol. She held her breath and squeezed the trigger. The two shots fired simultaneously, but the Mexican fell. Still holding her breath, she wrapped her fingers around the pistol and moved to the other window, where Chet had leaned his rifle to look like another stood guard. It occurred to her then. Chet only had one rifle.

Another shot fired, and the Indian fell. The third man stole around the barn entrance in the direction of the fallen Apache. Serena didn't see Chet, and a new set of tremors raced up her spine.

The third man stood in the clearing for a mere second before chasing around the side of the barn. Serena could wait no longer. Unlatching the door, she hurried outside. The man must have sensed her, for he whirled around, pistol aimed.

With a loud groan, the man fell face down with a knife in his back. Chet raced toward her.

"You crazy girl," he said, his voice hoarse. "He would have killed you." He caught her and pulled her into his arms.

Serena could not hold back the sobs. "I was afraid he'd shoot you. And you lied to me; you only had the rifle. I couldn't sit by and do nothing."

For several long minutes, he held her and stroked her hair. "It's all over now, Sweetheart."

Finally he released her and they looked behind them. The men were dead; no doubt entered her mind. Reality sickened her at what she'd done. . .they'd done. Chet stepped in front of her, blocking her view of the fallen men.

"Let's go see about your pa," he said, slipping his hand around her waist and urging her to the cabin. "You're still shaking."

She nodded, unable to speak until she garnered enough breath to calm herself. "I feel horrible, dirty, and yet relieved," she said.

He brushed a kiss in her hair. "I know. I feel the same way each time I finish a job. You did real well, Serena, but you have to put it past you. Think about what they'd done if you and me had not stopped them."

"Oh, Chet, I know, and I'm grateful God spared us." She took another glance behind them. "Would you pray with me?"

He turned her to face him and grasped both of her hands into his. They bowed their heads; even so, tears still trickled down her cheeks.

"Thank you, Lord, for delivering us from those men," Chet began. "They won't be hurting any more folks. Lord, I still don't understand the ways of war, but I know You protected us today just as You have done for me many times before. The cap'n is in bad shape, and we ask Your healing powers to mend his body. Amen."

"Thank you," she whispered, gazing into his treasured face. "I think we need to give them a proper burial."

"I will," he said firmly, "right after we check on your pa."

Hand in hand they walked into the cabin where Pa had gained consciousness. His head lay in Ma's lap, and she held his face in her hands. His side had been bandaged, but his leg still needed doctoring. The agony of pain layered lines upon his face, causing him to look years older.

"Go ahead and tend to my leg, Rachel. It won't get

any better like it is," he said through a labored breath.

She bent and kissed his brow, then glanced up at Serena and Chet. "Would you bind it? I don't want to let him go." Ma picked up his hand and wrapped her fingers around it, her lips braving a tender smile.

Together Chet and Serena cleaned the wound and bandaged it. Pa said nothing but gripped Ma's hand all the harder.

"There, it's done," Chet announced. "What do you say we get you into bed?"

"Not yet," Pa said, wetting his lips. Perspiration dotted his brow. "Let me rest just a minute. Besides, there's a thing or two I need to say."

Serena suddenly grew numb. Surely Pa would not run Chet off after he'd saved their lives.

"Chet, you saved my family today," Pa said, struggling with each word. "And I owe you."

"I didn't do anything you wouldn't have done for me."

"I know, but you and I haven't been on the best of terms lately."

Chet kneeled on the floor beside him. "Just some misunderstandings, Cap'n. We can put it behind us."

"Guess we can."

"You'd be proud of Serena. She got one of them," Chet replied, placing an arm around her waist. "I couldn't have licked them without her."

Pa attempted a smile. "She's a ranger's daughter. . .and I reckon. . ." His face distorted in pain, and he paused before speaking again. "She'll make a fine ranger's wife."

Serena gasped as the words graced her ears. "Oh, Pa, do you mean it?"

"Don't think I have much choice. You already know how hard this life is; I won't be disguising it." He grimaced and sucked in his breath. "Both of you got the best, so I'm giving you my blessing."

Chet squeezed her lightly, and she laid her head against him. "Thank you. I'll love her good and proper."

Pa raised a brow. "I know you will 'cause you won't want to tangle with me."

Chet chuckled, sparking a lopsided grin from Pa.

Pa peered into Serena's face. "Happy birthday, Little One. Guess you got a little more than what you bargained for."

"A husband, a blessing, and a palomino," Serena said, bending to touch his whiskered cheek. "Best birthday I ever had."

The Niall family joined them in the afternoon, with Dugan returning home for an Irish cure to soothe Pa's pain. By then, the three men were buried, but the tale only needed telling once. None of them felt boastful over the morning's happenings.

"I have an announcement to make," Pa said, long toward evening with the effects of Dugan's elixir easing the burning in his body. "Chet and Serena are fixin' to be married."

"When?" roared Dugan.

"I reckon as soon as we can get a preacher here to do the ceremony," Pa said. He cast an approving glance toward Serena and Chet. "Guess I'll have me a son and a lieutenant. Seems to me, I'm one lucky man."

Later on, after the celebration ceased and Pa slept,

Serena and Chet sat on the porch and watched the stars break through a night sky.

"I need to ask you in a fitting way to marry me," Chet said, his hand clasped firmly into hers.

She said nothing—but waited.

"You aren't going to make this easy for me, are you?" he asked with a nervous chuckle.

"No, I plan to savor every word, so speak nice and slow." She drew her knees up under her dress and rested her chin on them. She had long anticipated his endearing words and a promise of a life together. Now, at this moment, she wanted it all to last forever.

He cleared his throat. "Serena. . .what's your middle name?"

She straightened up and gazed into his face, wishing she could see his eyes. "Hope."

"Hmm. I like that; it's right pretty."

Another long minute passed as they were serenaded by a family of locusts and purple martins.

"Serena Hope Talbot, I love you—imagine I have for a long time, just didn't have sense enough to recognize it. I used to have this peculiar idea of what I needed in a woman. *Strength,* I called it, and I thought it meant physical strength. But I made a terrible mistake, for in many ways you are a stronger person than me. I need you, Serena, for now and always. I know God planned for us to be together as man and wife. So I'm asking if you will marry me—be a Texas Ranger's wife."

She sighed and formed a smile she could not conceal. "I've loved you since the first day Pa brought you home and introduced you as a new ranger recruit over two years ago. I knew I wanted to marry you then, and I've not changed my mind since. Yes, I'll marry you and be a ranger's wife."

He pulled her closer and lightly brushed a kiss across her lips. "Our lives won't be easy. Trouble is always springing up somewhere, and this feud between the Republic and Mexico over Texas's boundaries isn't going to be settled without fighting."

"I know. You're a ranger."

"And you'll still marry me, knowing I'll be gone for days at a time?"

"Yes, Chet. I agree to it all. I love you, but. . ."

"What?"

"Please, don't call me skinny."

He kissed her again. "I will never call you skinny, just my precious Serena."

"You've got me, Lieutenant Chet Wilkinson, and I'm never letting you go."

DIANN MILLS

DiAnn lives in Houston, Texas, with her husband Dean.
They have four adult sons. She wrote from the time she
could hold a pencil, but not seriously until God made it
clear that she should write for Him. After three years
of serious writing, her first book *Rehoboth* won favorite
Heartsong Presents historical for 1998. Other publishing credits include magazine articles and short stories,
devotionals, poetry, and internal writing for her church.
She is an active church choir member, leads a ladies Bible
study, and is a church librarian. She is also an active board
member with the American Christian Romance Writers
organization.

The Reluctant Fugitive

by Darlene Mindrup

One

West Texas, 1859

April Hansen set a glass of milk next to her twin brother's plate, then took a seat across from him. She studied the hard lines of his face and wondered just what had happened to him over the last two years.

The chilly November wind whistled eerily outside the cabin, the mantle clock above her fireplace chiming the hour of midnight. She shivered, waiting for the heat from the Franklin stove to warm the air around her.

"So tell me, Ted, what you've been doing with yourself. Did you find the gold you were looking for?" she asked, pulling her robe tightly around her to help ward off the chill.

He grimaced, tucking into the plate of stew, seemingly oblivious to the cold around him. "Not really. How about you?"

She pushed a strand of coal black hair behind her ear and shook her head slightly. Her sky blue eyes met an exact replica when they collided with his.

"Not really. I *am* making good money as a seamstress, though."

He smiled slightly, pushing the cleaned plate away and downing the glass of milk. "That doesn't surprise me. Mother always said you had real talent."

For a moment, his face darkened. He turned away, looking out the paned-glass window of her kitchen. The wind found its way through cracks in her small cabin where the chinking had dried and left small holes, causing the hurricane lamp to flicker slightly.

April laid her soft white hand on his darker, harder one and gently squeezed. "They're with the Lord now, Ted."

His blue eyes were like chips of ice when they met hers again. "Why? Because He needed them more than we did?"

Seeing the pain he caused her, he relented. "I'm sorry, April. I just can't help wondering if my life would have been different if only they had lived."

"We were sixteen when they died, Ted. If you didn't have their beliefs embedded in your heart by then, what makes you think you would have if they had lived longer?"

"It wasn't their beliefs that I needed!" He jerked his hand from hers, glaring a message she refused to heed. She hadn't seen her brother in two years, and she wasn't about to miss this opportunity. He needed to come back to the Lord if he wanted any hope of a normal life.

"You can't blame God for the way you choose to live your life."

He jumped to his feet, his hands clenching into fists at his side. There was a haunted, unhappy look about him that touched her sisterly heart.

"Can't I? Can't I just! Keep your God. I don't need Him!"

She got up and reached out to touch him, but he jerked away from her. Her hand fell uselessly to her side.

"Don't you, Ted?"

For a brief instant his eyes were filled with an intense yearning. April seized the moment.

"Don't you remember how good it was to go to church every Sunday and sit together as a family? Remember, too, the day you accepted Christ into your life?"

His lips twitched slightly. "I remember. It was October and the water in the river was *extremely* cold."

She smiled. "That day you were baptized, you said that God would be the master of your life."

The smile fled from his face, and he turned angry eyes to her. "Have you ever heard of the slavery in the South? When a master is mean, the slaves sometimes run away."

April's face paled. "Don't say that. God is never mean!"

She could see that her brother was rapidly losing control. He closed a fist and shook it at her.

"I *needed* them, and He took them away!"

"Ted. . ."

"No! I don't want to hear any more. Say another word and I'll leave!"

April closed her lips on the angry torrent of words begging for release. Tears threatened her composure.

"What about me, Ted? *I* needed *you,* and you left me."

She couldn't read the expression that flashed across his face. "You've never needed anybody," he disagreed, his voice lacking inflection.

How wrong could a person be? Had she seemed so self-sufficient to him? After her parents had died of the fever, she had quickly taken charge of their lives. Having been apprenticed to a wonderful seamstress at the age of twelve, by the time her parents had died four years later, she had developed quite a reputation of her own. She had an uncanny knack of mixing just the right colors and styles to make women look their best. Her business had thrived, bringing in the money they needed to survive.

It was only when Ted had started getting into trouble that she had listened to the advice of one of her customers and come west to Abasca, Texas. The woman had told her that it was a growing, thriving area yet still free of many of the vices of larger, more settled towns. Thinking to remove her brother from the temptations to which he had so readily succumbed, she had quickly made arrangements and left Chicago far behind.

She had hoped to influence her brother to make the right decisions, but somehow or another, she had failed miserably.

Having lived on his own in Chicago for four years, the constraints placed upon him by the remote location of Abasca had finally gotten to him. After two years here and thinking that he was man enough at the age of twenty, he had set out on his own to make his fortune. The loss of her parents had been devastating enough, but losing her brother as well was almost more than she could bear. Still, she had survived, though her lonely heart often ached with the need of someone to love.

That had been over two years ago, and she couldn't help but wonder what had brought her brother back now.

"Does it ease your conscience to believe that?" she asked quietly. He looked away, and for the first time, she noticed the Colt revolver holstered on his hip. Her eyes widened, lifting quickly to meet his enigmatic look.

"What do you need that for?" Her voice squeaked. "What have you been up to, Ted?"

Taking her by the shoulders, he tried to calm her. "It's for protection, all right?"

She wanted to ask him if that protection included killing people, but she didn't have the courage. Seeing the set look on his face, she was afraid to find out.

"I need your help, April."

The very words she dreaded hearing. How many times had she heard them in the past and lived to regret it.

"What. . .what do you need? I have a little money."

Tenderness filled his eyes, and he smiled. "I don't need your hard-earned money, Sis."

Releasing her, he pulled a handkerchief from his pocket and began to unwrap it. When he held it out to her, she drew back, gasping at the beautiful diamond necklace nestled among the blue and white folds.

"Where did you get that?"

"A friend gave it to me to keep. I want you to keep it in the bank for me."

April threw him a suspicious look. "This *friend*, why couldn't she keep it herself?"

He chuckled. "You sound almost like a jealous wife." The smile slid from his face and he became all at once grave. "She had to go somewhere in a hurry. The only thing she has left in the world is this diamond necklace, and she'll need it when she gets back."

April wrapped her arms tightly around herself, her teeth chattering with the cold seeping into the cabin. "W–why can't she j–just put it in the bank. . .herself?"

Seeing her shivering, Ted pulled her close, holding her against his warmth. She snuggled closer, as thankful for her brother's love as for the heat from his body. She had missed him terribly, even though he was forever causing her pain by his crazy shenanigans.

When her teeth finally stopped chattering, he told her, "I'll make up the fire and we'll talk."

They huddled around the cheerful blaze, neither one looking very cheerful themselves. There was something serious on her brother's mind, and April's suspicions were rising by the minute.

Ted told her that his friend, Darcy, was being hunted by a man who thought she owed him money. Since the man practically owned the town, she couldn't put her jewelry in the bank where she had been living. Afraid for her life, she had fled, leaving Ted with her necklace and a promise to reclaim it.

Though there were holes in Ted's story, April's heart went out to the young woman.

"So you want to put it in the bank here?"

He nodded, his look fixed intently on her face. "I know it will be safe with you."

"What about you?"

He shrugged, looking away. The rocking chair creaked when he rose, the only other sound the crackling of the fire as he added more wood and the soughing of the wind through the pine trees outside.

"I'll move on, too, once the necklace is safe."

"Why can't you just stay?" she asked him softly.

He lifted his head slightly, still not looking at her. She could see his shoulders tense. "Maybe I will."

April felt a little thrill of hope. If only she could reach her brother and remind him of the boy he had once been. The boy whose sole hope was in Jesus Christ. Surely he could still become the man the Lord meant him to be.

She dropped her gaze to the gold-and-green braided rug between them. "You are more than welcome to stay with me."

He looked at her then, something indefinable in his eyes. Again, there was that look of desperate yearning. He opened his mouth to say something, then quickly closed it.

"Thanks," he told her, his voice lacking emotion. "And thanks for letting me stay tonight and feeding me."

"You're welcome. Anytime, Ted. You know that."

His shining eyes smiled into hers. "Have I ever told you just how much I love you?"

"No, but there's always a first time," she told him, grinning impishly.

He got up from the chair and knelt beside her. Lifting a finger, he stroked her cheek. "Just in case anything happens to me, I wanted you to know."

At the husky tone of voice, April felt a prism of fear clawing its way up her stomach. What was he trying to say? Just exactly what did he expect to happen?

"I'll get my bedroll," he told her, "and camp out here in front of the fireplace."

He left her sitting there worrying over what he had just said like a dog worrying over a bone. When he returned, she pulled chairs aside so that he would have ready access to the floor in front of the fireplace.

She opened her mouth to ask him about what he had just said, but she noticed the weary lines graven into his face. She decided it could wait until morning.

" 'Night," he told her, and she heard the sluggishness in his voice.

"Good night. See you in the morning."

She went to the other side of the cabin, and placing her robe on the wall peg at the foot of her bed, she climbed beneath her double wedding ring quilt.

Though she had much to think about, the rattling of the shutters by the wind soon lulled her to sleep.

When they entered the bank the next morning, Mr. Dice, the bank manager, saw them coming and quickly rose to his feet. He looked immaculate in his business suit, his dark hair parted in the middle. It had surprised April when she had first met him to find out that he was so young yet held such a responsible position.

She exhaled softly. For several weeks now Jason Dice had been paying marked attention to her. At first she had been delighted, never having had much attention from the male set before, but then she had overheard Jason talking to another gentleman when he didn't know that she was just around the corner.

"Marry April Hansen? Sure. A man can overlook a woman's lack of good looks when she has a sufficient bank account."

His greediness had repelled her more than his thought-less words. Since she knew that she was not pretty like other girls, his remark had left her unfazed. She had enough confidence in her abilities not to worry about good looks. What were good looks when you had to make a living? Though she had never mentioned the conversation to Jason, she had studiously avoided him as much as possible. The trouble was, he didn't take subtle hints very well.

Now he crossed to their side, assessing Ted as he came. There was an ambiguous look to his face when he finally stood before them.

"Miss April. What can I do for you?"

April motioned to her brother who was carefully scrutinizing the other man. She could tell by the look on his face that he had appraised Jason's character in that all-inclusive look and found him lacking.

"Mr. Dice, this is my brother, Ted Hansen."

Looking relieved, Jason held out his hand. At first, April thought her brother was going to ignore it, but then a sudden sparkle lit his eyes and he suddenly crushed the banker's hand in a mighty grip.

Rubbing the offended appendage, Jason quickly moved to April's side and out of Ted's way. April gave her brother a reproving look.

"Mr. Dice, my brother has something he wishes to place in your vault."

"Indeed?" he glanced at Ted doubtfully, slipping his fingers into his vest pockets and puffing out his chest pompously.

Ted pulled the handkerchief from his own pocket and held it open for the banker to see. An avaricious light entered Jason's eyes. His demeanor changed instantly, becoming almost fawning in his attempt to please.

"Come this way. I'll help you fill out the paperwork myself, since April is such a good friend of mine."

April barely kept from rolling her eyes at the ceiling.

"If it's all right with you, Mr. Dice," Ted interrupted hastily, looking suddenly uncomfortable, "April has a few things she needs to attend to at home."

Both Jason and April glanced at him in surprise. "They can wait, Ted," April disagreed, frowning. "I'd like to spend time with you."

He looked from her to Jason, and April sensed his nervousness. His jaw tensed, the muscles working convulsively.

"That's all right, Sis. You can go ahead. I'll come straight home when I'm finished, and we can have that long talk."

The bell jingled over the door and a tall man came in. His dark, stringy hair looked like it hadn't seen a washing in many a long day. April saw her brother's face pale. He tried to push her toward the door.

"You go ahead."

April resisted. There was something mighty strange going on here, and she wasn't about to leave now.

"I think I'll just wait," she told both men inflexibly.

Quick anger fired in her brother's eyes. He gave Jason a forced smile. "Perhaps you can convince her, Mr. Dice."

Ignoring the undercurrent of tension between brother and sister, Jason smiled at April, his white teeth gleaming. "Oh, don't ask me to try to persuade April to leave. Her very presence adds sunlight to an otherwise drab day."

April hastily averted her eyes from the banker's proprietorial look. She noticed that the stranger caught

Ted's eye, flashing him a message, and April wondered how they knew each other.

Biting his lip, Ted tried once more to get her to leave. Again, she refused. Though she could tell he was angry with her, he said nothing more.

April sat quietly while the two men transacted their business, her gaze wandering around the bank. Few people were there this early in the morning.

Jason got up, motioning them to follow. There was an edginess about Ted that communicated itself to April.

"This way, please. Your trinket will be safe here, Mr. Hansen, I can assure you. Our safe is the finest quality steel. We have never been robbed."

Fumbling with the tumbler on the safe, he puffed out his chest proudly, turning to retrieve the necklace. He found himself looking down the cold barrel of Ted's revolver.

Two

Things happened so fast, April was caught totally unaware. When she finally realized what was happening, she grabbed for Ted's arm.

"What are you doing? Put that gun away!"

Wrapping a large arm around her shoulders, Ted pulled her to his side and held her firmly.

"Be still, April, and no one will get hurt."

The stranger had his gun out as well and was glaring menacingly at the bank's occupants. He waved his Colt threateningly.

"That's right. Everyone just take it easy and no one will get hurt."

The look of betrayal April gave her brother caused his lips to turn down at the corners. His returning look asked for understanding.

"I'll never forgive you for this, Ted," she told him coldly.

Jason stood frozen to the spot, his angry gaze flashing from sister to brother. "Don't try to make it seem as if you had nothing to do with this, April. *You* brought him in here."

Ted's look became more threatening, and the banker's eyes filled with fear.

"My sister had nothing to do with this. She knew nothing about it."

Though Jason said nothing, his expression was skeptical. April realized that she might possibly go to jail for something she had no control over.

The stranger pushed past the trio and entered the vault. "Let's get the stuff and get outta here."

After filling a bag with cash, the man motioned for Ted to take it. Ted released April and took the bag from him, avoiding her accusing glare. He reached across and grabbed the diamond necklace from Jason's unresisting fingers.

"I'll see you hang for this," Jason hissed. The hatred in his eyes filled April with alarm. Instinctively she knew that having his pride dented would make him a lethal enemy. It was obvious that his anger was directed at April as well. There was no way that he was going to believe that she had nothing to do with this fiasco. He had quickly changed from ardent suitor to impassioned foe.

"You'll have to come with us," Ted told her grimly, recognizing the threat to his sister.

"I won't," she answered defiantly. "Unlike you, I'll take my chances with the law."

Ted exchanged glances with Jason, the look in the banker's eyes bringing a swift frown to his face. Ted shook his head, never breaking eye contact.

"I said you're coming with me."

"We ain't taking no woman along," the stranger interrupted angrily. "She'll only slow us down."

Throwing the man a blistering scowl, Ted set his shoulders uncompromisingly. "She's my sister, Amos, and I'm not leaving her here to face the consequences alone."

So intense was their argument that neither man noticed Mr. Harris, the bank teller, lift a rifle from behind the counter. He pointed the gun at Ted.

"Drop them revolvers," he told them, his voice shaking slightly. His beetling eyebrows lifted to his receding hairline as he waited for compliance.

Everyone went still. A split second later, Amos whirled to fire at the teller. Seeing his intent, April lunged to stop him. The Colt revolver went off, the bullet missing Mr. Harris's heart, but imbedding itself in his shoulder. A woman screamed and fainted to the floor.

Amos looked shocked, then turned an accusing glare on April. "Let's get outta here!"

Grabbing April, Ted lifted her and threw her over his shoulder, striding out of the bank behind Amos. He unceremoniously dumped her on her stomach over his saddle. Climbing up behind her, he quickly turned the horse.

"Let's go!" Amos shouted, and from her upside-down vantage point, April could see a flurry of horses' hooves kicking up the mud. It was then she realized there were more men than just Amos and Ted.

As they thundered out of town, April heard shouts behind them. Bullets winged by her head, and for the first time in her life, she felt the very real presence of death.

When they were far enough from town, Ted briefly stopped his horse and helped April to sit upright. Her stomach was still heaving from the pummeling it had received from their fast escape, and she glowered at her brother.

"I'm sorry," he told her, and there was true contrition in his eyes. "I never thought this would happen."

"You never thought, period," she snapped. "You never do."

April heard a chuckle and turned to find Amos and two other men watching them with interest. The other two looked as disreputable as Amos.

"Shoulda left her behind," Amos smirked. "Women ain't nothing but trouble."

"Aw, now, Amos," one of the others disagreed. "They have their uses."

Gleaming eyes studied April thoroughly, and she cringed closer to her brother. She could feel him tense against her.

"Watch it, Chauncy. She's my sister."

The other man lifted his hat slightly, surprising April with his courtesy.

"Ma'am." He smiled. "I'm pleased to meet you."

April's reproachful silence met this greeting. Amos frowned. "Enough of this. We gotta keep moving. They'll be after us by now."

The others waited for him to take the lead, then rapidly set out after him in a quick gallop. April clung to the saddle horn, wishing that she would wake up and find herself in her nice cozy bed.

She tried to button her blue wool coat, but her fingers felt frozen, whether from cold or fear she wasn't quite certain. Only the fact that it was her brother's arms wrapped around her kept her from giving in to sheer hysteria.

Several hours later, Amos pulled to a stop. April's teeth were chattering with the cold, but it was her bones that felt like they had been jarred out of her body.

"Al," Amos commanded, "go back and see if you can catch sight of a posse. We'll head for the canyon. Be sure you take the back route to find us, just in case anyone spots you and follows you."

Al nodded once, turning his horse back the way they had come. He raced away like the hounds of fury were after him, his speeding horse churning up mud behind him.

They traveled on, but at a much slower pace. April was thankful for the reprieve from the bone-wrenching ride. Her mind was as numb as her body, and both refused to obey her will. Ted leaned forward so that he could whisper in her ear without being heard.

"I'll get you out of this somehow."

She said nothing. She heard him sigh in exasperation.

The sun had set hours before, and now April noticed that they were descending into a small valley. Entering it, the cold wind suddenly decreased. The freezing temperatures caused frost ringlets from their breath to swirl around their heads in a light mist.

Finally, they stopped at the entrance to a small cave. It was well hidden from view by the scrub brush around it and therefore made an excellent hiding place.

Ted helped her dismount, holding her while her shaky legs became accustomed to the ground beneath her feet once more.

Amos led the way into the cave, lighting a lantern

near the entrance. April wrinkled her nose at the smell of unwashed bodies mixed with rotting food. How on earth had her brother gotten so low in his life?

He cleared a place for her and motioned for her to have a seat while Chauncy made up the fire. Amos came and stood next to them. He grinned down at April, his tobacco-stained teeth making her stomach churn.

"How's it feel to be an outlaw?" he wanted to know.

Ted glared at him. "That's not funny, Amos. She wasn't supposed to be involved."

Amos shrugged his shoulders. "Hey, I wasn't the one offered to get us into the bank."

Flushing, Ted had no answer.

April glanced from one to the other. "So what happens to me now?"

"Well now, that kinda depends on you. You be a good little girl, and I'm sure we'll get along just fine."

He gave her a warning look, then turned and left them alone. April shivered.

"How could you get mixed up with someone like that? He's awful!"

Ted knelt beside where she sat stiff-backed on a wooden crate. The pleading eyes that normally wrenched her heart had no effect on her now. She deliberately ignored that tender spot in her heart that only he could touch.

"April, I can't explain now."

She studied his face. "What explanation could you possibly give for using me to commit a crime?"

His eyes flashed. "If you remember correctly, I tried to get you to leave."

Her brows lifted, hiding beneath her dark bangs. "And that's supposed to make a difference?"

There was a rustling at the entrance, and Amos and Chauncy spun, their guns already drawn from their holsters. Al came in, stopping short at the sight of the two gun barrels facing his way. He lifted his hands, palms facing forward.

"Hold on, fellers. It's just me."

Slowly they replaced their guns. Al joined them near the fire.

"So what'd ya find out?" Amos queried.

Squatting down next to the fire, Al held his hands out to the warming flames. "Well, since no one saw me in town this morning, I just moseyed on into town and hung around the saloon for a spell. Figured I'd hear the news better there." He grinned, his gleaming eyes speaking clearly of what he had done while in the saloon.

"And?" Chauncy interrupted impatiently.

"I guess it's just too cold for them town folks. They decided not to send a posse out after all."

Amos leaned back, sighing with relief. "That's good news."

Al shook his head. "Not quite."

Ted frowned. "What do you mean?"

"I mean," he told them, "that they called for a Texas Ranger instead."

Amos's face paled. Chauncy threw his coffee into the fire. "Blast it all!"

April glanced up at her brother and caught an odd expression on his face. "Who are they sending?" he asked quietly.

Al looked at each man in turn, his own face rather pale by the light of the fire.

"Yellow Wolf Jackson."

April settled down under the blanket her brother had provided for her and tried to sleep, but the sound of the hushed voices of the others unsettled her nerves. She could hear the conversation as clearly as though she were sitting among them. Her eyes were fixed on her brother, sitting quietly like a statue.

"He's like a wolf," Al muttered. "He slowly, methodically stalks his prey until he's ready for the kill."

"Learned his tracking skills from his Comanche father," Amos said, spitting into the fire. The hissing of it had barely faded before Chauncy took up the refrain.

"Everyone knows a ranger can shoot a fly off a fence a half mile away, but Jackson uses his bow better than most men use their gun."

Amos nodded. "Yep. That's what makes him so deadly. Least ways if you hear a trigger cock, you have time to draw, but you never hear that bow twang until it's too late."

A long silence followed this pronouncement.

"Why's he called Yellow Wolf?" Ted asked, his quiet voice startling the others.

"His ma was white," Al answered, "but his dad were Comanche. He's got his mama's hair, yellow as sun-ripened wheat."

The more she heard, the more alarmed April became. What if this Yellow Wolf caught up with them and killed her brother? She might be angry with him, more than angry even, but she would never wish him dead.

Chauncy sighed loudly. "We're in for it, that's for sure. He has a reputation for always getting his man."

Amos answered this with a snort. "There's four of us, ain't there? And some of us is pretty good at trackin' too."

"Did you ever hear of the Walton gang?" Chauncy asked without lifting his eyes from the fire. "They was ten of them. Jackson caught 'em all. Killed four of 'em with that bow before they had a chance to reload."

April's eyes widened. The man must be some kind of savage.

"Let's get some sleep," Amos commanded. He motioned Ted toward the entrance. "I need to talk to you."

When her brother returned, his face was pale and strained. He glanced her way, then quickly turned aside. April could hear him stumbling about for some time before he finally settled with the others for the night.

Exhausted from the torturous ride, she felt the tug of sleep's call, and too weary to do any more thinking, she finally succumbed.

She dreamed of galloping horses and a faceless man with golden hair chasing her across the hills of West Texas.

When she opened her eyes in the morning, the man sitting Indian style across from her was not her brother. His yellow hair hung long to his shoulders, and the two Colt revolvers strapped to his side gave away his identity before he ever said a word.

Three

April lay immobile, frozen with shock. Numerous thoughts chased themselves through her mind finally settling into one cohesive idea. She had to warn her brother.

Jumping to her feet, she ran for the entrance to the cave. She never reached it. Strong hands latched onto her upper arms, whirling her around. Her eyes were level with a broad chest housed in soft buckskin. She struggled against the restraining grip, pushing her small fists upward until she was able to pummel the intruder in the chest.

"Let me go!"

Grabbing hold of her wrists, he twisted them behind her until she was effectively pinned against his chest. She lifted frightened eyes and was surprised to find a smile on the man's face, although the smile was a decidedly nasty one.

"Just where did you plan on going?" he asked, a snicker in his voice.

Chocolate brown eyes roved her features, and April stilled beneath his careful scrutiny. He was a big man, tall and powerful. She felt a tremor of fear run through her when she remembered the comments of the others.

"Unhand me!" she commanded. She wanted to hurl the word *savage* at him, but realizing his size and power, she didn't dare.

As though he could divine her thoughts, his eyes darkened until the only thing she could see was her own reflection in them. His face turned grim.

"Where are the others?"

Glancing around, she realized that they were truly alone, just she and this savage. Her own brother had deserted her, leaving her to face this man alone. Pain unlike any she had ever known rose up to choke her. Although she was angry at her brother for deserting her, she was relieved that he had gotten away.

"I don't know." She could barely speak past the obstruction in her throat.

Again he searched her face, delving deeply into her eyes. A puzzled frown crossed his face, and suddenly he released her.

"So they left you here to divert me from the chase, huh?"

The nasty smile had returned to his face. He cocked his head slightly, assessing her critically from her tousled black hair to her black button-up shoes. Blushing profusely, she wrapped her arms defensively around her waist.

"I must say, I'm tempted."

The color multiplied in her cheeks until they resembled overripe cherries. "You, Sir, are no gentleman."

The smile turned into a full-fledged grin. He folded his arms over his chest, causing the buckskin to strain against him. April's eyes followed the line of his figure past long, lean legs wrapped in the same buckskin to feet encased by leather moccasins.

"Not like your brother and his cohorts, huh?"

She had nothing to say to that. If the truth were told, this man had a strong magnetism that reached out to her even from the distance she had removed herself to. If he was a savage, he was unlike any she had ever heard about.

"What are you going to do with me?"

His eyes flicked over her briefly. "Well, I've got to hand it to your friends, their little ruse worked. I can't very well take you with me, and I can't leave you here alone."

He went to the fire and lifted the coffeepot from the coals. Surprised, April watched him pour a cup and hold it out to her. She hesitated before crossing to where he crouched and took the offered cup.

"So, I repeat, what are you going to do with me?"

He glanced up at her from under a lowered brow. "I'm going to take you back to Abasca and then come back and follow the trail again."

April pulled her lips in between her teeth, pressing them together. She sat down on the crate she had vacated the night before. When she finally looked at him, she found him watching her.

"Look, Mr. Jackson." His eyebrows lifted at his name, and she stumbled to a halt. His eyes grew dark and stormy.

"How do you know my name?" he asked in a quiet voice that was frightening in its intensity.

She explained about Al's returning to town. His eyes began to gleam, and April felt real fear for her brother.

"So, it *is* Miller's gang."

Confused, April tilted her head slightly. "Miller?"

His eyes narrowed to slits. "You're good, I'll give you that. The perfect picture of innocence."

April felt her temper begin to rise. Trying to keep it in check, she took a deep breath before continuing.

"Mr. Jackson, I *am* innocent. I have no idea who this *Miller* is that you're talking about."

"Mm hmm."

Throwing all restraint to the wind, she snapped back at him. "Fine, then take me back to town. I'm certain no jury in the world would convict me if they knew the facts."

"And the facts being. . .?"

She was sorely tempted to smack that smug look off of his face. "I was unwittingly involved in that bank robbery." Something occurred to her, and she gave him a hard look. "How did you find this place so fast anyway? Surely you weren't just passing through the vicinity when they called for you."

A quick look flashed into his eyes and was just as quickly gone. "Hoping to have more time to get away?"

He was obviously going to ignore her question. "I told you. Just take me back to town and be off on your search."

His slow smile made her insides tingle. "No can do," he told her softly. "It's been raining for the last hour, and with the temperatures dropping, we're going to have an ice storm."

Panic robbed her of speech. To be lodged inside this small cave with this big. . .*man* suddenly shortened her breath. Her chest rose and fell in alarming rapidity.

"We can't just stay here," she finally managed to whisper.

"Woman," he told her in aggravation, shifting away from her until his back was against the cave wall. "If I wanted to do something to you I could have done it long before now. I've been sitting here for the past three hours."

The thought of him sitting there watching her sleep left her slightly rattled. She didn't know what to say.

"By the way," he said, lifting the steaming cup to his lips. "Did you know that you snore?"

Affronted, she forgot to be afraid. "I most certainly do not!"

He grinned, nodding his head. "Yep, you do. It's kinda cute, though."

Of all the compliments to receive, this had to be the worst. He was unlike any man she had ever met, savage or otherwise.

"Look, Mr. Jackson."

"You can call me Wolf. Most folks do," he interrupted.

With his slanting eyes gleaming at her, he certainly reminded her of one. The wolf from *Little Red Riding Hood* had been a sweet talker too. It was an analogy she would rather forget.

"Mr. Jackson," she reiterated and watched the slow smile curve his lips again. If she didn't know better, she would believe him capable of reading minds. "I don't mind a little rain and cold. We can't be that far from town."

His amused look made her feel like a foolish little schoolgirl. "We're a good forty miles."

Her mouth dropped open. "That can't be. We made it here in one day."

"Yep, hard, long riding will do it. I made it in six hours, myself. I'd say it probably took you the better part of fifteen."

She went to the entrance to the cave, but he didn't try to stop her. Peeking out, she watched the rain falling in torrents. The river at the floor of the canyon was already rising. She turned back to Wolf.

"Will we be safe here?"

He shrugged, refilling his cup. "Safe as anywhere, I expect."

Restless, she wandered around the cave noticing things she hadn't when she had arrived last night. This cave must have been used by Ted and the others for some time. There was a load of supplies in one corner, along with extra kerosene for the lamp that hung from a nail pounded into the wall. Ted had been so close yet hadn't come to see her until he was ready to use her in his crime. Her heart felt as though it were breaking into a million pieces.

She felt Wolf watching her and turned. He was regarding her warily now, no smile left on his face.

"You say you're innocent. Tell me what happened."

So she did.

Wolf noticed every changing emotion on her face, every nuance of her body language. He was tempted to believe her, but he had been this route before. It wasn't often his intuition failed him, but it *had* been known to happen. Especially where the *weaker* sex was concerned.

He studied her earnest face, noting the freckles speckled across her nose. She was neither attractive nor unattractive, but she *was* interesting, though he couldn't put a handle on why he thought so. He hadn't been attracted by any woman since Moonwater, and he didn't relish the idea now.

But then maybe that's why this woman was so attractive to him in the first place. She had the same coloring as the Comanche. If anything, she looked more like an Indian than he did, though her skin was much fairer and her eyes were the color of the summer sky. Even her scent was unlike any he had come across, soft and fresh like the spring rain. His mouth twisted wryly at his decidedly poetic thoughts.

She finished her story and stood looking at him, expecting him to believe her. And strangely enough, he did. Still, he wasn't taking any chances.

"That's all very interesting," he told her. "Now when you tell it to the judge and jury, maybe they'll believe you."

She glared at him. "But you don't, do you?"

He leaned back against the wall of the cave, one eyebrow lifted upward. "It doesn't really matter what I believe, does it?"

April got up from the crate and stormed across to her blanket. For some reason, it bothered her that he held such a low opinion of her. Throwing herself down in a huff, she shifted the blanket to make herself more comfortable. If she was going to have to stay there with this giant of an Indian, she might as well make herself as cozy as she could.

She heard something rattle, and lifting the blanket, she found a piece of paper lodged between two rocks on the floor of the cave. She picked it up and unfolded it, recognizing her brother's handwriting at once.

Sis,

I had to leave you. It's for your own good. I'll be back for you as soon as I can.

Ted was coming back. Her heart leaped with joy at the realization that he hadn't deserted her after all, but just as suddenly she was seized with fear. If he came back now, he would come face to face with Yellow Wolf. She had to get the ranger out of there somehow. Crumpling the note in her hand, she casually crossed to the fire. When she reached out to drop it into the flames, a large hand wrapped around her wrist. Though the hold was gentle, she knew he could crush her bones if he wanted to.

Prying her fingers open, he retrieved the paper. After reading it, he glared at her.

"So you're innocent, huh?" He placed the paper carefully in his pocket, noting her attention. "Evidence," he told her coldly.

"It's not what you think," she argued.

"Sit down."

She wasn't certain why she felt she had to justify herself in his eyes, but she couldn't let things stand the way they were.

"Mr. Jackson. . ."

"I said, *sit down.*"

April sat. If other Indians looked that ferocious when they were angry, no wonder they were called savages.

Wolf rummaged through the supplies stacked in the corner until he found what he was looking for. Using his knife, he pried open a can of beans, his silence profound.

He wasn't exactly sure why he was so angry, although maybe *disappointed* would be a better word.

He dumped the beans into a small pot and set it over the fire. This woman might look like a Comanche, but it would seem she hadn't the honor.

"As God is my witness, I am innocent," she told him clearly.

He lifted one eyebrow arrogantly without looking up from his work. "God? What would you know about God?"

She knelt on the ground across from him, her eyes beseeching. "I'm a Christian, Mr. Jackson. I don't lie nor do I steal."

He dumped half of the pot of beans onto a tin plate and handed it to her. His enigmatic eyes met hers.

"You ever hear of John Brown, Miss Hansen?"

She had. The man was a notorious abolitionist who wasn't beyond killing to further his cause, and all in the name of Christianity.

"I'm not John Brown," she told him scathingly.

He took up his own plate of beans and began to scoop them into his mouth. He politely chewed and swallowed before answering.

"Maybe not," he told her, his eyes traveling over her slowly. "But in my eyes you're about the same caliber of Christian."

Hackles rising, April set her plate on the floor untouched. Her appetite had deserted her.

"And what exactly would a man like you know about Christianity?"

His look was so dark she shivered. "A man like me? You mean a half-breed?"

Horrified at his train of thought, she shook her head vehemently in denial.

"I didn't mean that at all! I meant your profession."

He got up, reaching for her plate. He scooped the contents up with his own spoon until the plate was empty, then took both and disappeared outside. When he returned, the plates were clean. He set them with the other supplies.

Coming close, he knelt beside her, and she shrank back from the anger in his eyes.

"I'm a lawman, Miss Hansen. I keep and uphold the law. What about you?"

"I'm the same," she told him, her voice softly supplicating. "I'm telling you the truth."

He pulled the slip of paper from his pocket. "This tells me otherwise."

They stared at each other for a long time, searching for the truth in each other. The atmosphere between them grew tense with suppressed emotions. Nostrils flaring, Wolf moved away first.

The thought that April could so move him that he wanted only to believe her, to deny the evidence, made Wolf angry. Being close to her clouded his thinking, and he didn't fully understand why. It wasn't like him to accept a woman so quickly.

She returned to her blanket, sitting cross-legged across from him. Dirt streaked her face where traces of tears had been the night before. Something wasn't right here. He couldn't believe that his judgment was *that* faulty.

For three hours he had watched her sleep, her face innocent in its repose. Back and forth, his emotions had surged. Something about her touched his icy heart, and he felt it slowly begin to thaw. And that was before she was even awake. Now, after talking with her, he was even more confused.

She had been more hurt by his denial of her Christianity than by anything else he had said. It was there in her face, as plain as day.

The day passed with turtlelike slowness, their cramped quarters making them both edgy. They made desultory conversation some of the time, at others falling into a silence fraught with unanswered questions. Each of them thought of what would happen when the rain stopped, but neither broached the subject.

When April next spoke, her words scattered Wolf's thinking to the four winds.

"Did your mother love your father?"

April regretted the words as soon as they left her mouth. What on earth had possessed her to ask such a personal question in the first place? The anger in his voice when he had said the word "half-breed" told her clearly that it was a sore spot with him. Maybe she had wanted to hurt him as badly as he had hurt her, but then, she really did want to know.

Wolf's body went so rigid, it seemed as though he had turned to stone. His dark eyes glittered dangerously.

"He didn't rape her, if that's what you mean."

April dropped her gaze to the floor. "I'm sorry," she whispered contritely, knowing that if her purpose had been to give him pain, she had succeeded.

"My mother was the daughter of a missionary to the Comanche people. She was a child when her parents came to try to teach the people about the white man's God."

April lifted her head at this. "He's not a white man's God," she interrupted.

"I know Who He is," he answered harshly. "My mother taught me all about Him. How His people love and care for one another."

His biting sarcasm caused April to flinch. She remained silent.

"When my mother's parents died, the Comanche took her in and raised her as one of their own. She and my father fell in love, and he chose to marry her."

Curious in spite of herself, April leaned forward. "Do you have brothers and sisters?"

She could see him tense. He got to his feet and walked away from her, as though her very presence disturbed him. He stared out at the wet landscape, watching the sun slowly sink below the horizon.

"No. My parents were killed when a group of white settlers attacked their village in reprisal for an attack on their own town by renegade Comanches."

Appalled, she could think of nothing to say except to tell him that she was sorry. He smiled at her, a smile that didn't reach his eyes.

"Don't be. If what you believe is true, then they are with your God."

Four

April awoke the next morning slightly disori-
ented. It took her a moment to get her bearings,
rubbing sleep out of her eyes as she did so.

She glanced around the cave and noticed that it was
empty. Her heart plummeted to her toes. So Yellow Wolf
had gone after her brother after all and left her there
alone. Would he come back for her? She had no horse,
and the thought of the long walk to town in the freezing
cold was a daunting one.

But maybe he hadn't gone far. Maybe she could still
catch him. And then what? He had already said that he
wouldn't take her with him, but could she possibly get
him to change his mind?

Stumbling over her blanket, she got up and rushed
out of the cave. She hadn't taken more than two steps
past the entrance before she found her feet flying out
from beneath her. She would have plunged over the edge
of the trail and catapulted to the rushing river in the
canyon below if not for a long arm snaking out and
pulling her back to safety.

Her back was against Wolf's chest, and she thought

surely he must be able to feel the pounding of her heart against his arm. He bent his face forward until their cheeks almost touched.

"Going somewhere?" he wanted to know.

She tilted her head back slightly, bringing her face even closer to his. The fresh scent of the cold outdoors clung to him, but he seemed totally unaffected by the cold. Her heart slowed its thundering pace.

"I. . .I thought you were gone."

One corner of his mouth tilted up on the side. "What, and leave you here alone?" His eyes twinkled down into hers, laughing at her. "But then, I'm not a *gentleman*, am I?"

He slowly released her, keeping one hand on her arm to give her support. Only then did April notice the landscape around her. Prisms of rainbow light were reflected all over the small canyon from the ice clinging to every surface. She caught her breath sharply.

"Oh! It's beautiful!"

He nodded, watching her carefully. "Beautiful and *dangerous*."

She moved slightly, and her feet slipped again. His hold on her arm tightened fractionally until she steadied herself.

"I see what you mean." She peered over the edge to the canyon below. "We'll have to be very careful leaving here."

He lifted one brow, the twinkle back in his eyes. "We're not going anywhere. At least not for awhile. It would be suicide to try to make it out of here just now."

Her eyes flew to his. "When can we leave?"

Wolf shook his head, picking up the cup of coffee he

had sitting on a rock beside him. He took a swallow and grimaced. In the short time April had been out there, it had already grown cold.

He had been standing there drinking his coffee and marveling at the beauty around him when she had come plunging out of the entrance to the cave. Only his quick reflexes had averted a near disaster.

He had felt her heart drumming in her chest and knew that his was pounding in equal rhythm. He looked at her again. It was odd, but he wanted to take her back into his arms just to feel her nearness, to know that she was truly safe. She aroused every protective instinct in him that he had thought long ago dispelled.

With his feelings in such chaos, he knew that it was not a good idea to stay there another night, but he also knew that he had no choice. Were he alone, he would manage it, but with April in tow, he couldn't take the chance. His horse would have to pick his way carefully back up to the top of the canyon as it was, but he couldn't walk his horse and hold on to April too. And he couldn't let her ride, just in case the horse did slip.

"Mr. Jackson."

He brought his attention back to the matter at hand.

"I said, when *can* we leave?"

He threw the cold coffee over the ledge. Without looking at her, he told her, "Another day or two, probably."

Her appalled look brought a quick frown to his face. "As the day warms, the ice will melt, but by then it will be too late to travel. We can't camp out in the open in this kind of weather. It would be foolish."

Her throat worked convulsively. She crossed her arms,

shivering against the cold, and met his look. He could see the fearful uncertainty in her eyes. What was she afraid of, anyway? Hadn't he proved himself trustworthy?

"You mean we have to stay here?"

Without realizing it, his face took on the immobile mask that the Comanche used to hide their thoughts.

" 'Fraid so."

She carefully pulled out of his grip and moved cautiously toward the cave. She threw him one last look before ducking back inside. Wolf lifted his head upward, closing his eyes. Somehow, he just knew this was not a good idea.

April stood in the entrance to the cave, her lips pressed tightly together. Closing her eyes, she rubbed her forearms to relieve herself of the chill. She couldn't stay there another day. She just couldn't. There was some kind of force at work here, and she was very much afraid it wasn't godly. Why else would there be such undercurrents of emotions between her and a perfect stranger? *Well,* she thought wryly, *not* quite *perfect.*

Her eyes flew open. Could it be that God had brought her to this point to show this heathen the way to Him? He knew about the Lord, but she sensed that it was an area of his life he wished to ignore. Much like her own brother.

She shook her head slightly, frowning at her thoughts. Wolf was no heathen. She could tell that it bothered him not to be considered a gentleman in her eyes, but she no longer believed that to be so. He was everything a gentleman should be, more so than her brother's friends.

He came into the cave, bumping into her from behind. He grabbed her arms to keep her from tumbling forward.

"What are you doing standing here in the doorway?"

he asked, his voice laced with exasperation. "You'll catch your death."

"Sorry."

He dropped his hands and she moved quickly away. He went to the fire, and picking up the coffeepot, he lifted it enquiringly in her direction.

She retrieved her own cup and held it out to him. While he poured, she studied his face. He had the high cheekbones of the Indian, the proud tilt to the head. His skin was darker than most men she was used to, but he was definitely handsome.

He caught her staring at him and lifted a brow in inquiry. April flushed brightly, dropping her gaze.

"Thank you for the coffee." She managed a smile. "You make it rather well." ·

He grinned. "For a man, you mean."

Her smile came more naturally. She seated herself on the crate, lifting her gaze to meet his eyes.

"Tell me more about yourself," she encouraged.

He met her look, and both found themselves unable to look away.

"Why do you want to know?" he asked quietly.

"Because I'm interested," she answered softly, realizing that she really was. He fascinated her more than anything had in a very long time.

He glanced away. She thought he was going to ignore her request, but he seated himself in his usual spot, leaning back against the cave wall. He turned to her, but it was some time before he spoke.

"I told you about my mother and father. What else do you want to know?"

April shrugged. "What was your childhood like? Where did you live? How did you become a ranger?"

His mouth tilted into a half smile. "I lived as a child among the Comanche. My mother was a typical wife—feeding her family, caring for her child and husband, visiting with other female friends. For the most part, it was a good life." He stared vacantly at the wall opposite, and April knew that his mind had gone back to that world so different from her own.

"I was taught to hunt and track and kill. I made my father quite proud of me with my prowess with a bow. When they were killed. . ." His voice tapered off. He glanced at April then, his eyes dark and haunted. She saw in him the same yearning that she had seen in Ted. They were so very much alike in their pain.

"I was never accepted by the Comanche as one of their own, nor by the whites either. I found it better to become a Texas Ranger and live my life alone."

April's heart went out to him. She could picture the lonely little boy he must have been. What agony it must have caused his mother to watch her child being shunned by others.

"You said your mother was a missionary's daughter?"

He nodded, staring deeply into her eyes. She wondered what, exactly, he was looking for.

"She taught me of Jesus and His love, and for a time I believed. Maybe that's why the Comanche never accepted me. When they danced to their gods, I sat aside. When they gave offerings, I only watched."

April wet her lips, hesitant to ask. "Did you ever marry?"

Wolf jerked his gaze back to hers, wondering what had provoked such a question. Just idle female curiosity? Somehow, he doubted it. She didn't seem the nosy type.

"No, I never married."

The set look of his face warned April not to further probe that area of his life. He tilted his head to the side. "It's your turn," he told her, smoothly changing the subject.

"There's not much to tell. Actually, we have something in common. Both of my parents died when I was young, too."

His face became inscrutable. "At least they weren't murdered."

"No," she agreed softly. "But my mother also taught me about Jesus and His love."

"What about your brother?" he asked, refusing to be sidetracked into a theological discussion.

"We were both raised to believe the same things, but somehow he's gotten away from them."

She didn't like his smile. "Life has a way of changing us."

He got up and went to the cave entrance. He took a deep breath of the clean air. April joined him, and he glanced down at her briefly. Again, there was something strange that seemed to be pulling them closer together. They could read it in each other's eyes, though neither would mention it.

"The ice is melting," she suggested cheerfully, turning away from his look. He said nothing, continuing to watch her.

"I need to go outside," she finally told him in embarrassment. "Is it safe yet?"

He nodded. "But don't go far," he warned.

She went past him, staying only as long as necessary. Although the temperatures were rising, they were still too cold to stay outside for very long.

When she returned, she found Wolf bent over the fire with a fry pan. He took some flour and water, mixed it together, then poured it into the sizzling hot lard.

"Can I help?"

He shook his head. "There's not much to do. I'm just making some fry bread to add to the beans." He grinned up at her. "Not exactly hotel cuisine, but it'll keep us from starving."

She was surprised by his reference to a hotel, and she had noticed that his English was as proficient as her own. Again she found herself wondering about his life.

"I think I'll go crazy if I have to stay cooped up in here much longer!" she exclaimed, dropping to the seat across from him.

"Solitude is good for the soul."

The look she gave him spoke volumes. "Well, I'm not exactly alone, am I?"

"Bored with my company, huh?"

She could tell he was laughing at her. His eyes crinkled at the corners, though his mouth merely twitched into a smile.

While they ate, Wolf told April about attending college in Boston. There was much he left unsaid, and she thought she could read between the lines. After living among the Comanche most of his life, city living must have been very difficult for him. Although he didn't mention it, she suspected that being half Indian had probably caused him much grief at school.

After they ate their impromptu meal, Wolf rummaged through his saddlebag. He brought out a small piece of wood with an intricately painted design on it.

"How about a game?" he asked, and April narrowed her eyes at him suspiciously.

"What kind of game?"

"Well," he told her in a wickedly amused voice, "actually we'll have to modify it somewhat. It's usually played by a group of people."

He explained how the Comanche used the piece in a game both men and women alike enjoyed. "There are two teams. Each one takes a turn trying to fool the other by passing, or not passing, the wood. Someone from the other team will finally call out which man he thinks has the piece."

She watched him warily. "Then what?"

"You keep score. The one with the highest score wins."

"Just what exactly does he win?"

His look made her grow warm all over. "That depends on the bet," he told her softly.

Her eyes widened, and she drew in a shaky breath. "I don't gamble," she finally told him in a quavery voice.

He looked disappointed. Sitting back, he smiled ruefully. "That's all right. We can play the game anyway."

"How?"

He closed his fist around the wood, then began shifting his hands back and forth. When he stopped, he grinned at her.

"Pick one."

She returned his grin. "This is like hide the button."

Her forehead puckered in concentration as she studied his hands. Finally, she reached across and tapped his left hand.

"That one."

He turned his empty palm over. "Wrong. That's one for me." Reaching over, he drew a mark in the sand with a twig.

He handed her the wood. "Your turn."

Giggling like a child, she followed his example. He tapped her hand, and she turned over the palm with the piece in it.

She frowned at him. "How'd you do that?"

Ignoring the question, he took the wood piece again. After almost an hour, he had far more marks in the sand than she did. She looked at him, clearly puzzled.

"How do you always seem to know?"

His eyes roved her face slowly, and she felt her stomach begin to churn.

"It's your face," he told her softly. "It gives you away."

Her eyes widened until they were so large Wolf thought he could walk right into them. He smiled slowly.

"You're wondering what thoughts I can read on your face."

April sucked in a sharp breath. That was exactly what she had been thinking. Over the past hour she had found herself wondering what his bet might have been. The look in his eyes made her breathless, and she had wondered if he would have demanded a kiss. Paradoxically, she had hoped that he would.

He leaned across, placing one large hand behind her neck and pulling her gently forward.

"I'll take my winnings now," he told her quietly.

She placed her hands against his chest, pushing firmly. "I told you, I don't gamble."

"But I do."

His lips closed over hers, and she forgot every reason she had for refusing him.

Five

Wolf stood outside the entrance to the cave castigating himself severely. That kiss had to have been the stupidest thing he had ever done in his life! What on earth had gotten into him anyway? He had only known the woman for two days.

He pulled the slip of paper from his pocket, reading it yet again. He tried to use it to bring his anger to the surface, but somehow, he just couldn't do it. No matter how hard he tried, he couldn't reconcile April's innocent face with a desperate gang of outlaws.

He was confused by the strange rush of emotions she invoked in him. This was something far beyond his experience, especially where women were concerned.

Most white women shunned him, though there were those who followed him with longing in their eyes. Those women he avoided. Indian women were more lenient, but he was too white to fit into their way of life. The education his mother had insisted upon set him apart from most.

Being around April just that short period of time had set him yearning for things he wasn't even aware that he wanted. But she was far too different from him, also. She had a faith in a God he had long ago abandoned. Though his parents had served Him almost their whole lives, He had chosen not to protect them when they needed Him most.

The sun was setting and it would soon be dark. An eagle screamed high above the trees, circling ever downward toward its nest and its young.

Would he one day have a nest of his own, with children and a loving wife? Was it possible any woman would want him? And even if it were, could he do that to a woman that he truly loved? Could he subject her to the same kind of prejudice his mother had faced all her life? The same kind of prejudice *he* had faced all *his* life.

Gritting his teeth, he forced himself to return to the cave. Though the cold air had cooled his ardor and his thinking, the tense atmosphere remained.

April watched him warily, sitting cross-legged on the blanket she used as a bed. Her blue dress had long ago taken on a dusty hue, leaving her looking a bit bedraggled. He lifted an eyebrow slightly.

"An Indian woman would never sit like that. It's not considered proper," he told her, hoping to lighten the mood. It had the opposite effect. Her forehead twisted into a frown.

"I'm not an Indian woman," she returned coldly, her frosty eyes raking over his beaded buckskins.

He sighed heavily. "I'm sorry. I was only teasing." He crossed to her side and knelt on one knee before her, careful to keep some distance between them. "I'm sorry, too, for kissing you." He reached out to touch her, the fringe on his buckskin shirt swishing with the movement. He saw the trepidation return to her eyes, and he dropped his arm, his hand curling into a fist. His lips tilted into a half smile, and a twinkle entered his normally serious brown eyes. "Well, not really. I guess I'm sorry I kissed you without your permission."

April stared at him, confounded by his honesty. "Do you always go around kissing women you've known for such a short time?"

His look became at once sober. "Only when their eyes ask me to."

April's mouth dropped open. Snapping it shut, she turned her eyes away, unable to deny what he said. "You think too highly of yourself."

"Maybe," he agreed, unruffled by her sarcasm. "Anyway, I wanted to tell you that you needn't be alarmed. It won't happen again. I give you my word."

She gave a small sigh of relief, which quickly fled at the temerity of his next words.

"That is, unless you want me to."

She got to her feet, glaring down at him. Dark tendrils of hair that had escaped her bun hung around her face. She brushed them back with an impatient hand. "Don't hold your breath!"

He rose to stand before her, towering over her by at least a foot. She prudently moved backward a step.

The emotion in his eyes caused her heart to start fluttering irregularly.

"We'll see. In the meantime, you might as well get some sleep. We'll be leaving in the morning."

April was surprised at the reluctance she felt at this disclosure. When her eyes met his, she found the same feelings reflected there. Nodding, she began to prepare her bed for the night.

They ate their supper in silence. After Wolf had again cleaned the plates, they settled down on their respective bedrolls. The crackling of the fire was a soothing sound as the darkness and cold descended outside the cave.

April leaned up on one elbow and looked across to the other side of the cave where Wolf had his back to her. "Wolf?"

"What?"

His testiness did little to encourage her, but she had to know.

"Did you turn from God when your parents were killed?"

By the dim light from the fire she could see his back and shoulders tense. "That was part of it," he finally replied.

"And the other part?"

He rolled over to face her, his dark eyes glittering through the dimness. His voice was filled with anger. "I watched people claiming to be representatives of God murdering, stealing, and lying to a race of people they thought inferior. Many thought they were doing it in the name of God. *Manifest destiny* they called it," he spat. "I saw little children lying in the dirt, shot through the heart, their mothers lying beside them, dead. Their last act one of motherly devotion in trying to save their children."

The images his words elicited filled her with horror. She didn't know what to say.

"Grant you, the Indians have dealt with the whites just as badly, but at least they don't do it in the name of God."

"Not all whites are that way," she rebuked softly. "Just as not all Indians are."

His eyes met hers. She found it hard to read the message in them.

"So I'm beginning to find out."

She lay back down, turning her back to him. She wanted to say more, but she didn't know how. It was hard to share a faith that she didn't understand herself. Hard to explain *why* she believed the way she did.

"April?"

She looked over her shoulder. "Yes?"

"What has God ever done for you?"

She turned fully toward him, wondering how she could put into words such a feeling.

"It's hard to explain, Wolf," she told him softly, "but I'll try. When my parents died, I had to take care of myself and my brother. There were times when things were bad, but no matter how bad they got, I knew that God was there watching over me. Crying with me. Laughing with me. It gave me strength to go on. Perhaps that's the best way to explain it. He gives me strength and courage when I need it most. Even if I die, I know I'll always be with Him. It's like the Apostle Paul once said. 'To live is Christ, to die is gain.' If I live for Him, I have everything. If I die for Him, I still have everything."

He seemed to be pondering what she said. Again, there was that longing in his eyes.

"I wish I could believe that," he whispered. Turning back to the wall, he effectively ended the conversation.

The next day dawned bright and clear. April joined Wolf

outside, her eyes darting away from him in embarrassment. After yesterday, she found it hard to look at him without remembering that kiss and his words about her wanting it reflected in her eyes.

Though cold, the air was fresh and invigorating. April crossed her arms and rubbed them vigorously.

"It's a beautiful day," she greeted cheerfully.

There was a frown on his face. His head was tilted to the wind, and his eyes scanned the blue expanse overhead.

"Something's not right," he answered absently.

Suddenly frightened, she glanced all around her but could see nothing. The hair prickled on the back of her neck at his mantic voice. "What do you mean?"

He took a deep breath, letting it out slowly. "There's something in the air. It might not be wise to leave just yet."

Now April was really frightened. To stay here with him in such close proximity was unthinkable. "The ice has melted, and the sky is clear. I think it would be best if we left now."

Wolf's eyes met hers then. He could read the uncertainty and the fear. Was she so afraid of him that she would risk her life, and *his*, to be away from him? Or was it something else? Perhaps she knew more than he believed about her brother returning for her. Maybe he was on his way even now.

Still, she had a point. The way his feelings were escalating, it wouldn't be prudent to remain there much longer.

A crackling in the underbrush brought him whirling around, his Colt whipped from his holster. A small rabbit came from the bushes, startled at their presence. It froze in fear, then turned and skidded away.

Wolf turned back to April and found her staring fixedly at his gun. She lifted terrified eyes to his, and he quickly holstered his weapon. He could read the questions racing across her uneasy features.

"Get your things together," he ordered gruffly. "I'll get my horse."

She watched him walk away and saw what she hadn't noticed previously. A small cleft in the side of the canyon formed a natural indented shelter. Wolf had lashed pine branches together to form a covering against the wind. He pulled them away, and a beautiful pinto was revealed to her eyes. It nickered softly when it saw Wolf.

"Hey, Boy," he responded, patting its sides. "Ready to go?"

He carefully moved the horse backward out of the little shelter, turning him until he faced back up the canyon.

April stared at the two of them, wide-eyed. "Has he been here the whole time?"

"Yep."

"But I never saw him or heard him when I came outside."

Wolf grinned at her in amusement. "Not very observant, are you?"

April ignored his comment. She came closer, stroking the animal's soft nose. "He's a beauty. What's his name?"

"Sky Dancer. I call him Dancer for short."

Wolf entered the cave, returning moments later with their packs. He glanced at April's shoes.

"I hope you can make it up the canyon in those."

Surprised, April studied the trail they were about to take. "Aren't we riding the horse?"

He shook his head, strapping the packs to the horse. "Not until we get out of this canyon. There's still ice clinging to many of the surfaces. It's too dangerous." He took the horse's reins and began moving forward carefully. "Watch your step."

April took one last look at the cave. It had been a refuge of sorts for the past two days, and she was suddenly reluctant to leave its comfort.

When they reached the top of the canyon, the wind hit them with its full force, taking April's breath away. Her blue wool coat did little to dispel the cold. She shivered.

"It seems colder up here," she yelled.

Without turning, Wolf yelled back at her. "It is. There's nothing to block the wind."

When he attained a safe distance, he turned and reached to help April into the saddle. Climbing up behind her, he settled himself comfortably, stretching around her to hold onto the reins.

April tensed at his nearness, then slowly relaxed against his warmth. "Are you sure Dancer can carry both of us?"

"He can, but not as quickly as he can carry one. We're going to have to camp out tonight."

She jerked her look back over her shoulder. "Outside? But we'll freeze!"

His intense eyes met hers. "It was either that or stay until the weather warmed."

Unable to hold his knowing gaze, she turned forward.

"Although leaving might just have been the second stupidest mistake I've ever made," he continued, his voice dangerously low.

"Why?"

The question barely left her mouth before the sun was blocked by moving clouds. She looked up and saw the sky growing leaden gray.

"It's going to snow!" she said in surprise.

His look flickered around the sky, his face growing grimmer by the minute. "I'm afraid so."

As they plodded along, April sucked in a deep breath of the cold air. The distance between them and the cave increased, and she became more relieved with each passing mile.

"A little snow won't hurt us," she encouraged.

His silence made her curious. She looked over her shoulder and caught the quick frown on his face. Her heart began to hammer with dread. "What is it?"

"This isn't going to be a little snow." He shook his head in disgust. "I knew this was a bad idea."

Wolf stopped the horse in a stand of trees. Getting down, he pulled April off after him.

"We need to make a shelter."

April looked around at the forest of pines. "Can't we just go back to the cave?"

He shook his head, retrieving a small ax from his saddlebag. "We've come too far. It would take too long."

He started hacking away at small pine trees. "Help me get these over there to that spot beneath those three large pines."

They worked together as quickly as possible, but even so, by the time they had cut enough saplings, the snow had started to fall.

Using some rope from his saddle, Wolf made a crisscross section using the three large trees as poles. He then wove the saplings between the rope until there was a small lean-to, while April gathered their blankets and some of the supplies.

Finding some dry kindling, Wolf started a fire in the middle of the area and motioned April to have a seat. She hurried inside, watching as Wolf began putting more saplings against the front, finally closing them inside.

"What about Dancer?"

He shook his head. "He'll be fine." He scooted over until he was close to the fire. "We should be all right here 'til the storm passes, though I'm not certain how long that will be."

Although it was far from warm in their little shelter with the wind blowing through the cracks and branches, it was much better than being outside. April was thankful that she was with Yellow Wolf. His survival instincts would keep them alive, she knew without a doubt. Oddly enough, despite his earlier amorous attitude, she felt remarkably safe with him.

"How far did we come?" she asked.

"About five miles."

Amazed, she turned a shocked face to him. "You mean we still have thirty-five miles to go?"

He looked at her, laughter in his eyes. "Yep."

"How long do you think the storm will last?"

"I'd say until tomorrow morning, at least," he told her, without looking at her.

April swallowed hard. If this man was so attractive inside the cave where she had some room to move around, what was he going to be like sitting three feet away?

She caught his glance and saw his slow smile. He knew what she was thinking, she was certain of it. If he was dangerous in the cave, she decided, here he was going to be absolutely lethal.

Six

For two days, they were buried by an avalanche of snow. Periodically Wolf would push his way free of their shelter and check on Dancer. April stayed huddled near the low-burning fire.

During this time, they were able to talk. The tension between them crackled like the burning embers of the fire, but Wolf kept a respectful distance. April wasn't certain if she was grateful or disappointed. She had never experienced such a strong attraction to anyone in her life, and she didn't know what to do about it.

Periodically, April caught Wolf studying her and wondered what he was thinking. His thoughts were hidden by his set, immobile face.

April shared with him the story of her life. Whenever she talked about her brother, Wolf could hear the love and devotion in her voice. He wondered again if she was as innocent as she claimed. Perhaps her brother had used that devotion to convince her to help him. Still, it was hard for him to believe.

When they finally rose from their shelter, snow had fallen to a depth of several feet. Wolf had never seen anything like it in his life. He'd lived most of his life in these parts, and while snow was common, this one was definitely out of the ordinary.

He was lashing what was left of their supplies to his saddle. He glanced over his shoulder at April.

"In my saddlebag is some twine. Could you hand it to me, please?"

April hurried to do as he asked, anxious to get moving. Her feet crunched through two feet of snow, the cold seeping up her legs and into her already numbed feet.

She delved into the bag, her fingers encountering a small, hard object. Curious, she pulled it out. She stared at the Bible in surprise.

Wolf glanced up at her, his mouth open to hurry her. He stiffened when he saw her standing there, his Bible open in her hands. He crossed quickly to her side, his long legs making short work of the distance.

He jerked the Bible from her hands. "I said *twine*," he grated, moving to put the book back in his bag.

She placed a detaining hand over his. "Wait!"

His set look was forbidding.

"Please, there's something I would like to show you."

He didn't stop her from taking the book, but the glare he gave her was uncompromising.

"It was my mother's. That's why I keep it, no other reason."

"Wolf," April countered, "you and Ted have something in common besides the death of your parents. You both blame God for their deaths."

He lifted a supercilious eyebrow. "And I shouldn't?"

She looked into his eyes, trying to impart a small

measure of her faith. He recognized the sincerity behind her look and stilled.

"For two years I've wanted to show my brother two special verses in the Bible, but I didn't have the opportunity until just lately. I missed that opportunity." Her blue eyes were serious. "I don't want to miss that opportunity with you."

She flipped the pages of the Bible to the book of Hebrews. Sliding her finger down the page, she finally stopped at chapter two, verse fourteen. She lifted it for him to read. His eyes skimmed it, then lifted to hers.

"And?"

She then flipped the pages until she reached the book of Matthew. She had him read the twenty-eighth verse of chapter ten.

"Wolf," she told him, "Satan has the power of death. You blame God, but there is another entity with the power to destroy lives. It's Satan you should be angry with, not the Lord."

His eyes darkened in anger. "The book of Job talks about God allowing Satan to use that power. He could always say *no.*"

Surprised, April studied his tense face. He knew far more of the Bible than just a casual reading would allow. It was obvious that at some time he had studied it.

"Tell me," she asked him sharply. "Are you angry with God because He didn't serve *your* purpose instead of His own? Maybe you think you have a better understanding of the universe!"

Her sarcasm stung. Wolf's nostrils flared. He pulled the twine from the bag and turned to leave. April called after him, desperation in her voice. She *had* to make him see.

"If Satan killed your parents, then why do you serve him? *He's* the one you should be angry with, and you should be doing everything in your power to deny him instead of following after him."

He turned sharply, his face unusually pale. His hands folded into fists at his side.

"Get your things together, and for your own sake, *shut up!*"

April's eyes widened at his ferocious look. She swallowed hard, staring at him in impotent fury. She turned quickly and disappeared inside the lean-to.

Wolf released his breath slowly, his hands uncurling at his sides. The thing that bothered him most was that she made perfect sense. One could only serve two masters, either the god of the world or the God of heaven. And it was not the God of heaven who had brought sin into the world.

He finished his preparations to leave in heavy silence. April came and stood next to him, her look wary. He lifted his gaze to her face.

"Don't worry. I'm not about to scalp you."

Her lips twitched slightly. "I *had* wondered."

Ever so slowly his lips curled into a smile. The darkness of his eyes lightened as the anger drained from him.

"Are you ready to go?"

She nodded but said nothing.

"We're going to have to walk. The snow's too deep for Dancer to carry us through." He lifted an eyebrow. "It's gonna be tough going."

April looked around, then sighed. "Well, we can't

stay here, can we?" Moving past him, she began trekking forward. Wolf's sharp whistle pierced the air, and she turned to him in question. His hand snaked out, his forefinger pointed in the opposite direction.

"That way."

Flushing, she raised her nose slightly and headed in the direction of his pointing finger. Grinning, he followed her.

It took them a whole day to travel only a few miles. That night Wolf once again rigged them a small shelter.

"Tomorrow we should make it out of the snow, then we'll be able to travel faster."

April laughed, though she felt no humor. "Can't wait to be rid of me, huh?"

His eyes met hers, and at the look in them, her breathing grew labored. She ducked her head, sorry that she had spoken.

"What will happen to me?" she asked quietly.

Folding his tongue behind his teeth, he glanced away. "You'll have to stand trial."

The color drained from her face. "But I didn't *do* anything!"

Still not looking at her, he told her, "That'll be for the jury to decide." When he finally looked at her, she could see uncertainty in his expression. "Would it help if I told you that *I* believe you?"

She smiled slightly. "I'm glad for that, but somehow I don't think it's going to help me much. Jason will want to see me hang."

He frowned. "Jason?"

April told him about the banker. He glowered at her. "If he's any kind of a man at all, he'll want to see justice done."

"Maybe."

The unrestrained fury in his eyes unnerved her. She settled down to try to sleep, exhausted by the day's travels. The snow had been brutal to try to travel through, and even Dancer stood a few feet away with head hung down.

Wolf lay a short distance away from the fire listening until he heard April's deep breathing. He turned his head slightly until he could see her by the light from the fire. She lay on her side, her blanket clutched tightly against her. Her dark hair spilled in a mass around her head, and he found himself wanting to run his fingers through its silkiness.

Shaking his head, he forced himself to concentrate on his next move. Within two days, he would hand April over to the sheriff at Abasca. His insides went cold at the thought. Was it possible that she would really hang?

He glanced back at her sleeping form. For the first time in his career, he wanted to take a prisoner and run. Get her as far away as possible. But he knew that was not the way. He had to trust in the law to make things right.

April, he knew, trusted in God to make things right. But what if it wasn't in His will to let April live? She knew the possibilities, yet she seemed so secure in His love. What if He chose to let her die, just like his parents? Pain lanced his heart at the thought.

How could one woman so consume his thoughts and feelings in such a short time? Was it just the fact that they had shared hardship and danger together and so naturally grew closer by doing so? He thought not, for April was not the only woman he had ever been sent to capture. The problem was, she had instead captured him. Whatever happened, he was irrevocably tied to this woman in his heart. He sighed heavily, rolling away and forcing himself to crawl into the arms of Morpheus.

Three days later they topped the ridge that led to Abasca. Wolf pulled Dancer to a stop, suddenly reluctant to continue.

April's quiet voice startled him.

"Wolf, do you think we could go by my cabin first so that I might clean up some?"

She glanced up at him over her shoulder, and his mouth went dry. Could he do it? Could he actually turn her over for trial?

"Sure," he answered gruffly, thankful for the reprieve.

They plodded into her yard, and April sensed the emptiness. Had it only been six days? It seemed more like a lifetime.

Wolf pushed himself backward over Dancer's rump and came around to help April dismount. His hands rested on her waist long after her feet touched the ground. Their gazes were locked together, and April found herself unable to look away. She placed her hands against his buckskin-clad chest and felt his heart racing against her palms.

In a few short hours, this man would hand her over to the sheriff. After that, he would be gone. If he caught her brother and his cohorts, he would bring them back for trial, but what if he was killed? Or what if she was hanged before he returned? Despite what he said, she had no faith in seeing justice served when so much was stacked against her. Still, with God, she knew that she was loved and protected. Whatever happened, He was there for her.

"Wolf?"

He said nothing, continuing to stare into her eyes.

She knew he would never break his promise. She surprised herself with her boldness.

"Please kiss me."

His eyes grew so dark, they reminded her of her mother's black onyx stone necklace. He pulled her close, crushing her into his arms. His kiss told her that he felt the same, as though this might be the last time they saw each other again. The kiss went on and on until April's legs grew weak beneath her. She finally pushed away, but Wolf refused to release her. His fingers grazed her jaw ever so lightly.

"As God is my witness," he told her roughly, imitating her own words, "I will *not* let you hang."

She lifted her hand, allowing her fingers to stroke the several day's growth of whiskers on his chin. "Trust in Him," she whispered. "Just this once, trust in Him."

His look moved over her face, imprinting its picture on his memory. "I do."

Wolf flinched as he heard the door of the jail cell clang with finality. April curled her fingers around the bars, looking out at him. Such faith shone in her eyes that it softened his heart.

The sheriff glared at her in disapproval. "Miss Hansen," he barked, "I never would have thought it of such a fine upstanding young woman like yourself."

Anger rose up in Wolf. "Sounds like you've appointed yourself as judge and jury already. Are you going to be the executioner too?"

The sheriff's cheeks turned ruddy with embarrassment. "She'll get a fair trial," he snapped.

"She'd better."

The sheriff's eyes grew large at the softly implied threat. His face lost some of its color. There wasn't a person in the territory who hadn't heard of Yellow Wolf Jackson. The sheriff's eyes slid to the Colt revolvers resting at his sides.

April's cool voice lifted some of the tension in the room. "It's all right, Sheriff Baker. I know you'll do your duty and do it well. You always have."

Disconcerted by her show of faith, the sheriff coughed slightly. "Yes, Ma'am."

Wolf glared at Sheriff Baker. "I need to speak with the prisoner alone for a few minutes."

Glancing from one to the other, the sheriff nodded and left the room. Wolf wrapped his hands around April's, leaning close against the bars.

"I'll be back, I promise you."

She moved her mouth through the bars, and he kissed her again.

"I believe you," she told him softly.

Reluctantly, he turned to go.

"Wolf?"

He turned back.

"Please don't kill my brother."

His expression clouded. "I never kill unless there's no other way."

"Then I'll be praying for you both."

Her quiet words hung in his mind long after he had departed the jail.

Seven

The judge's gavel rapped twice on the desk. Silence finally settled down over the room with only a whispered comment rupturing it from time to time.

Since Abasca didn't yet have a town hall, the trial was being held in the one-room schoolhouse. There was standing room only, and it seemed as if the whole town had turned out for April's trial.

Jason sat to the side, his dark look filled with malice. If anyone hoped she would hang, it would probably be him, April decided.

The attorney seated at her side gave her hand a reassuring squeeze. She smiled at him, relieved that Mr. Cord had decided to stand in her defense. He was a well-respected member of the community, and what was more, he was firmly convinced that April was innocent.

He pulled his watch from his vest pocket, frowning. He might be in a hurry to get the show on the road, but April was certainly not.

The circuit judge from San Antonio glared out over the courtroom, and April felt her heart sink. Mr. Cord noticed her frightened expression and smiled reassuringly.

"It's all right, April. Judge Bonner is a very fair and honest man."

Relaxing slightly, April sat back and allowed the lawyer to take over. He rose to present his case to the court, his well-groomed appearance giving him credence as an esteemed member of his profession.

He brushed a hand back through his iron gray hair and cleared his throat. "Your honor and members of the jury, my client wishes to plead not guilty to the charges of aiding and abetting a robbery."

There was a brief tittering in the room. The prosecution counselor, Mr. Myers, rose to his feet also. Giving Mr. Cord a slight nod, he suggested to the court that he would prove beyond a shadow of doubt that April Hansen had, indeed, participated in the robbery on Abasca's bank.

When Mr. Harris, the bank teller who had been shot, was called to the stand, he walked by April and gave her a shy smile. April smiled back. She had always liked Mr. Harris. Not only was he the teller in Jason's bank, but she sewed dresses for his wife.

Mr. Myers tucked his hands into the armholes of his vest, his grave look making him rather intimidating.

"Now, Mr. Harris, tell us what happened on the morning of November third."

Mr. Harris related everything he could remember from that morning. He motioned to April with his arm in a sling. "And if it weren't for April Hansen, I'd be plugged six foot under right now. She saved my life!"

The crowd broke out into excited chatter, and Mr. Myers frowned. Obviously, that was not what he wanted to hear. The judge rapped his gavel to quiet the crowd again.

"Be that as it may, Mr. Harris," Myers continued, "she was there with her brother, was she not?"

Mr. Harris agreed that she was. Myers ended his questions.

Mr. Cord rose to his feet to cross examine. "So, Mr. Harris, is it your opinion that Miss Hansen was trying to thwart the robbery?"

Myers got quickly to his feet. "Objection, your honor. Mr. Cord is asking the witness to speculate."

"Sustained." The judge gave Mr. Cord a warning look. He apologized.

"Let me rephrase the question. Mr. Harris, did Miss Hansen's quick action help to thwart the robbery?"

Wrinkling his face, Mr. Harris cocked his head to the side. "Well, the robbers got away with the money, but no one got hurt. So I'd say, yeah, she did."

When Jason was called to the stand, April's heart sank. His malevolent look focused on her, and she shivered.

Mr. Myers crossed the room and stood next to Jason's chair.

"Please tell the court your name."

Without taking his eyes from April, Jason answered, "My name is Jason Dice. I am manager of the Abasca Bank, the one *she* helped rob."

The crowd came alive again. Mr. Cord frowned at Jason. "I object, Your Honor."

"Sustained." Judge Bonner glared at Jason. "Kindly refrain from making any more of those suggestive remarks, or I will have to declare you a hostile witness and remove you from the courtroom."

Jason subsided, his lips curled out into a childish pout. He answered the questions of both Mr. Cord and Mr. Myers, still trying to implicate April with the robbery.

Mr. Myers called as his final witness the woman who had fainted. She made her way hesitantly to the front of the room and, after swearing on the Bible, hastily seated herself.

Mr. Myers smiled reassuringly. "Now, Mrs. Winston, suppose you tell us just what you saw and heard on that morning."

She basically confirmed the stories of the others, but she added one final clause.

"I heard Miss Hansen try to stop her brother. She told him she would never forgive him for what he was doing."

The silence was once again disrupted. Mr. Cord refrained from questioning, knowing that Mrs. Winston had already made his point for him. The judge dismissed the jury and told the room that court would resume after three o'clock.

April was returned to her jail cell, where she quietly prayed, not on her own behalf, but for Wolf and her brother.

When they returned to the courtroom several hours later, the judge asked the jury for its verdict.

The jury foreman stood to his feet. "Well now, Judge, the law says you don't condemn a man unless there's no shadow of a doubt about his guilt." He glanced at the other members of the jury. "We all feel that Miss Hansen is a good, upright young woman. We have our doubts about whether she's guilty of such a crime. Therefore, we find the defendant not guilty."

The room erupted in cheers. April sank bank into her chair, exhaling her breath in relief.

No one noticed the tall figure clad in buckskins who exited the room at the back.

Wolf slipped out of the courtroom, his heart light with relief. Through the whole trial, he had been praying that God would spare April. Now he realized that if God had done so, it wasn't because of him, Wolf, but because of April's faith in the Lord Himself. Still, she was right, and he was through serving the devil who had killed his parents. From now on, he would give his all to fight Satan here on earth in any way he could.

He had found the trail of the Miller gang. Three had gone in one direction, one had circled back. Hansen was in the vicinity, he knew, and he had no doubt that he would be waiting to talk with his sister. Wolf would be ready.

April climbed down from the buggy, turning to smile at the man holding the reins. "Thank you, Mr. Cord."

He returned her smile. "You're quite welcome. I knew you were innocent."

"Well, thank you again for having such faith in me."

She stepped back from the buggy, but Mr. Cord didn't move on. He frowned at her. "Are you sure you won't come and have dinner with Mrs. Cord and me? I hate to think of you spending this day alone."

Her lips tilted wryly. "Solitude is good for the soul,"

she quoted. "Right now, I think I *want* to be alone."

He nodded in understanding. "Well, don't be a stranger. You're always welcome in our home. Besides," he grinned, "you owe Mrs. Cord a dress."

"Are you sure you don't want more payment than that?" she asked softly. "I *do* have some money, you know."

He lifted a brow. "Not until that Texas Ranger gets it back, you don't."

At the reference to Yellow Wolf, April felt her breath lodge in her throat. Where was he, anyway? Had he found Ted and the others? Was Wolf alive, and if so, had he had to kill Ted? These torturous thoughts had been with her the entire past week since Wolf had left. She longed for him to finish his job and return to her as he had promised, but she also knew that to do so would more than likely be to condemn her brother.

"Good-bye, Mr. Cord, and thank you again. Tell Mrs. Cord to let me know when she wants to start on her new dress."

He nodded, tipping his hat. "Will do."

April watched him leave, then slowly turned and headed for her small cabin. She entered the house, dropping her bonnet by the door. Her whole body was filled with lethargy from the anticlimax of the past two weeks. The whole thing seemed like some surrealistic dream.

Jason's glare when he had passed her on the way out of the courthouse had left her just a little shaken. His look promised retribution. She shook her head sadly, going to the fireplace to ready a fire.

She stopped short. The logs and kindling were already set, just waiting for a match. Who would have done such a thoughtful thing? Mr. Cord? Glancing quickly around the room, she froze when a figure rose from her bed in the corner. She could barely make out the figure in the dim light coming through the small glass windows. With a glad cry, she flew across the room.

"Ted!"

She ran into his outstretched arms, and they folded close around her. He laid his cheek against the top of her head.

"Oh, April, April! I thought you would never speak to me again. I'm so sorry for the hurt I've caused you."

She pulled away slightly, staring up into his face. "How could you, Ted. How could you leave me like that!"

He pulled her over to the bed and sat down next to her. Taking both her hands in his, he squeezed gently.

"I had no choice. Amos told me that we either had to leave you behind or kill you. Since there was three against one, I was afraid to take a chance on you getting hurt." His hold tightened. "I've never prayed so hard in my life."

"Oh, Ted! Then it was all worth it."

He pulled back, looking into her face. He stroked his fingers down the side of her face. "I'm so sorry for all the pain I've caused you. I realize how much I've hurt you, especially by rejecting God." His smile was rather lame. "But I never could get away from Him. He wouldn't let me go."

"He never will," she told him softly.

He noticed her shivering and crossed to the fire. Striking a match, he soon had a roaring blaze and motioned her to join him next to it. The look he fixed on her was intent.

"I take it the ranger found you?"

Flushing, April watched the fire flickering in the stone hearth. "Yes," she answered him quietly. "He found me."

"Did he. . .were you treated good?"

She swallowed hard, still not looking at him. "Yes, he treated me well." Her voice softened on the last word, and her brother's brows rose.

"What aren't you telling me?" he demanded, pulling her around to face him.

"She's not telling you that we fell in love."

April spun around at the same time as her brother, his hand instinctively reaching for his gun. He pulled it from his holster so quickly, April stared in amazement. The only problem was, Wolf stood in the doorway, his gun already pointed at Ted's heart.

Eight

W olf!"
April barely got the word out of her
mouth before Ted shoved her behind him.
Neither man was willing to drop their weapon.

"You don't want April to get hurt, do you, Hansen?"

Ted glanced over his shoulder at his sister huddling
behind him. She lifted terrified eyes to his face. Slowly he
dropped his Colt to the floor.

Glowering, he glanced up at Wolf. "What do you
mean you fell in love? In a few days? That's impossible!"

"It's been known to happen before," Wolf replied, still
not holstering his own weapon. He moved carefully across
the room until he could pick up Ted's gun.

"Wolf, please!"

April tried to push past her brother, but he snaked
out an arm to hold her in place. He glared at his sister. "Is
what he says true?"

For the first time, Wolf totally ignored Ted. His dark
eyes were fixed intently on April. "I knew it as soon as I
left you," he told her softly. "I didn't want to love you, but
I do."

Ted's angry voice lashed out at April. "You can't be in love with a. . .a. . ."

"Half-breed," Wolf supplied, his eyes glittering angrily, and he heard April's swift intake of breath.

Ted turned to him, anger rising in his own eyes. "I wasn't going to say that. I don't want my sister involved with a ranger. That's no kind of life for a woman."

April was staring fixedly at Wolf. She knew she had been attracted to the ranger, but she hadn't realized just how deep those feelings ran until he walked out of her life. She looked at her brother standing defiantly against Wolf, still trying to protect her. She loved him too.

Her gaze clashed with Wolf's. "Let him go, Wolf, please."

What did she see in his eyes? Disappointment?

"I can't, April. I have a job to do, and I've given my oath."

They both were surprised by Ted's soft voice. "You know he's right."

April turned a pale face to her brother. "They might hang you!"

He shook his head. "Not for robbery. That's just jail time."

Wolf studied him closely, his thoughts hidden behind a granite mask. "Amos Miller's gang has killed eight people. April's right. If convicted, you'll probably hang."

Ted flashed him a look. "She didn't need to know that."

April didn't know what to do. She had always gotten her brother out of his scrapes, but this one was beyond her. "Oh, Ted," she lamented softly. She didn't know what else to say.

"Where are the others, Hansen?" Wolf demanded.

Ted gave him a strange look. "I think you already know, Jackson."

Wolf's puzzled look moved over Ted slowly. "I only tracked them as far as Hilton's ledge, but you're right. I'll find them. But it would sure save me a lot of time, and possibly help you, if you cooperated."

April tugged on his sleeve. "Tell him, Ted."

Ted shook his head, still watching Wolf intently. "I don't think so. Let's just see how good you are, Jackson."

Wolf sensed a double meaning behind the words. His lips pressed into a tight line. Without saying anything, he fastened a pair of handcuffs to Ted's hands, while Ted watched him impassively.

April looked from one to the other, wringing her hands in agitation. She tried to get her brother to see reason one last time, but he still refused.

Wolf found Ted's horse where he had hidden it behind the cabin. He helped him to mount, then mounted Sky Dancer.

April laid a hand against his saddle, and he frowned down at her. Her blue eyes pleaded with him, and despite himself, he felt his heart soften.

"I want to come too," she begged.

He looked like he was about to decline, but then giving a quick nod, he reached down and lifted her to the saddle in front of him. Wrapping his arms around her securely, he noticed Ted's uncertain look flicking from one to the other.

Wolf led the way back to town, reluctant to open April up to any more censure. Still, Ted was her brother, and she loved him. It was only natural that she wanted to be with him.

He glanced once more at Ted, and the other man met his eyes. There was a message in them that he couldn't quite interpret. Wolf pulled April closer, thankful for the time he could hold her in his arms.

April's silence made his heart ache with sympathy. She loved her brother so much. What would it do to her if he did hang? And how could he live with himself if he was the cause of that pain in her life? At times like this, he almost hated being a ranger.

He handed Ted over to the sheriff, leaving April alone with her brother. He filled out the necessary paperwork to submit to his captain and quickly left the building. The sooner he got on the road, the sooner his job would be finished. And when this job was finished, he was coming back for April.

Although he had wondered if he could make any woman go through the prejudice his own mother had been through, he knew that he couldn't go on without at least offering April the chance to give them both a life full of love. After today, though, he was no longer confident of her feelings in the matter.

He had just mounted his horse when April hurried outside. The cold wind caused her gray wool dress to wrap around her legs. Shivering with the cold, she wrapped her arms tightly around herself. "I need to talk to you, Wolf."

His hands tightened on the reins. He thought he knew what she had to say, but he wasn't certain he wanted to hear it. After consigning her brother to almost certain death, how could she help but hate him?

"Not now, April. When I get back."

"No! I have to say this now."

Staring into her determined blue eyes, he slowly dismounted. Taking her arm, he pulled her to the side of the building, out of sight and sound of others who might be passing by.

He folded his arms across his chest, his look wooden. "Go ahead."

She studied his face for some time. Sighing, she laid a hand gently on his arm. "What Ted has done, he has to pay for. He made his own choices."

Slowly, his shoulders relaxed. "April, I—"

She placed her fingers over his lips. "It's all right, Wolf. You did what you had to do. I don't hold that against you." A sad smile curled her lips. "If you hadn't, you wouldn't be the man that I love."

He pulled her close, his large hand pressing her head against his chest. She could hear the thundering of his heart against her ear, and her smile widened. She looked up into his face, and blue eyes filled with love met brown eyes filled with adoration.

"I'll be back," he told her huskily, and she knew he was making her a promise.

"You better," she agreed just as huskily. Her eyes grew solemn. "Be careful, Wolf."

He kissed her with a kiss so full of promise, her legs threatened to buckle beneath her. She watched him climb back on Dancer, and giving her one last look, he wheeled about and headed out of town. Heavyhearted, April watched him leave.

She made her way slowly into the sheriff's office, not

certain she was up to her brother's upcoming interrogation. The look in his eyes told her that she had a lot to answer for.

The sheriff allowed her into his cell, and she seated herself on the bunk next to him. His look roved her features, and lifting one dark eyebrow, he asked, "Jackson gone?"

Flushing, she dropped her gaze to the dusty floor. "Yes."

"Do you really love him?"

She looked at him then, her eyes sparking with resolution. "Yes, I do."

He sighed heavily. "I hope for your sake that you're not disappointed."

"Why should I be?"

Reading the look on her face, his own face darkened. "Don't even think that! I am not referring to the man's race. If you remember correctly, mother hired a black nanny for us when we were younger, and we both loved her. You're not the only one who can see beyond skin color. I have no problem with his race." He got up and curled his hands around the cell bars. "But there are things you don't understand."

"Such as?"

Instead of answering, he yelled for the sheriff. Sheriff Baker took his time answering the summons, and when he finally meandered into the room, Jason Dice was with him.

"What do *you* want?" the sheriff snapped.

Jason's look was nasty. "He wants to hang, don't you, Mr. Hansen?" The look he threw April was full of loathing.

"I have something for you," Ted told the sheriff, surprising everyone. He reached down and took off his boot.

Turning it over, he pried open the heel with his fingers and pulled out a piece of paper. Unfolding it, he handed it to the sheriff.

Curious, April joined him at the bars. She tried to see past his broad shoulders, but all she could see was the stunned expression on the sheriff's face.

"What is it?" she asked.

The sheriff looked at Ted, his face a curious mixture of disbelief and awe. "It's a letter from the commander of the Texas Rangers, Mr. John Ford. It's cosigned by the president of the United States, James Buchanan."

April's startled gaze flew to her brother.

"It says here," the sheriff continued, "that Mr. Ted Hansen, Texas Ranger, is acting under the auspices of the federal government and the State of Texas, and that he is to be afforded every vestige of legal rank."

Jason grabbed the paper from his hand. "Let me see that!" He quickly scanned the note, his face blanching. "It's a forgery," he declared vehemently.

The sheriff took the paper, studying it. "Not with the president's seal, it's not."

The color drained from April's face. "You're a ranger? But. . .but why didn't you tell Yellow Wolf?"

He avoided her searching eyes. "I need out of here, Sheriff. Now!"

Sheriff Baker hastily retrieved his keys and opened the door of the cell. Ted quickly exited, April following more slowly. Jason followed behind, his manner suddenly subdued. He stalked past them angrily and left the office.

"I need my guns," Ted barked at the sheriff.

"Ted!"

He turned to her then. Taking her by the shoulders, he bent until he could look into her eyes.

"Listen to me, April. I don't have time to explain things now. You'll have to wait until I get back."

"*If* you get back!"

He cocked her a grin. "Have a little faith, will you?" Strapping on his holsters, he returned the paper to his hollowed-out boot sole, tapping the leather back in place. Putting his boot back on, he told her solemnly, "Pray for me."

He dashed out the door, jumping to his horse tied to the rail. Whipping the reins loose from the post, he turned and galloped after Yellow Wolf.

April watched him leave, her heart in her throat. Swallowing convulsively, she decided that he was right. It was time to pray.

❧

Amos Miller had been decidedly sloppy in leaving a trail to follow, and Wolf was more than a little suspicious.

He watched from the confines of a green shelter belt of trees as the trio ambled around their shanty in preparation for leaving. They were tying bundles to their horses, and he suspected it was probably the loot from their recent escapades. That they were cold-blooded killers warranted caution.

He pulled his bow up, knocking an arrow onto the string. Two other arrows sat on the ground beside him. He would have to be fast, because Amos was a notorious quick draw.

He located each man, and with quick precision let fly three arrows, one right after the other.

The first pinned Chauncy to the side of the shanty, his gun arm arrested by the piercing of the arrow. The second arrow struck Al in the right arm, effectively ruining his gun hand. The third arrow missed its target, Amos's quick reflexes causing him to drop to the ground to allow the arrow to fly over his head. Still, it gave Wolf the time he needed to get quickly to his feet and draw his two revolvers.

Amos, reaching for his holster, froze to the spot. The other two did the same. Seeing Wolf clad in buckskins, his bow slung over his back, reminded them of all the stories they had heard about him.

He carefully descended the hill until he was on level ground with them.

"You're getting sloppy in your old age, Miller. You left a trail a child could follow."

Amos cursed, spitting on the ground. "That's a lie. We took care to cover our tracks."

"It were that pup, Hansen," Al growled. "You told *him* to disguise our trail."

"That's right, you did."

Wolf tensed, recognizing the voice from behind him. He could hear Ted climbing down the hill at his back. If he let off three shots at the others, would he have time to turn and fire on Hansen?

With his mind off center from his opponents, Wolf missed Amos's quick draw. A shot rang out from behind him, and Amos's gun fell with a thud.

Ted drew up beside Wolf, his cocky grin a bit disarming. A wisp of smoke from his gun added the smell of burning powder to the air. "Hi ya, Jackson. Glad we're on the same team."

Snarls from the men greeted this statement. Puzzled, Wolf threw Ted a quick glance.

"I'll explain on the way. Right now, let's get these desperadoes behind bars where they belong."

Ted passed him, going to the others and cuffing them. He then searched the saddlebags and bundles. "Looks like it's all here."

Wolf waited passively while Ted got the three hoodlums onto their horses. Ted turned to him, shifting uncomfortably under his steady regard.

"You don't have much to say, do you? Aren't you curious?"

Wolf crossed his arms over his chest, feet spread apart. His look was enigmatic.

"Ford sent you, didn't he?"

Startled, Ted turned to him, his mouth slightly agape. "How'd you know?"

Wolf took Dancer's reins and swiftly mounted. Though his face was inscrutable, his eyes sparked with anger.

"It doesn't take a genius to figure it out. Rip Ford hates Comanches, and I'm half Comanche."

Ted had to hurry to catch up with him. "It's not like that at all. Rip found out that there's a bad ranger, one who is helping robbers for a piece of their profit. Since Miller and his gang have been so hard to track, he knew they must be getting help somewhere."

Wolf cast him a wrathful glance from the side of his eyes. "And since I'm part Indian, of course it had to be me."

Color mounted to Ted's cheeks. "I'll grant you that probably had a part in his thinking, but you aren't the only one who is under suspicion. You *have* been trekking around out here where we knew Miller's hideout to be. And since the Comanche have been giving settlers and reservation Indians so much grief this past year trying to implicate them in crimes, well. . ."

"You needn't explain. I understand perfectly." Wolf glanced at him again. "I've been tracking Miller for some time on my own. I knew if anyone could find him, I could," he suggested, totally without conceit. He tilted his head slightly. "What about you? What changed your mind about me?"

"April."

Wolf jerked his head upward. "What about her?"

The look Ted gave Wolf spoke volumes. "My sister couldn't love someone the way she loves you if they were bad. It's just not in her."

"She deserves better," Wolf growled.

A small smile tilted Ted's lips. He reached forward, patting the neck of his gelding. "She couldn't find better, and I'll be telling Rip so."

Wolf's features hardened. "You can also tell him that I'm resigning from the Rangers."

Ted sighed heavily. "I can't blame you, but are you sure you want to do that? The Rangers need men like you."

"I'm doing it for April."

April heard hoofbeats outside her cabin and hurried to the door. She flung the portal wide, breathing a sigh of relief when she saw her brother and Wolf come cantering into the yard.

Though Wolf dismounted, Ted stayed seated on his mount. April's eyebrows lifted in question.

Ted smiled wryly. "I have some things to do. I'll return in a few days."

"What kind of things?" she asked, coming across the yard to his side. Looking up at him, she studied him to see if he was well.

"Well, I have to return that diamond necklace to the bank in San Antonio, for one thing. They only let us borrow it with a guarantee of return."

April placed her hands on her hips, her forehead wrinkled. "There was no Darcy, was there?"

He shook his head, smiling. "I'm sorry about all the lies. It was necessary." Seeing the questions about to come, he told her, "Wolf can fill you in on the rest." He leaned down and touched her cheek, his eyes meeting hers. "He's a good man, Sis. Keep him if you can."

She smiled, quick tears coming to her eyes. "Come back soon."

He returned her smile, then gave Wolf a quick nod. Turning, he trotted out of the yard. April watched him until he was out of sight.

"I like your brother," Wolf said, his hands coming to rest on her shoulders.

April turned slowly until she was facing him. His arms wrapped around her.

"I'm glad," she told him, placing her palms against his chest. "And he likes you."

Wolf smiled wryly. "It always helps if you can get along with your in-laws."

He looked deep into her eyes and saw the answer to his question before he ever asked it. He asked it anyway.

"Will you marry me, April Hansen?"

"In a heartbeat," she returned quickly.

His smile turned into a full-fledged grin, but it slowly faded, his eyes becoming serious. "It could be difficult."

"Aren't all marriages?" she quipped.

He frowned. "April—"

She stopped him with a quick kiss. "People have survived it before. I suppose we can too. I love you, Wolf. Like Ruth said so long ago, wherever you go, I'll go." She wrapped her arms around his neck, waiting to see if he would break his long-ago promise.

His eyes grew darker with each passing second, but he still refused to move.

Realizing that he would never break his oath, no matter the incentive, she sighed. "You're a very stubborn man, Yellow Wolf Jackson! Would you please kiss me? Now and every day for the rest of our lives."

He readily complied.

DARLENE MINDRUP

Darlene is a full-time homemaker and home-school teacher. A "radical feminist" turned "radical Christian," she lives in Arizona with her husband and two children. Darlene has written several novels for Barbour Publishing's **Heartsong Presents** line. She has a talent for bringing ancient settings like the early Church in the Roman Empire and medieval to life with clarity. Darlene believes "romance is for everyone, not just the young and beautiful."

Saving Grace

by Kathleen Y'Barbo

Dedication

This novella is dedicated first and foremost to
my Heavenly Father who reigns on high
and to my earthly father who now lives with Him.
Also, to the men in my life:
David, my real-life Texas hero,
and Josh, Andrew, and Jacob,
the source of much inspiration, irritation,
and indescribable joy.
And finally to all the strong women
before and after me who,
through their courage and convictions,
have been the roots out of which my family tree
has flourished, especially
Mom, Mimi, Granny, and of course, Princess Hannah.

*"For by grace are ye saved through faith;
and that not of yourselves: it is the gift of God."*
EPHESIANS 2:8

One

Texas, on the trail between Santa Fe and the Brazos River
October 1854

Nine times out of ten, Ranger Captain Jedadiah Harte listened to the Lord and acted without questioning Him on the finer points of His plans. Today, however, he felt like maybe he'd misunderstood.

Many times on the ride from San Antonio, he'd been tempted to slide his trusted matched Walker Colt revolvers from their resting place beneath his King James Bible and slip them back into his belt where they used to belong. Always he'd felt the strong pull of the Lord's hand keeping his fingers on the reins and his heart on the straight and narrow.

To the surprise of everyone but the God who knew him well, Jed had turned over leadership to his second in command and hit the trail. The talk around headquarters gave him six months before he came riding into town and reclaimed it, but Jed knew better. A part of him would forever love being a ranger. The thrill of the chase and the triumph of good over evil never failed to satisfy.

In nearly fifteen years with the Rangers, "Heartless Harte," as he'd become known, had amassed an impressive list of criminals dispatched to the afterlife, a testament to the deadly accuracy with which he could aim his Walker Colts. He'd been proud of his record, and more than one newspaperman had trailed Heartless Harte to write about it later in gory detail.

Then last spring he'd been tracking a couple of rustlers when he came across a camp meeting south of Gonzales. Normally he would have steered clear of the place in favor of a warm bedroll and a shot of red-eye, but something he later realized to be the hand of the Lord caused him to stay.

First thing, the circuit-riding preacher asked him where he planned to spend eternity. The question left him madder than a peeled rattler, and the answer left him frightened for the first time since he'd been out of knee pants.

Right then and there he gave his life over to the Lord and promised Him He'd be first in command. Baptized in a little creek in the middle of nowhere, the infamous Heartless Harte became just plain old Jed Harte, citizen and soldier for the cross.

No more killing and no more use for the Walker Colts; he'd promised the Lord. His rifle would shoot all the game he could eat and his bowie knife would skin the carcasses. He'd lived by his senses before he'd become a ranger, and he sure could do it again, although with fall nearly past and winter coming on, he had his doubts on exactly how.

Besides handling a firearm, he'd been pretty handy

with a hammer and nail. If carpentering was a fine enough profession for his Savior, it sure was good enough for him.

His prayers had led him to believe his true calling came in winning souls, and someday he hoped to do just that. Heading for Galveston by way of the Brazos River, he felt he might have some luck gathering a following for Christ amongst the roughs on the dock. After all, those were his people; the ilk from which he'd come. What better place to finish his life than where it all started?

Jed shifted positions in the saddle and stretched to loosen the kinks. With an eye to the fading sun, he urged his mount into a gallop. A little luck and he'd make it by sunset. He'd camp there, maybe near a landing owned by a fellow he knew from his ranger days.

A decade ago, he'd helped him build a house to bring his bride home to. Now maybe Ben Delaney would return the favor by putting him up for the night. Tomorrow he'd catch a passing steamer downriver at first light and be off on the mission the good Lord had created him for.

Ducking his head to pass beneath the low limb of a spreading pecan tree, he thought about what he'd be doing right now if he were still back in San Antonio. The Lord knew what lay ahead, but Jed would never forget what he'd left behind. Someday, though, maybe he'd bring enough souls to the Lord to earn His forgiveness.

A lazy butterfly teased the rust-colored mane of his sorrel mare and landed on the horn of his saddle. For a few minutes they rode together in companionable silence, only the hoofbeats and the gulls' cry breaking the peace.

Then, from out of the blue came a loud crack, and his whole world went black.

"So much black."

Grace Delaney looked down at the yards of black muslin covering the rise in her belly. It spilled across the quilt and gathered in a dark pool at her feet on the chilly wide boards of the oak floor. Two months, three at the most, and her child would make an entrance into the world. A world filled with a future just as black as the widow's weeds its mother wore.

Only five-year-old Bennett and little Mary-Celine, her precious children, kept Grace from shedding the prison of her widow's clothing to disappear for good into the muddy swirls of the Brazos River. She fingered the heavy muslin of her skirt and banished the awful thought.

How little time had passed since she'd worn crinolines and whalebone corsets and attended the French Opera House in New Orleans and danced at the finest planta-tions along the river? Could it be less still since she'd come to Texas and settled at Delaney's Landing as the seven-teen-year-old bride of the dashing Ranger Ben Delaney?

Some days it seemed like just yesterday. Other days, it seemed like an eternity had passed since she and Ben had taken up farming together and built the landing that now supplied foodstuffs up and down the Brazos.

From the ruins of a burned plantation, they built a farm big enough to meet their needs and feed the family they planned. Bennett Delaney, Jr., came first, a strapping boy with a shock of dark hair like his mother and a fierce streak of stubbornness like his father. Three winters passed after Bennett's birth, and with each one they buried a small blanket-wrapped bundle together and mourned the loss, only to find in the spring another child would be on the way.

Her husband loved babies, as did she, and what Texas took from them, they bore with the knowledge that the children were in a much better place. Finally, two summers ago, Mary had been born. Theresa, the former slave who now served as Grace's friend, confidant, and house help, presided over all the births with concern. At the last confinement, she had stood toe to toe with the oversized Irishman and declared to Ben that Mary should be the last of the Delaneys.

No more babies or Grace would suffer for it.

Grace let the folds of crisp cloth slip from her fingers and slowly squared her shoulders. As much as she would love to give in to the bitter tiredness in her bones and the inescapable pain in her heart, she had no time for such luxuries. The steamer *Lehigh* would arrive at the landing mid-morning tomorrow. With only Uncle Shaw and the day help to fill the order, time would be tight. She and Theresa would have to see to the garden, a job that would make for a long afternoon under the best of circumstances.

Today, with the ache in her back and the heaviness in her belly, it would be downright unbearable. And yet, she would manage.

She always seemed to manage.

"Oh, Ben, why did you have to leave me like this?"

A question she'd asked a thousand times, of him and of God, and yet no answers had been forthcoming. Dead men don't speak, and obviously the comforting arms of the good Lord didn't reach as far as Delaney's Landing anymore.

He hadn't been with her husband the day lightning struck him and knocked him off his horse to die alone in the dirt at the age of thirty-two. And now, with more work to do before tomorrow than half a dozen men could perform in a week, He couldn't possibly be with her either.

No, the Lord of Theresa and her husband, Uncle Shaw, was not the Lord she knew. Their Lord showed patience and kindness and offered them peace and comfort. Only the blackness of exhausted sleep offered Grace comfort anymore.

Shaking off the thought along with the chill that had gathered in the small room, Grace stood slowly. Theresa met her at the door with a wool cloak and a tin cup filled with hot coffee.

"You tell those folks they'd best be treatin' you right, Miz Grace, or they'll have the Good Lord and me to deal with."

Grace mustered a weak smile and shrugged into the cloak. The faint scent of wood smoke still clung to it from yesterday's work in the fields.

Unfazed at her lack of response, Theresa slipped the tin cup into Grace's hand and frowned. "Now don't you mind what they say about a woman running Delaney's Landing. Womenfolk, they's a lot stronger than men, anyhow." Her dark gaze settled on the curve of Grace's belly. "Just let one of them try and push a young 'un into the world."

With a nod, Grace pressed past her to emerge onto the broad front porch of the home Ben built long ago. The door shut with a resounding crack, and in an instant the thick, cold air swirled around her, almost visible in the first shimmering lights of dawn.

As she'd done every morning since Ben's death, Grace left her coffee untouched on the porch rail and made the trek down the path along the edge of the fence until she reached the giant pecan tree that marked the southeast corner of the Delaney property. Beneath its spreading limbs stood four simple wooden crosses, one newly planted and bearing the name Bennett Delaney, Sr.

Ignoring the protest of her sore muscles, Grace knelt at the edge of the fresh soil and smoothed the edges of the ragged blanket covering the mound. The quilt had been Bennett's idea, a way to keep his pa warm when the weather turned cold a few weeks back. Already the sky blue blanket had begun to dull a bit, and the edges of the white lamb Grace had embroidered on the center square showed evidence of fraying.

She leaned forward a bit to touch the corner of the quilt and allowed her mind to tumble back in time to her son's birth. The baby inside her shifted and pressed against her in protest. A moment later, the familiar pains shot up through her back and settled there. With difficulty she sat back on her heels to seek a measure of relief.

"Be patient, Little One," she whispered. "There's much to do before you come."

And there was much to do. A garden to tend, orders to fill, and books to balance—these were just a few of the items she knew she must attend to before she could sink back into the blissful oblivion of another night's sleep.

If only she had help. Uncle Shaw and Theresa had both become indispensable, each in their own way, but neither could ease her burdens completely.

Already news had traveled up and down the Brazos,

and more than one captain had bypassed Delaney's Landing in the mistaken impression that without Ben Delaney in charge, the landing would be closed and the warehouse shuttered. Those who did stop were surprised to find Ben's widow had taken over the running of the warehouse and the filling of orders.

None of them were pleased.

Many refused to deal with her. Some made lewd comments or ignored her outright when she tried to conduct business as she'd seen Ben do. A captain by the name of Stockton had even suggested she pack up and leave Delaney's Landing, offering her what he called a first-class deal for the property. She'd called it something else entirely and sent the man on his way with a few choice scalding words and a request never to return.

Only afterward did she give any thought to the danger she would have been in had the captain not gone willingly. Uncle Shaw, while strong of body, was getting on in years and could have done little to stop a man who didn't want to be stopped. The day help, a dozen during harvest and less most of the time, were hired out from neighboring plantations and held a loyalty that was doubtful at best.

"Oh, Ben, what am I going to do?"

The silence rumbled thick around her, broken only by the occasional call of a gull. Her gaze skipped from Ben's grave to the three others lined up beside him. Her husband and her babies, all waiting for her in heaven.

Heaven? Since when had she given the mythical place any consideration? Surely Ben's death had caused some small bit of concern about it, but to give it any serious thought?

There had been no time.

Nudged by another insistent kick in her belly, Grace shifted to her knees and bowed her head. The north wind teased her hair and lifted the edge of her cloak to blow a chill air across the black muslin she wore.

It would be so easy to give up, to let the land win and let Delaney's Landing become a thing of the past. Her family in New Orleans, if any of them still remained, had never quite forgiven her for leaving polite society to marry a Texas Ranger. Ben, on the other hand, had no family left on this side of the ocean. Besides, she could never leave Texas and the landing Ben loved.

On the wind came a thought, one more frightening than the threat of an angry steamboat captain. "Face it, Gracie, old girl. You're on your own. At least as long as you're able."

What about the children? Like it or not, she had a family to take care of. Bennett and Mary depended on her, as did Theresa and Uncle Shaw. If she gave up, what would happen to them?

Too soon her time of confinement would come. Theresa already looked at her with baleful eyes, concern brimming on her face when she thought Grace couldn't see.

And if the unthinkable happened and Theresa proved right?

"What will I do?" she repeated.

You will pray, came the soft yet insistent answer.

"Pray?"

Surprisingly, the idea seemed to set right. She tugged at the strings holding her cloak together and tried to conjure up just the right words to speak to the Lord. After all, it had been quite awhile since she'd made the attempt.

"God," she finally managed, "I'm not asking this for me, because I can handle whatever life gives me. I'm asking for the babies." She touched the gentle rise of her belly. "This one included," she added.

Her eyes searched the sky, now fading from dark gray to a silver blue as the dawn gave way to morning. The distant whinny of a horse alerted her to the presence of a rider coming up the main road, most likely one of the day workers.

"Lord," she whispered, "if You're up there, I'd be mightily obliged if You'd send me a man to give me some help."

Her boldness surprised her, and yet again, it felt right. She touched the back of her hand to the sky blue blanket.

"He'd need to be strong of health and a dead aim with a pistol. A ranger like Ben would be fine if You've got one. Just to keep the babies safe and the landing going until I'm up and around again. Amen."

She sat back on her heels once more and waited for the answer. The limbs of the old pecan tree rustled and a squirrel skittered across the clearing ahead, but nothing earth shattering happened.

No answer came.

"Silly, I suppose," she said as she rose with difficulty and shook out her aching limbs.

Grace wrapped her cloak around her and turned to take the long, slow walk back to the house. In a few hours the sun would stand high in the sky and the steamer would dock at the landing. No amount of wishful thinking would get the ship loaded and the bill of lading in order.

She looked up at the sky, barely visible through the canopy of dark green leaves overhead. A profound sadness settled around her like a mist. With a weak wave of her hand, she attempted in vain to push it away.

Mindful of her tender state, she stepped gingerly over a fallen limb and headed toward the fence line and the grassy path. What had seemed like a short walk earlier now felt like an almost impossible hike.

If only she could go home and fall into the soft feather bed she'd only just left. If only the Lord heard her pleas and answered.

"What did you expect, Grace?" she asked as the sound of horses' hooves grew louder. "Did you think the Lord, if He exists, would hear your pitiful prayer and send someone just like that?"

Of course not, came the answer. *First you must have faith.*

"Faith?" She shook her head. "Lord, if that's You talking to me, You ought to know I'm trying. For the babies, if not for me."

A moment later, a sorrel mare stepped out of the brush into the path in front of her. Its rider, an oversized dark-haired man in dusty, trail-worn clothes, lay slumped over the saddle horn, a ribbon of blood flowing down the end of his outstretched arm.

As she crept closer to the horse and recognized the man in the saddle, she realized the Lord had sent her a ranger. Unfortunately, it looked like He had sent her a dead ranger.

Two

The morning sun had climbed over the porch rail and now brightened the front parlor with ribbons of gold shimmering across the flowered needle-point carpet. At the center of the light lay the ranger, silent, solid, and most likely bound for his reward at any moment.

Matted hair covered one eye and a dark purple bruise the other. His skin wore a paleness even the many layers of Texas trail dust couldn't hide.

Grace tried to remember what Ben had said about Ranger Harte. They'd ridden together as new recruits, and Jed had stayed on at the landing long enough to see to it that Ben Delaney's New Orleans sweetheart, should she agree to marry him, would come home to a real house and not a tent, like so many ranger wives.

He'd fussed over the porch rail so many times Ben had declared him soft in the head. When she arrived at her new home, she had been greeted by a hand-lettered note on the back of a reward poster asking them to please be careful of the rails until Ranger Harte could return to finish the job.

True to his word, he'd come back a week later to mend a wobble in the posts only he could see and ended up staying until past the last frost. Harte had claimed it was the carpentering that kept him there, but Ben had declared it to be Grace's cooking.

Grace smiled at the memory. She hadn't seen Jedadiah Harte in almost a decade, although Ben had spoken of him on occasion. While her husband had been content to stay near the landing and nearly give up the life of a ranger altogether, Jed Harte had pursued justice and glory until he reached the rank of captain and led his own group of men.

"Oh, Ben."

Why could she go for hours, even days, once, without feeling the grief, then out of nowhere, it would return? She felt it now, the blinding abyss of dark hurt chasing her, threatening her, nearly engulfing her. Only Theresa's sudden movement kept her from tumbling in.

"Let's git him comfortable, then I kin see what's what." Theresa eased a rolled blanket beneath Ranger Harte's neck, then began matter-of-factly to undress the lawman, starting with his boots, which she handed to Uncle Shaw. "Wonder who he is?"

"Harte," Grace said, almost numb with grief. "Jedadiah Harte."

"The ranger?" Uncle Shaw whistled softly and held the boots at arm's length. He wrinkled his nose. "Been on the trail awhile too, I'd guess."

Grace nodded and took the coat from Theresa. Waves of nausea threatened at the smell of the trail-worn woolen garment and the sight of the blood staining the collar and sleeve. Quickly she draped it over Uncle Shaw's arm and stepped back to sink onto the stiff cushions of the rosewood settee.

"See that these are taken care of, please," she managed. "If we don't have enough to feed him, we can at least make sure he's clean."

"Shame on you, Miz Grace." Theresa bent over the patient and eased his blue flannel shirt off a broad shoulder caked with blood. "You can't be worrying about whether we can manage. You know the Lord'll provide."

Grace looked away, suitably chastised. Still, concern bore hard on her. When she petitioned the Lord for a ranger, she thought she'd made it clear she needed a healthy one who could wield a revolver and maybe scare up some game or plow under a row or two in the garden. She certainly hadn't bargained for the one now lying half dead in her parlor.

"Looks like it went clean through." Theresa lifted Mr. Harte's shoulder and examined his wounded upper arm, causing him to groan softly. "Sure did, and that's to the Lord's glory, I'll say for sure."

Grace handed a strip of clean cloth to Theresa. "So he's going to live?"

"He might. I 'spect the chill air's hurt his chances a bit, though."

Theresa began to bind his wound, lifting his arm each time to reach beneath it. Throughout the process, he showed no indication of noticing.

"It don't take but one bullet to stop a feller, even one as big as this 'un." She made a soft clucking sound. "Looks like he hit his head on somethin' and near put his eye out. Probably done it after the bullet got him."

The ranger's good eye flickered, and his lips, parched and cracked, began to move as if he were trying to speak. With strong hands and soft words of comfort, Theresa settled the man and covered him with several layers of quilts. She reached for a cloth and the basin of water warming near the fire. A noise above made her look up sharply.

"Them young 'uns are awake."

Grace sighed and climbed to her feet. Too many things demanded her attention—the landing, the farm, and the complaints of her tired body—but her children came first. They always would.

"I'll see to them, Theresa," she said slowly. "You'll let me know if there's any change with Mr. Harte."

Theresa shook her head. "I'll get the babies. You don't have no business climbin' those stairs no way. When I get back we gonna talk about the help what's comin' this mornin'."

"Help?" Her hopes rose. "With the landing?"

Theresa shook her head. "With the chilluns, Miz Grace."

Yet another mouth to feed; not what she'd had in mind when she asked the Lord to send help. Grace opened her mouth to protest, but Theresa waved it away with a sweep of her hand. Handing her the cloth and a razor, she pressed the basin in her direction.

"I love those babies like I birthed 'em myself an' you know that, but your time's a comin'. I can't worry about them and take care of you." She hefted her bulk off the floor and started toward the staircase. "The Lord's so good, Miz Grace," she tossed over her shoulder. "I asked

Him for help, and out of the blue He answers my prayer by sending my grandbaby, Ruth."

Grace nodded meekly and eased to her knees beside the patient. It was hard not to compare whatever help Theresa got with the help He had sent her.

While Theresa's heavy steps sounded on the stairs, Grace set to work on the ranger, determined not to allow her stomach to rule her hands. She did not have the luxury of illness.

Resolutely, she lifted his head into her lap, or at least what remained of her lap, and began to shave away the dark beard. As she worked, a ruggedly handsome face began to appear, first with the firm, square jaw and finally with the soft curve of a set of cheekbones that could have been chiseled in granite. When she dropped the razor in the basin, his features contorted into a tight grimace and a lovely amber-colored eye flickered open only to disappear once more beneath a frame of thick black lashes.

"Pray for me," came in a thick whisper between cracked lips.

"Pray?" She wrapped the muslin over his injured eye and settled his head gently on the blankets. "Is that what you said?"

Wouldn't the Lord be surprised to hear from her again so soon? What would she say? She shook her head. "I don't know if I can, Mr. Harte."

His good eye opened again, and after a moment, his gaze settled on her. "You must," he said with what sounded like the last of his strength.

"Of course," she said. Lowering her head, she cleared her throat and cast about her somewhat addled brain for the appropriate words. "Lord, I ask You to come and help the man You sent us. I know my aim was to ask for a body to protect us and see that the babies do fine no matter what happens to me. I'd be much obliged if You would see to it that this ranger—"

"No." He began to thrash about beneath the blankets. "Not ranger. . ."

His declaration startled her, and only her hand on his forehead stopped the man's movements. "What is it?" she whispered.

"Pray," he said, obviously struggling to keep his eye open. "For Jed Harte."

"I tried," she said, exasperated. "I asked the Lord to take care of you and heal you so you could ranger again and maybe—"

"No," emerged from his lips like the howl of a wolf.

"What in the world is going on here?" Theresa appeared at the door with Mary on her hip and Bennett at her side. At the sight of her, the children wriggled away and ran to her.

"Mommy, why is the man on the floor?" Bennett asked, wide-eyed.

"Big man hurt?" Mary added.

Ranger Harte settled into a quiet calm and stared at the children. The children, in turn, stared back.

Grace glanced up to see that Uncle Shaw had returned. In place of his usual bland expression, he wore an uncharacteristic look of worry.

"S'cuse me, Miz Grace, but you be needed real bad down at the warehouse."

The story unfolded on their walk to the landing. Ruth

had arrived only moments earlier. Sadly, trouble had tagged along in the form of the obstinate steamboat captain Stockton, the same man who'd given Grace trouble a week ago. Shaw told him of the lawman's arrival and led him to believe Harte would be running things soon. Stockton left in a hurry, although Shaw had a suspicion they hadn't seen the last of the man.

Grace responded with a nod and a word of thanks, seating herself behind Ben's desk to begin yet another long day of work.

When she finally pushed away to begin the short walk to the house, she wondered where the day had gone. Her stomach complained at the emptiness and her muscles ached. Only a meal and a few hours' rest stood between her and repeating the whole process.

She thought about the ranger's Bible, retrieved from his saddlebags, and the words she'd seen circled there when she opened it. "Create in me a clean heart, O God; and renew a right spirit within me," she whispered as she trudged the last few steps to the back door.

Shame flooded her as the meaning of the words emerged. Should the Lord come today, neither her heart nor her spirit would stand the test of His all-knowing mind. Right there in the middle of the dusty path, Grace knelt and opened her thoughts to the Lord.

"Oh yes, Lord, I do need a clean heart. Forgive me for losing sight of You and blaming You for all my troubles. Ben and my babies are in a better place, and I know I've got a long way to go to get there." She paused and lifted her gaze to the purple twilight as Ben's child shifted and squirmed beneath her ribs.

"I love You, Lord, and I love my Ben. Don't let me forget him, but please, if You could, teach me how to live without him."

The back door slammed and Grace looked over in time to see Theresa running her way, skirts held high and her petticoat rustling. Grace's blood ran cold at the wide-eyed look on the older woman's face. "What's wrong, Theresa? Did something happen to the babies?"

"Oh, Miz Grace, I done thought your time had come, and you couldn't make it t' the door." She fanned her ample bosom despite the chill air and seemed to have trouble catching her breath. "I declare you scared the life right outta me."

"You mean that's why you came running out of the house?" Grace stifled a grin as her racing heart slowed to nearly normal. "I thought something had happened to one of the children."

"Oh, lands sakes no," she said with a chuckle as she reached to help Grace up. "My Ruth, she's already got those sweet angels fed and nigh t' sleep. Don't you worry about them, not at all."

Grace took the hand Theresa offered and stood gingerly, allowing her body to settle and the baby to stop moving before attempting to walk toward the house.

The mention of Ruth caused her to remember the Bible she'd forgotten on Ben's desk. This sent her thoughts reeling to the ranger, and a stab of guilt reminded her she hadn't given his health any concern. She'd only thought of herself and the selfish pity she'd wallowed in. The shame of it burned deep. *A clean heart,* she repeated to the Lord. *Please teach me, Father.*

Theresa slowed her pace to allow Grace to catch up. "You worried about Mr. Harte?"

The question pressed further the point of her guilt. "Any improvement?" The baby shifted positions to jolt her insides.

Theresa gave Grace a sideways look. "No," she whispered. What a cruel irony that she'd asked the Lord to send this ranger to her, and now he, too, could die. At least it seemed that way to her.

Grasping the stair rail for support, Grace shook her head. "I'll tend to the ranger tonight."

Theresa opened the door and held it wide so Grace could enter, then closed it softly before hurrying to the stove to stir the pots left simmering there. "I've known you too long to argue, Miz Grace, so I won't even try. Set yourself down and see to that baby of yours with some supper afore you tend to the ranger. That's all I ask."

Grace nodded. Satisfied, Theresa reached for the sassafras root and began to chop it into the mixture bubbling in the pot. Grace inhaled a deep breath of the exquisite smells of Theresa's cooking and sank into the slat-backed rocker by the fire, resting on her elbows to relieve the pain in her back. It would be gumbo tonight, Theresa's way of using the last of yesterday's hen in a meal along with the meager contents of the pantry, but it would be good. It always was.

As the flames licked and jumped beside her, the tiredness seeped into Grace's bones and settled there. The baby protested her bent-over position with a swift kick to her insides, so she accommodated him by shifting to a less confining position.

Instantly the little one stilled, although Grace's back muscles began to protest. Stifling the complaint she wanted to voice, she turned her thoughts back to Ranger Harte while Theresa began to slice the corn bread.

How could she consider offering to spend her precious sleeping hours taking care of a man who might die before morning? Yet, under the circumstances, how could she not?

"Renew a right spirit." The verse from the ranger's Bible came tumbling back to her, along with the surprise that Jed Harte even owned a Bible, much less read one. What had happened to her right spirit? Had she ever had it in the first place?

A shiver of guilt snaked down her spine. She and Ben had a Bible, a beautiful book Ben had brought in his trunk from Ireland. She'd accepted the Lord based on that book. Now she would be hard pressed to know where it was.

A forlorn wail punctuated the silence, followed by a crash. Grace struggled to her feet despite the screaming protest of her muscles.

"Oh, Lord preserve us, that's the ranger." Theresa bustled out of the kitchen. "He done hurt hisself, I just know it," she said as she disappeared into the hallway and headed toward the parlor with Grace trailing more than a few steps behind. "Sakes alive, would you look what he's gone and done?"

Grace pressed past her to see Jedadiah Harte half sitting and half lying across her rosewood settee. The blood seeping from beneath his bandaged arm had already begun to stain the cushion a bright crimson. Her rosewood side table, now reduced to splinters, lay in a heap beneath one long leg.

"Lands o' Goshen, Ranger Harte," Theresa said as she eased him into a sitting position on the settee. "You done gone and made a mess of yourself for sure. Why in the world you wanna be a doin' that?"

Three

Why *indeed?* Jed took in his surroundings through one eye, in a haze of pain and a swirl of faces. Two faces, one dark and the other light. He blinked and the pain sharpened. His head tilted and the world went with it.

"Whoa there, Mr. Ranger," the dark one warned. "You ain't gonna break yourself along with the missus' table. Not if I have somethin' t' say about it."

"Break?" He caught the word and tossed it around in his addled brain until he made sense of it. Beneath his feet came the crunch of the most perfect piece of rosewood he'd seen this side of New Orleans.

"Excuse me, Mr. Harte. How do you feel?"

Jed blinked again, and the lighter of the women came into focus, robbing him of his thoughts. She touched his forehead with the back of a pale hand, and he nearly reeled backward with the cool relief it offered.

"Mr. Harte? I asked how you felt."

He licked his lips and shut his eye, then thought hard to make out the words and understand them. Formulating an answer seemed to take forever. "Weak as a newborn calf," he said slowly.

When he opened his good eye, the woman smiled and removed her hand from his forehead. "The fever's broken."

"Praise the Lord," the dark one exclaimed.

Jed nodded, confused. The pain swirled around him in a thick fog with his shoulder and left arm at the center. Atop the source of his discomfort lay a thick pad of muslin and a wrapping of red-stained bindings.

"What happened?" he asked, attempting with clumsy hands to investigate the situation.

The woman's pale fingers stopped him. "You've been injured," she said softly in the honeyed tones of a woman of culture. "Shot, actually." Her hand led his to the spot of greatest irritation and gently set it upon the bindings. "The bullet went through your left arm just below the shoulder."

In a few simple words, the woman told him of how he came to be in her parlor. Understanding dawned along with a white-hot burning beneath his brow. The events began to roll back in a slow progression beginning with his ride out of San Antonio and ending with a shot, which must have taken him down near the Delaney property.

"Ben's wife," he murmured.

She acknowledged the fact as if it pained her. Worry etched lines across her face where age did not. When she pulled a chair next to him and sank into it, he saw the evidence of the babe she carried.

"Well, well, old Ben's gonna be a daddy," he mumbled, a mixture of envy and pain flooding his heart. "Grace, isn't it?" he managed.

She nodded, stiffly rising to accept a bundle from the dark woman. "And this is my friend Theresa." She began to tear off a length of fabric. "You'll need to let me change the bandages now, Mr. Harte."

Jed watched Grace Delaney as the bindings loosened and the bandage fell away to reveal a decent bullet wound. What kind of ranger was he to be blindsided by a stray bullet? Then it came to him. He was no ranger at all; he'd given himself over to the Lord and promised to put away his weapons. The Lord had made him clean.

How long ago now had he given up the life that had carried him off the docks and into the law? Not long enough to put the past behind him. Straining to fight the blackness chasing him, he leaned forward, then fell back when the blinding pain hit him between the eyes like a runaway steer.

"God bless you for coming to save us, Ranger," were the last words he heard before he gave in to the dark waters of sleep.

He'd come to save them, beckoned by desperation and prayer. Many times during the busy daylight hours, Grace felt a pull of worry concerning the ranger but could do nothing about it. The duties at hand kept her mind tossing back and forth between the patient in her parlor and the never-ending chores.

Morning work in the garden had given way to afternoon work at Ben's desk when the pains began. She pushed away from the desk and stood in the hopes they would leave as quickly as they arrived.

When standing didn't alleviate them, she began to walk, first a few halting steps around the desk and eventually, after tucking the ranger's Bible under her arm, across the warehouse and out into the remains of the daylight. Still the discomfort chased her. Grace held a hand to her brow and squinted into the sun to find the distance to the house.

"You're an impatient one," she whispered through gritted teeth to the child in her womb. At least her other two children were not a worry tonight. With Ruth and Theresa, they were safe and well taken care of.

Grace lifted her gaze skyward and said a word of thanks for the two women, telling the Lord just what they meant to her. Later, when she managed the trek to the house, she made a promise to tell Theresa and Ruth at the first opportunity.

Ignoring the plate left warming on the stove, she left the Bible on the kitchen table and went upstairs in search of her children. To her delight, she found them sitting at Ruth's feet, eyes wide and listening to a tale about two birds and a squirrel in a pecan tree.

When Ruth saw her standing in the hall, she ended the story with a promise to tell another in the morning after breakfast. The children began to protest but squealed with glee when they saw Grace.

"These children sure love their mother," Ruth said with a smile.

"I love them too," she said as she eased onto the floor and gathered Mary into her arms, then settled Bennett beside her. The children smelled of soap and sunshine, a heavenly combination. "And I couldn't manage without you, Ruth," Grace added.

The girl offered a shy smile. "It's me who's blessed, Ma'am," she answered softly. "And it is you and the good Lord who should be thanked."

Unable to answer, Grace sent Ruth downstairs while she took over the duties of readying Bennett and Mary for bed. After listening to the stories of adventures they had during their afternoon walk in the woods, she kissed the children good night, tucked them in, and read to them from a book of their favorite tales from Ireland.

Mary fell asleep first, her two middle fingers planted firmly in her mouth. Grace kissed her daughter once more, gently removing the tiny fingers from her pink, bow-shaped mouth. Quietly, she moved to Bennett's bed, where, true to his nature, the boy lay awake.

Grace sank heavily onto the bed and kissed his forehead. Sometimes it seemed as though the Delaney men had perfected stubbornness. Tonight this one wore it all over his face.

"Mama, Ruth says I can't sleep in the parlor." He pronounced his dislike of the statement with a face intended to convey the sentiment.

As she had done so many times before Ben's death, Grace climbed onto the bed next to her son and stretched her legs out, feeling the strain of her muscles and the pull of her belly. "You've got to listen to Ruth," she said while she fussed with the blanket, then smoothed her son's curly locks. His nose wrinkled in protest, and she pressed it lightly with her fingertip. "Go to sleep, Precious."

Grace curled her arm beneath her head and reclined, feeling the baby inside her begin to dance a jig in protest. At least the pains had stopped. For that she could be grateful.

Silence fell in the little room, only the usual chatter of the forest to keep them company. By degrees Grace felt her eyes slide shut and her body become heavy. Even the babe settled. Just before sleep overtook her, Bennett tugged on her arm with a soft whisper of "Mama."

She blinked and shifted positions to see him better, then instantly wished she hadn't. In the long shadows, with only the flicker of the lamp to light him, Bennett bore so much resemblance to his late father that it made her want to cry.

"Mama," he repeated.

She gathered her memories into a tight ball and shoved them into the corner of her mind. Later, in the privacy of her room, she might take them out again. Better still, she might not.

"Yes, Darling," she answered softly, hoping her son missed the catch in her voice. "What is it?"

"It's about Ruth."

Ah, the Delaney stubbornness again. She sighed. "Remember how we talked about her being in charge when I'm out at the landing or working in the garden?"

Bennett nodded, but his frown told her he remained unconvinced. "The ranger's sleepin' in the parlor, and if I'm gonna be a ranger someday, I gotta learn how to make do too."

"Boys belong in their beds, Darling," she whispered. "And I'm sure that if the ranger had a choice, he'd be sleeping in a soft bed like yours."

"Your mother's right. A man always picks a mattress over a bedroll if he gets the choice, ranger or not."

Grace nearly jumped out of her skin as she turned to look over her shoulder at the doorway and the man who filled it. She stifled a gasp and scrambled off the bed, covering her legs and her embarrassment as best she could. To her horror, she nearly stumbled before she caught hold of the bedpost and righted her ungainly body. A shaft of pain sliced across her abdomen and nearly buckled her knees.

"Mr. Harte, what in the world are you doing up?" she said, when she could manage words.

Bennett bolted upright, and his cry of glee caused little Mary to stir in her bed. Grace limped to her and smoothed the blankets beneath her daughter's tiny chin, hoping to send her back to dreamland without the drama an early wake always caused. Despite her best efforts, Mary shook off the blankets and frowned while Bennett began a barrage of questions directed to the ranger.

"Mama?" she asked in a sleepy voice. "Is the big man all better?"

"I'm just dandy," Ranger Harte said quickly.

Too quickly.

She looked over her shoulder to see the ranger sway, then catch hold of the door frame to remain upright. Intuition told Grace something was very wrong, something beside the fact the ranger shouldn't even be up and walking, much less all the way upstairs.

Proper folk didn't go exploring a house without an invitation. Ben had always said she had an active imagination, and she gave it free reign as she worked to settle the children as quickly as possible.

"You two hush now," she said. "Our guest ought to be plenty tired."

Mary began to complain, while Bennett put his stubborn look back on. The ranger leaned forward slightly, and the dim yellow glow of the lamp illuminated his features. Like Mary, he wore a frown. Unlike her, his looked to be etched with worry.

Imagination gave way to intuition. Something was definitely wrong. His uncombed hair and disheveled clothing gave him the look of a man up to no good, but his reputation as a ranger said otherwise. Even in the semidarkness, she could see the glint of amber in his one good eye and the promise of it in the other. It sent a shiver up her spine.

Lord, please protect the babies from whatever harm might come, she prayed, as she firmly slid the blankets over Mary's kicking legs. One look into her eyes and the child lay still. A glance at Bennett produced the same result.

"Mr. Harte, I suppose you'll be wanting some supper since you missed yours. Why don't I go and see what Theresa has left on the stove?"

He nodded. "That would be just fine, Ma'am."

"I'm hungry too, Mama," Bennett said. "I didn't get to—"

"A ranger learns to make do, Son," Mr. Harte said as his gaze met Grace's. He slowly cut his gaze to the right. "Your gut might be telling you to eat, but your instincts are telling you there might be somebody right behind you that you'd miss if you were set on having vittles."

"That happen to you much?" Bennett asked.

"Occasionally," he said as he looked first at Bennett and then to his right again.

Grace's gaze followed his, and she saw the shadows. Where there should have only been one, there were two. It seemed as though the second person stood even taller than Mr. Harte. Her sharp intake of breath did not go unnoticed by the ranger.

His lips curved into a smile that didn't quite reach the rest of his face. "If you hombres don't mind, I'm going to borrow your mother for a minute," he said, his voice laced with a deadly combination of calmness and coldness. "You just close your eyes and dream about breakfast, little man."

She opened her mouth to refuse, to tell him she would never leave her babies no matter how many men he'd brought with him. Before she could protest, a silent warning passed between them like a chill in the night. Almost imperceptibly, he shook his head. Slowly, he lifted his index finger to his lips in a request for her to remain silent.

"Father, forgive me," she thought she heard him whisper.

The second shadow moved, and Grace jumped in surprise. Split seconds later, the ranger slammed the door. The sound of men scuffling in the hall echoed through the room, and Bennett cried out in surprise.

"Climb into the bed with your sister and stay there," Grace ordered as she pressed her ear to the door in an attempt to hear something, anything, over the pounding of her heart. Out of the corner of her eye, she saw Bennett race for Mary's bed.

As the sounds of struggle continued on the other side of the door, Grace spied the rocker and made a grab for it, one hand still firmly on the doorknob. With the last of her strength, she pulled the heavy chair toward the door, while the babe in her womb kicked in protest.

Wedging the back of the rocker under the knob, she stood back to test her handiwork and a spasm of sheer agony knocked her to her knees. Like flames licking at her nerves, the pain sharpened and splintered, then came to rest in her abdomen. Something wet and warm spilled onto the hem of her gown, and she looked down to see a deep crimson stain had begun to form at her feet.

Outside, the men had fallen mysteriously silent. Behind her, Grace heard the rustle of bedcovers and the soft voices of her children.

"Mama?" Bennett whispered. "What's happening?"

Then came the ear-splintering shot.

Four

J ed looked down at the body slumped against the door and waited while his breath caught up with his mind. With his heart still thrumming a furious beat, he kicked the Colt—his own stolen revolver—away from the dead man's hand.

"Thou shalt not kill," he said under his breath as the gun slid across the slick wooden floor and landed with a crash against the opposite wall.

His arm ached where the bandages wrapped his wounds, and in the semidarkness of the hallway, he could see a tinge of pink had begun to stain the fabric. At least he still had a cool head and a clear mind.

Clear enough to see that, even with only one eye, he'd sent another one to the undertaker.

Disgusted, he turned away and knelt in the shadows, closing his good eye and covering the other with a trembling hand. "Heavenly Father, forgive me. I didn't mean to shoot him. It was. . ."

He paused, the truth too horrible to repeat. But the Lord knew him inside out. He knew what lay in his heart. Jed Harte might have been washed in the blood of

Jesus and bathed in the cold waters of a creek-side baptism, but inside he was still the same Texas Ranger who'd learned with pride a thousand and one ways to deliver a man to death's door.

"It was instinct," Jed finished, knowing the full depth of his sin was that he hadn't changed one bit from the man he used to be. "I shot him because that's what I do. I kill people."

In the silence of the hallway, with the smell of death bearing down hard on him, Jed Harte knew he would forever be Heartless Harte, the ranger who let no man live who'd crossed him. He was a sorry sinner and not worth spit.

Never would he be worthy of the grace the Lord had bestowed upon him. Never would he earn the forgiveness He so generously had offered on the banks of that creek such a short time ago.

"For by grace are ye saved through faith; and that not of yourselves: it is the gift of God: Not of works, lest any man should boast."

With a cry of anguish, Jed pushed the familiar verse from his mind. He'd contemplated the meaning of it once too often on the ride from San Antonio and had come up with nothing more than a headache.

How could the Lord send His Son to die for a man who made killing his business? How could He forgive a man who seemed to keep on running back to the old ways like a baby to his mother?

"Mr. Ranger," a child's voice called from the other side of the closed door. "My mama needs help."

Scrambling to his feet, Jed pushed the dead man out

of the way and yanked on the knob. It refused to turn. Focusing his good eye on it, he tried again.

Still stuck tight—not a good sign.

Jed swallowed the bile climbing in his throat and assumed the amiable tone he'd perfected on the job. The last thing he needed was to be on the wrong side of a door with a scared kid on the other.

"What's wrong with your mama, Little Man?"

No answer.

Jed struggled to remember what Ben's wife had called the lad. "Bennett, is that your name?"

"Yes, Sir," the wavering voice responded.

"Well, that's a fine name." Again he tried the knob and found it locked tight. "So Bennett, do you suppose you could come on over and open this door?"

"No, Sir," the boy answered.

Sending a prayer for patience skyward, he eased his good shoulder into the door and pressed, hoping the door would budge. It didn't.

Perfect. He scowled at the dead man, the busted knob, and finally at the weak shoulder, which kept him from knocking the door down.

"Bennett?"

"Yes, Sir?"

The panic in the boy's voice slid under the door and lodged in Jed's heart. Irritation took a turn toward uneasiness. "If you want me to help your mama, you're going to have to open the door."

He waited, hoping the kid would cooperate. Once again, nothing happened. A thousand anxious thoughts converged and separated in his mind. Shaking his head to clear the noise, he tried again.

"Little Man, open the door."

"I can't," he finally said. "I tried and I can't reach it."

Jed leaned against the door and listened to the scampering of feet across the carpets. Obviously the boy was busy doing something. "Yes, you can."

"Nope," slid through the door on a loud whine.

The situation threatened to slip out of control. Just as he'd done countless times before, Jed met the situation head on and demanded results. "Open this door now before I shoot it open. Do you hear me, Kid?"

Bennett Delaney's wail echoed across the hallway. So much for taking control of the situation.

"Your mother," Jed called when the boy had settled some, "where is she?"

"By the door. Mr. Ranger, you have to help my mama," he said as he dissolved once more into tears. Moments later, a second set of cries joined the chorus, most likely the little girl's.

Now neither of them could hear him, nor would they do anything to help him get the door opened. Frustrated beyond description, Jed sent a prayer to his Maker.

Lord, this isn't working out like I planned, so do You think You could step in and give me a little help with these young 'uns?

When no answer seemed forthcoming, Jed returned to his investigative training for a solution. Kneeling once more, he leaned over until his ear touched the floor and peered into the space between the floor and the bottom of the door.

Through the opening he could barely make out the

shape of a woman's foot partially covered by the same sort of white linen as his shoulder. By shifting positions, he could see more of her. She lay on her side with an arm beneath her head as if she'd fallen asleep or possibly been knocked to the floor.

Then he saw the blood.

"Mama!" came the plaintive cry from the other side of the door.

"She hurt," the little one added.

"Hang on to your sister, Little Man," he shouted over the din. "I'm going to save your mama."

He stood and brushed off the sense of foreboding along with the lint decorating his shirt. "Once a ranger, always a ranger," he said as he stepped over the corpse to fetch the Colt from the corner of the hallway.

Retrieving the matching gun from the belt of the criminal, Jed took a second to get his bearings. The mantle of ranger settled easily on his shoulders, although the prick of his conscience was something he'd have to settle later.

The throb in his shoulder had long since ceased to matter, and the meaningless hum in his brain had refined and shaped itself into a command. He was a Texas Ranger, always had been and always would be. Maybe there was a way he could please God and the great state of Texas at the same time.

Right now, he had to worry about Ben's wife. Later, the Lord willing, he would take the rest of his dilemma up with Him and see what He had to say about the matter.

Taking the steps two at a time, he hung on to the stair rail for dear life. At the bottom of the staircase, blackness met him and brought him to a quick halt.

"Lord, I can't do this in the dark," he said as he felt his way around the carved newel post and stumbled over something hard and immovable. His toe ached and he longed to say the scalding words that had once come tripping so easily off his tongue. "I'd be much obliged if You would shed a little light on this for me."

"Mr. Harte, that you?"

Jed blinked at the brilliant light accompanying the familiar voice. "Thank you, Jesus," he said under his breath. "Follow me," he commanded to the dark-skinned woman he'd come to know as Theresa.

With the light of a single candle, Jed managed to navigate a path through the fancy parlor, across the center hall, and out the front door. On the porch, a chill wind blew out the flame and sent Theresa scurrying for another.

"Forget the candle. Go upstairs and wait by the bedroom door," he shouted. "Mrs. Delaney will need you."

Theresa stopped short, one hand on the door and the other clutching the dark cloak at her throat. "What's wrong with my Grace?" she asked.

Jed stepped out into the yard and looked up at the window where the woman and children waited. He reached across to test the porch rail, pleased his work had lasted all these years.

"If the Lord wills it, there won't be anything wrong with her that can't be fixed," he said slowly. "But I reckon I'm gonna have to get to her first to find out for sure."

The door slammed shut on Theresa's cry. Bracing himself for the return of the pain and weakness that had dogged his days and turned his nights into a string of foggy memories, Jed climbed the steps to the porch and threw a leg over the rail. His shoulder complained a bit when he threw the other leg over and stood, but by the time he'd caught the edge of the roof and begun to pull himself up, the pain disappeared.

Somehow Jed climbed onto the second floor roof and slipped the window open enough to climb in. As he slid inside the bedroom where the children lay crying together in a small bed, he could only give thanks to the Lord he'd made it that far.

Jed whirled around to see Ben's wife in a heap on the floor beside a rocker. He deduced the woman must have wedged the chair under the knob to keep the door from opening, most likely thinking it would serve to protect her babies from the ruckus in the hall.

A small pool of blood had begun to darken the flow-ered carpet and her gown had soaked up much of it. With a harsh glance over his shoulder, Jed pressed a finger to his lips to silence the racket, and to his great surprise, it worked. He turned his attention back to their mother.

"Mommy sick?" an angelic voice asked.

Jed turned to see the wide eyes of the youngest Delaney staring at him from her brother's lap. All freckles and curls, the little girl seemed to be holding up better than her sibling.

"She'll be fine," he said to both of them, hoping the fear he felt hadn't seeped into his words.

It wasn't right, this situation. He'd only rejoined the Rangers a few minutes ago, and he'd already been forced to climb a building, let himself in through a window, and comfort a couple of scared kids.

Next thing you know he'd be delivering babies.

"Ranger Harte, you in there?" Theresa asked. She knocked on the other side of the door to punctuate the question.

Shaking away the absurd thoughts, Jed shoved the rocker out of the way and knelt beside the bleeding woman. Her eyelids fluttered open, and she stared at a point past him. The stare of a dead woman, he thought with a shudder.

He'd seen it before.

"Open the door, Theresa," Jed said, easily lifting Ben's wife into his arms. Stepping back, he waited for the door to swing inward.

While the woman outside fumbled with the knob, Jed let his gaze wander to the beauty in his arms. Under other circumstances, if he'd seen her walking down the street in San Antonio or sitting in the pew across the aisle at church, he would have given her a second, more discreet look. Now he just stared.

Her hair cascaded over his shoulder and lay in a dark, shimmering curtain against the worn flannel of his winter shirt. The eyes that had peered back at him before were now shut, and the color he remembered from her face had drained away.

A knot wrenched in his gut when her lips parted and released a soft complaint. Jed shifted her to lean against him, sliding her head to rest on his shoulder. The door swung open with a protest from hinges in need of a good oiling. Theresa stifled a gasp as her gaze traveled from the woman to the carpet, then back again.

"Ruth, come quick."

The girl slid past the older woman into the circle of candlelight. Thinking on her feet, she pasted on a smile and strode across the room to gather the frightened children into her arms. "We're gonna finish that story now," Ruth said with a cheery brightness.

Theresa turned her attention back to Jed. "You aim to help or just stand there gawkin', Ranger?"

He peered down at the feisty female through his good eye. "I thought I was helping, Ma'am."

"Not unless you know how to deliver a baby," she said, worry etched along the lines in her face.

In his time, he'd delivered his share of calves, foals, and even a set of piglets once during a lightning storm, but babies were out of his realm of experience. "I believe I'll leave that up to the womenfolk, if you don't mind."

"Then git her downstairs and don't you be hurtin' her, you hear?" she declared.

For the first time in his adult life, Captain Jedadiah Harte willingly took orders from a woman.

Five

Ben's wife felt as light as a feather and delicate as the good china at the capitol building as he carried her down the hall toward the stairs, Theresa a half step behind him.

"Watch your big feet goin' down them steep stairs. She ain't no sack of corn."

"You just keep the light where I can see, and I promise I won't drop her," he said with a glibness he didn't feel.

Her husband ought to be told about whatever was going on here. If he knew his old buddy Ben, he most likely wouldn't stray farther than a day's ride. Two at the most.

One thing about Ben Delaney. He'd never liked leaving his wife for long, even for the Rangers. Jed hadn't understood it then. He envied it now. Given the fact he'd spent the better part of a week under the man's roof, he ought to be seeing him directly.

"You expecting Ben any time soon?" he asked as he turned the corner and sidestepped an especially ugly chair.

"I don't 'spect you heard 'bout Mr. Ben." She stepped ahead of him through the open door and readied the bed.

Arms folded, she turned to face him with a softer look. "We ain't expectin' Mr. Ben at all, Ranger." She looked away. "Lightnin' kilt him nigh on two month ago. He layin' under the pecan tree at the corner of the property."

The weight in Jed's arms began to slip, and he realized he still held Ben's wife. Ben's widow, he corrected, as he adjusted her in his arms.

"Jest set her nice and easy on those pillows. I don't reckon you can hurt her much more than she's already done been hurt, but see if you can be gentle."

Jed complied and watched helplessly as Theresa handed him a length of toweling and indicated for him to use it to wipe the blood off himself. "Now git," Theresa said when he'd done the best he could with the toweling. "This ain't the place for menfolk."

Numb, he shuffled toward the door and mumbled something in agreement. The least he could do was to make himself useful by removing the vermin in the upstairs hallway. If he had to dig all night, he'd make sure Ben's place didn't carry the stench of evil come morning.

It was the least he could do.

"Ranger?" Theresa called softly.

He cast a glance over his shoulder. "Yes?"

"Thank you," she mumbled. Her voice strengthened, and even in the dimness of the candle's glow, he could see a tear fall. She wiped it away with the corner of her apron and straightened her shoulders. "You're the answer to a prayer. More'n one, actually."

Jed ducked his head and made a quick escape as the walls threatened to close in on him. He attempted a prayer of his own several times during the night's work—

work he did with the help of Theresa's husband, a fellow by the name of Shaw—but mostly he busied his hands and tried to keep his mind as empty as possible. Once they had the dead man buried, Jed said a few words of prayer but kept his own thinking out of it.

At daybreak, the thoughts finally caught up with him. He walked with them swirling around him to the river, where he watched the Brazos until the first of the day laborers arrived along with Shaw to open the landing. Jed's shoulder pained him and his good eye scratched with the lack of sleep, but he could find no reason to rest.

Instead, he watched with interest as the first of the barrels were carried to the dock. Soon he joined the workers, handling small repairs and filling barrels—all he could manage with only one good shoulder. He continued laboring long past the time the others had stopped for water. At midday, Theresa found him and saw to his wound, fussing as she changed the bandage, then handed him his lunch.

"How is she?" he managed to ask, all the while pretending to concentrate on the chicken leg he held in his hand.

"Same," she answered as she pressed a cold cloth to his useless eye.

His nod met her gaze, and no more words were necessary. She walked away and left him with the food still held in his fist. Unable to muster an appetite for anything but work, he tossed the best fried chicken he'd ever smelled over his shoulder and went back into the warehouse.

Over the next few days the pattern continued. While Jed worked his worries into submission, Grace Delaney lay behind a closed door Jed dare not open.

For all he knew, his idiotic plan to get rid of the intruder by luring him upstairs into what he thought were empty rooms had put Ben's wife in that bed. Womenfolk were delicate and confusing creatures, and what went on in that hall probably caused her troubles.

Just another cause to believe he should do something to make up for his sins. To his mind, working his way out of the trouble at hand was the only thing he could do for her, so he spent all the time he could making himself as useful as a one-eyed man with a bad arm could.

The man called Shaw now ran things at the landing, although few along the river realized this. Most thought Jed had assumed the job, and the traffic began to increase. Men who refused to deal with a woman now returned, perfectly happy to do business with a man, especially one who happened to be a Texas Ranger.

In the back of his mind, as Jed hauled what goods he could and worked the small garden behind the house, he held out the possibility of making things right with the Lord and returning to the work he felt that God had called him to do. Someday he'd take care of himself, but for now he could only do this for Ben.

He spent Sunday morning in the ugly chair by the stairs reading the Bible and contemplating those scriptures that didn't affect him personally. The others he skipped over, promising the Lord he would return to think on them soon.

Returning to the passages proved to be more difficult than he thought. Before the noon meal could be placed on the table, Theresa left to see to the missus, then returned to Jed and sent the family out of the house with a warning not to return until Ruth came for them.

Giving thanks to the Lord for the unusual warmth of the day, Jed led the children to the garden plot and set them to the task of pulling weeds. As he knelt beside the boy who bore his father's stubborn expression and his mother's good looks, Jed felt the urge to pray.

Not just the simple words he'd said over the past few days, phrases he'd once knew meant something but now doubted. While his fingers worked the loose, dark soil, his mind turned over the ideas he'd once believed in so strongly.

The Lord. The Bible. His call to ministry. His duty to the Texas Rangers. Each was given much consideration. Finally, he formed the words to speak to God about them.

Lord, I'm coming to You a broken man. I had You written all over my heart, but then I went and killed a man. I took his life into my hands and I shot him dead. Even if he did mean to hurt Ben's wife and those babies, he was one of Your children and I ought not to have passed judgment on him. That's Your job, not mine and I was wrong.

"Somethin' wrong, Mr. Ranger?" the boy beside him asked.

"Wrong, Little Man?" he cut his glance to the side. "Naw."

"All right, then." The kid nodded and moved farther down the row to continue pulling weeds while his sister busied herself stacking twigs and leaves into some sort of creation.

Jedadiah Harte, you are one of My children too, came the soft answer without warning. *It is not up to you to pass judgment on yourself.*

"But Lord, I. . ." The children both looked up in surprise and he shook his head. "Don't pay any attention to me."

Mary, the angel in muddy red curls, toddled toward him and settled against his side. "I talk to God too." Smiling, she messed up his precise lines with a chubby hand.

"You do?" he asked as he tried to repair the damage.

She nodded. "Sometimes He talks back." Walking away, she took an oak leaf and buried it under a rock at the edge of the plot.

"Yeah, He does, doesn't He?" Jed asked under his breath.

"Mama says I'm 'sposed to listen when He tells me somethin'," the boy commented as he tossed something over his shoulder that looked more like a vegetable plant than a weed.

"Do you?" he asked.

To his surprise, Bennett Delaney, Jr., smiled. "I try," he said slowly. "But Mama says I'm stubborn like my daddy."

"Mine used to tell me the same thing," Jed said, remembering the words of loving chastisement that would trail him until his dying day. "You need to be more like your Heavenly Father and less like your earthly one," his mother had said. Always, he'd pretended he hadn't heard her. Never would he forget, though.

With those words in mind, he bowed his head and squeezed his good eye shut. *Father, let me be more like You. Change my contrary nature and fix my heart so I can be the man You intend.*

"You gonna stay with us, Ranger?" the boy asked, interrupting his prayers.

"I don't rightly know," was the only answer he had, and it surprised him. Until that moment, staying had been the last thing on his mind. He'd come to Delaney's Landing on his way to go to work for the Lord. After he'd broken his promise to the Lord and turned his gun on a man, he'd pretty much decided he'd go back to San Antonio as soon as he was able and take back his captain's job. Suddenly a third option loomed large. He could stay.

Lord, I need to know what You want me to do, so I'm going to need a sign. Tell me who needs me more, You or these kind folks.

Jed ducked his head and rubbed at his good eye. When his vision cleared, he saw Ruth running toward them across the field.

"Come quick, Ranger. Miz Grace be a needin' you bad."

Jed raced back to the house, unable to believe the Lord would make his path clear so soon. He burst through the door and down the hall, slowing only when he arrived at the closed bedroom door.

"Lord, make me ready for this," he said under his breath as he resolutely pushed on the solid wood door.

Theresa stood beside the bed, hunched over a figure he hardly recognized as Grace Delaney. "He's here, Honey," she murmured as she adjusted the wrinkled blankets and smoothed the woman's hair away from her face. "I'll be close by if you need me," she said softly.

Like a man walking to the gallows, Jed approached the bed. He stood near enough to touch her, near enough to watch her breath catch and her eyes close. Despite the chill in the room, beads of perspiration dotted her forehead and turned her hair slick and shiny.

She opened her mouth, possibly to speak, but instead began to make faint sounds, little whimpers like a child. Eventually her eyes opened. She fixed her gaze on him, making him feel like he'd just trespassed on a private moment.

"Ruth said you were in need of me," he said, painfully aware of just how inadequate those words were.

This time she managed a complete nod. "Yes," she whispered. "My children. Send word to my father."

"Your father?" Jed shook his head. "About what?"

Grace shifted onto one elbow and made a swipe at the table beside the bed, knocking a paper to the floor. Jed bent to retrieve it. In a shaky hand, someone had written a name, The Honorable Thomas Edwin Beaudry, and a New Orleans address.

Jed offered the paper to her, but she waved it away. "You want me to see that this gets to your father?"

She reached for his hand and caught his wrist. He stared at the pale fingers encircling his arm, then slowly shifted his vision to her eyes. Feral, that's what she looked like. Once on the trail Jed had run across a mama bobcat in the middle of birthing a brand new litter. She'd worn the same look.

"If I die, you see to these children, Ranger." Panic seemed to lie just beneath the words. "Don't let my babies be orphans."

Pure terror struck deep in his soul. His heart clutched at what he knew he had to do. He was a ranger, first and foremost, and a missionary of God to boot. He still hadn't worked out how he would hold onto both these jobs, much less add another to it.

"Ma'am, I can't—"

"You must. And if my father or brother refuse to come, you have to raise them. Theresa and Shaw will help. Ruth too." The grip tightened. "Before God, you have to swear it."

Six

Jed closed his eyes, terror swimming like ice water in his veins. *Father, I can't even figure out what I'm supposed to do with myself, much less with a mess of strangers.*

Instead of a clear answer, Jed heard the laughter of children in the distance and felt a deep peace descend, only to leave a moment later. He opened his eyes. Grace Delaney looked back expectantly.

"I'll stay," he said, unable to believe he'd voiced the words.

"Thank you," she whispered. For a moment, she lay back on the pillow as if all her worries had left her.

Something poured from those eyes besides the tears shimmering there, and whatever it was, Jed felt the impact right down to his boots. It seemed as if this woman had curled up behind his heart and settled there when he hadn't been looking. A crazy thought, considering the only thing he knew about her was she'd been a mighty fine cook in her younger days.

He felt the need to say something, anything, to shift the focus from him, possibly to keep her from thinking he meant what he'd said. "But you're going to be just fine, so there's no need to worry about those babies of yours. Come spring, this one here's going to be running around, and you'll have three underfoot."

"I can tell. . ." Her words trailed off as a wave of what must have been pain washed over her, tightening her features into a nearly unrecognizable mask that seemed to remain in place an eternity before it slowly ebbed away. "You haven't been around many babies," she finished.

"No, I haven't," he said, instantly grateful for the change in conversation. "See, I was the youngest of a mess of boys, and my mama said if I'd been first, I'd have been an only child." Grace almost managed a smile, so he continued. "We were a lively group, and I'm sure we sorely tried my mother's patience."

"Your mother," she whispered through parched lips. "Is she still alive?"

He shook his head. "The fever took her back in forty-one."

"Mine too." A gut-wrenching scream tore any further conversation from her mouth.

Theresa came running, and he fully expected to be sent from the room immediately. Dashing his hopes, the woman ordered him to a place near the head of the bed.

"Grab her by the shoulders and shove hard when I say the word. This baby's got to come or else we're gonna lose her."

In his lifetime Jed had seen many a man suffer. Never had he seen anyone in such a shape as this woman. Never did he intend to see it again, not even through one eye.

"The children," she managed. "You promised."

He slid into place behind her and rested his hands on

shoulders too thin and delicate to bear the weight of her present troubles. The position pained his own shoulder a bit and made his wound ache, but he knew it was nothing compared to what the woman bore.

From deep within his soul came the urgent call to pray, which he answered with a desperate plea for help. After a moment, Theresa leveled a hard stare at Jed, interrupting his prayers.

"What did you promise about those babies?"

Grace's cry of agony prevented his answer. What came next robbed him of the power to do anything but breathe, and he almost forgot to do that. From beneath the heavy quilt emerged something wet and bloody. It looked to be about the size of a fair to middling puppy, but without the hair and tail.

It was still and colored a pale blue.

Theresa swirled a length of toweling around it and thrust it toward Jed, her face without expression. Grace's eyes slid shut, and her body relaxed as if all the life had gone out of her. Easing damp shoulders onto the mattress, Jed accepted the bundle and followed Theresa's silent direction to take it and leave the room. On his way out, he slipped the letter in his pocket.

He met Shaw on the porch. "Ruth fetched the children down to pick pecans," the older man mumbled.

Jed nodded and shifted the bundle to rest against his chest. Instinctively, he wrapped the jacket he realized he'd never taken off around the lump of toweling.

With his free hand, he fished out the letter and handed it to Shaw. The elder man's dark gaze scanned the writing, then looked up to lock with his. A wave of recognition passed between them.

Shaw looked away to study the porch rail. "I believe I'll saddle up and ride to town," he said as he placed the letter gingerly in his coat pocket. "Ain't no boats today, and the hands can manage what might come. Lord willin' I'll be back by breakfast."

"That's a fine idea," Jed answered. "Did you say Ruth had the children down by the pecan tree?"

Their eyes met, and understanding dawned on the gentleman's wrinkled face. He allowed his gaze to fall to the bundle in Jed's arms.

"I believe I'll have her fetch them back to the house. They can busy theyselves upstairs here jest as well as they can play at pickin' pecans."

Jed passed by the elder man, studying first the ground and then the horizon as he went. It looked to be a few hours before sunset, plenty of time to lay this soul to rest while there was still light left in the day.

Pulling his coat a little closer against his chest, Jed set off. From his wanderings, he knew where to go with the child, and from his dealings with the inquisitive Bennett and Mary, he knew to be careful to stay out of sight lest they be nearby.

The wind blew across him, then abruptly shifted and stalled just as he entered the clearing where the pecan tree stood. Warmth flooded his bones and made his weary heart want to lay down his burdens right where he'd stopped. Instead, he clutched the bundle of blankets tighter to his chest and hit his knees like a preacher late for church.

"Lord, I aim to give this little one over to Your care." The prayer seemed lacking in something, and frustration brought tears to his eyes. Or maybe it was the body in his arms. He cleared his throat and tried again. "You took him before he even got started, but if You could, give him a warm bed and a full belly tonight in heaven because he's a scrawny little thing."

Carefully, he unwrapped the bundle a bit to show the Lord. Shock rendered him speechless when he saw two dark blue eyes looking back at him from a tiny face just as pink as the evening sky.

The war whoop he'd perfected riding with Jack Hays's First Texas Division during the Mexican campaign back in forty-six echoed across the trees and seemed to shake the very ground on which he knelt. The babe he held in the crook of his arm began to cry, and so did he as he raced toward the house and the woman busying herself at the stove near the window.

"You hush yourself. Can't you see Miz Grace is trying to—" Theresa flung the back door open and froze when she heard the baby's cries. "Oh praise the Lord! Ranger, you done saved us again."

"I didn't do anything," he said though he knew she took no heed of his words as she collected the child and ran to reunite him with his mother.

Bone tired and weary beyond description, Jed sank into the rocker beside the fire and let the warmth seep into his soul. A floor above him, the children played, while down the hall, women wept aloud.

But there in the kitchen, Jed sat alone with his thoughts. He'd promised the state of Texas to be a ranger, the Lord to be a mouthpiece of the gospel, and Grace Delaney to be the keeper of her children until her father came to claim them.

Only a miracle would allow him to do all three.

And if anyone could be counted worthy of a miracle, it sure wasn't him.

It was a miracle, pure and simple. Through the agony of childbirth, her baby boy had been taken away, and through the grace of God and the work of a single Texas Ranger, he had been returned.

Grace blinked back the tears to focus on the man who'd brought her son back. Every evening for more days than she could count, he had come to her room bearing his leather Bible, just as he carried it now.

At first, he merely sat quietly in the corner, dragging her favorite Empire chair from the parlor to sit quietly and read. Theresa said he'd maintained the habit of guarding her door during the dark days following Adam's birth, a birth she had little more than a dim memory of.

As she improved, he continued to visit, always bringing the Bible and the Empire chair. Nearly two months later, they still held evening visits, only now they spent the time talking across the kitchen table. The one topic they never seemed to cover was how long Jed would continue to visit her table or how long he would carry on the charade of running the landing.

Soon the new year would dawn, and on its heels would come the spring. Grace smiled and gave thanks for living in Texas, a place where the icy winds of winter merely teased but did not linger. If only she could be certain the ranger would be there to share in the joy of it. He'd become a part of the family in the months since his arrival, and even the baby sometimes quieted to the ranger's touch when Grace's did not satisfy.

She pictured the dark-haired ranger with the children and smiled. For such a big man, he certainly had a way with her babies. He'd begun to teach Bennett tales from the Bible, and Mary, ever the tagalong, had insisted he teach her as well.

Indeed, they'd all become quite attached to Captain Harte. He would never replace her precious Ben—nothing ever would—but he had somehow managed to carve a tiny spot in her heart and a huge place in her life.

This evening, as Jed settled across the table from her, she noticed a paper half hidden in the pages of the Bible. It looked to be a letter, although only closer inspection could say for sure. If Jed noticed her interest, he gave no indication.

Resolving to put curiosity out of her mind, Grace threaded a needle and picked up one of Mary's gowns from the mending basket. Now, if she could just keep her attention on her task and off the ranger. She cast a quick glance beneath her lashes.

Tall and arguably easy on the eye, Jed Harte made a figure to be reckoned with, despite the lopsided grin on his face. Lately, although she took great pains not to let it show, that lopsided grin had begun to set off butterflies in her stomach.

As he'd done so many times, Jed began to thumb through the pages. "Grace, I've been giving a lot of thought to something, and I'd be obliged if I could ask your opinion on it."

She nodded and continued with her mending.

"I'm wrestling with something I can't get a rope

around. That ever happen to you?" He removed the paper—definitely a letter—and let the Bible fall open.

"Of course," she answered, looking away with a start when he caught her staring.

"Well, this is new territory for me. I reckon it all started back when the Lord caught up with me." He reached for the knife and cut off a large slice of fresh pecan pie. "I figured my ranger days were behind me." Pausing to eat a bite, he gave her an expectant look.

"Why?" was all she could think to ask.

"Because when I took the Lord into my life, He washed me clean." Jed cut a slash through the air with his fork. "No more killing; just preaching."

Grace paused and rested the needle in the cloth. "But now?"

"But now I've gone and made other promises." He paused to chew another bite of pie. "And I've killed."

She winced at the reference. "You shot a man to protect us, Jed."

They'd never spoken of what happened that night, and Grace sensed now was still not the time. She searched her mind for another topic to discuss.

"Did I ever tell you that the day I found you I had just asked God to bring me a ranger to help?"

To her surprise, Jed closed the book and pushed away from the table. With his big feet thundering across the floor like a herd of elephants, he stormed out the back door and into the night, leaving the Bible and his plate of barely eaten pie on the table.

Grace dropped her mending into the basket and picked up the Bible. The temptation to open the book and read the letter tugged at her, but she refused to give in. On a whim, she grabbed the plate and set off to find the ranger.

He'd taken to sleeping in one of the empty shacks behind the house, or at least that's what she'd overheard Uncle Shaw telling Theresa. As soon as she rounded the corner past the summer kitchen, she saw the light shining in a derelict dwelling some distance away.

Bypassing the cozy cottage Theresa and Shaw called home, Grace headed toward the dim light, holding the plate of food on top of the Bible. Before she could knock, the door flew open and the ranger appeared, gun drawn. The Bible, the plate, and the pie clattered to the ground, and she whirled backward, landing in a very unladylike heap on the soft ground.

"What are you doing here?" Jed stuffed the gun into his belt and lifted her easily to her feet, retrieving the Bible as well.

A chill danced across Grace's spine that could be only partly blamed on the temperature. "Well, I, um—" she began.

"I could have killed you, Grace," he said on a rush of breath smelling faintly of sugar and pecans.

"Oh, I hardly think so." She attempted a smile. "Besides, you didn't even have time to aim."

In an instant, the chill went out of the air. Suddenly there were only two people in the world, and one of them could have melted into a puddle at any moment. The other, the ranger, looked rightly aggrieved.

"I don't miss," he said evenly.

"Oh," she said, which came out sounding more like a squeak than a word.

For a moment, time stopped while the night sounds swirled around them. Her mind raced to put words to the conflicting thoughts, only to realize they could all be summed up in a single prayer. *Lord, what am I doing here?*

Abruptly, he released her. "I appreciate the pie," he said. Without so much as word of good night, he disappeared inside the cabin and promptly extinguished the light.

"I appreciate the pie," she grumbled under her breath. "I don't miss," she added in a voice several octaves lower than her own. "Well, neither do I," she said as she tossed the remains of the dessert, plate and all, into the pig trough and stormed inside the main house.

The next morning she still fumed about it, although her anger had been tempered by the fact she'd very nearly had some quite unacceptable thoughts about the testy ranger. Well, tonight when he came to sit and discuss the Bible with her, she'd be ready.

"Let's just see what Ranger Captain Jedadiah Harte has to say about the Golden Rule," she whispered as she placed a sleepy Adam in the rush basket where he slept.

Through the kitchen window, she noticed the ranger working in the garden, and she longed to be recovered enough to do the same. "I may still be mending, but I don't have to do it all indoors," she said to Adam.

She fetched her sewing and took it outside along with the baby and his sleeping basket. Settling into the rocker, she ignored the ranger and resumed her sewing until the sound of a horse and rider coming up the road drew her attention. She watched as the dark-clothed rider dismounted near Jed, and the two men began to speak in earnest before turning to walk toward the house. Putting aside her needle and thread, she cast a quick glance at the basket where her angel continued to sleep soundly, then straightened her skirts and went to meet them.

"Grace, this is Reverend Spivey." Jed paused to smile at the stranger. "The man who led me to the Lord."

Jed's gaze locked with hers, and Grace felt the collision straight down to her toes. Despite her anger over his unexplainably rude behavior last night, the familiar butterflies threatened to return.

"Reverend, this here is Grace Delaney," Jed continued.

The slight, well-dressed gentleman stared at her with the brightest blue eyes she'd ever seen. "Welcome to Delaney's Landing," she said.

"Thank you, Young Lady," he answered, removing his dusty hat to reveal a thick shock of gray hair. He turned his attention to Jed. "So this is the woman you wrote me about."

The woman you wrote me about. Grace swallowed her surprise and replaced it with a smile, while Jed's discomfort showed plainly on his face.

"I reckon," Jed said slowly, studiously avoiding her gaze.

"Captain Harte indicated you might be amenable to allowing me to intrude on your hospitality."

"Of course," she managed.

"I'll not be a bother, and I don't plan to stay but one night," he added as he turned to place a hand on Jed's sleeve. "I've got business in Galveston, and I must confess I had hoped you might make the ride with me, Captain. Especially in light of the fact the Rangers have offered to let you operate out of the office there while you preach."

Seven

W ell, now," the ranger said, although his face spoke volumes more.

Obviously he hadn't intended for her to know this, although he'd certainly been busy making plans. She gave him what she hoped would be an I-don't-care look. The lopsided smile she'd come to love emerged, and Grace felt what little breakfast she'd eaten threaten to rise at the sight of it.

"It would be my pleasure to have you here," she said quickly, hoping the numbness she felt couldn't be heard in her voice. "You're welcome to stay as long as Mr. Harte does."

Grace plastered on a bright smile and watched Jed's fade. If the ranger could consider leaving, then at least he would leave with no idea she would miss him terribly.

"If you'll excuse me, I'll just go have Theresa set another place."

She turned her back on the men and concentrated on walking slowly toward the house until a hand on her wrist tugged her backward. Whirling around, she came face to face with Jed Harte.

The lopsided smile had vanished completely. Hers disappeared as well. Even the satisfaction of having him think she wouldn't miss him had left, replaced by a yawning cavern of emptiness. Not since the dark days after Ben's death had she felt such a sense of dread.

"I'm sorry, Grace, I know you're surprised but—"

She held up her free hand to stop him. "Your friend seems like a nice man. I'm sure the two of you will do just fine in Galveston."

He nodded. "I reckon he is, and I'm sure we would but—"

A sharp tug released her hand, and she turned to take the first of five porch steps. "But he's going to be hungry after his ride," she tossed over her shoulder. "Why don't you show him where he can stable his horse?"

"I already did," he said. "Stop, Grace," he added, then picked her up by the waist and set her on her feet in front of him. "Stand still and listen, Woman," he said roughly. "This is important."

Shading her eyes from the sun, Grace bit back on her anger and disappointment and said a quick prayer for the right words to come. "All right," she said slowly as she watched the preacher lead his horse toward the barn. "Speak your mind, Ranger."

He ducked his head and glanced toward the porch and the basket where Adam had begun to make little cooing sounds. Sunlight danced on the inky darkness of Jed's hair and turned some of the strands a deep golden color. The gold, she realized with a start, matched the amber of his eyes.

Slowly, he turned his gaze on her. A sane woman would

have walked away. Grace stood stock-still and stared.

"I'm a man of my word, Grace Delaney," he said in a low voice. "I told you I'd take care of things around here until your family could show up to claim you, and I don't reckon that's something I'd walk away from."

As his meaning penetrated her heart, it threatened to soar. *Lord, please give me the words to answer him,* she again prayed.

"Say something," he said, his voice ragged and laced with what sounded like a thread of desperation. He caught her wrist once more. "Say anything."

Say good-bye to him, came the answer she hadn't wanted to hear. She took a deep breath and let it out slowly. With care, she pulled out of his grasp to take his hand in hers. "You were forced into that promise, and I'll not have you bound to it."

"Doesn't matter how I agreed to it." The lopsided smile returned. "Until I know you and the young 'uns are taken care of, you're just going to have to get used to having me around."

Happiness bubbled to the surface and emerged in a broad grin. "Is that so?"

"Yes, Ma'am, that's so." The ranger dipped his head as Adam's whimpering increased. "You'd better go fetch the little feller."

"Miz Grace," Theresa called from the kitchen. "We be havin' company for lunch?"

She cast a quick glance over her shoulder at the woman in the doorway. "Set one extra place at the table, please."

"Just one?" she asked. "Then what're you gonna do 'bout those other folks?"

Grace turned to question Theresa, then caught a glimpse of the riders coming toward the house. Her heart sank when she recognized the well-dressed gentlemen. It had been more than a decade since she'd seen them, but she would have known her father, Thomas Beaudry, Sr., and her brother, Tom, anywhere.

Before she could catch her breath, the two riders reached the clearing and the house. "Father," she whispered, "it's really you."

"Grace Mary-Celine Beaudry," Thomas, Sr., said in a rush of breath. His face paled, and for a moment he looked as if he might slip off his horse. "Your letter said. . ."

"You're a sight for sore eyes, Gracie," Tom said. "And seeing you for myself sure beats a letter."

Her gaze shifted from the stiff-backed silver-haired judge to her brother, seated casually in the saddle. From Tom's thick shock of dark curls to his stubborn jaw and soft brown eyes, he looked much as she remembered him at age fourteen. The difference came in the breadth of his shoulders and the length of his legs.

He'd already eclipsed her height before she left, but now, as he climbed out of the saddle, she could see he'd continued to grow until he'd passed the judge as well.

The judge.

Grace swallowed her fear and stared directly into the eyes of her father. Still seated atop a bay mare, the look in those eyes seemed to match the feelings in Grace's heart. True to his nature, Judge Beaudry returned the stare without comment, leaving Grace to finally look away.

Never had she expected to see him alive. Obviously, he felt the same. Her mind raced as she watched him dismount and stand uncomfortably beside her brother. His eyes scanned the landscape as if he were looking for something.

She cast a glance over her shoulder to the little basket where Adam had been fussing only a few minutes ago. Thankfully, he seemed to have settled back to sleep. When her gaze returned to the men, she saw Tom studying her intently.

"I sure missed you, Gracie."

Knees weak, Grace tilted to look into her brother's eyes, and her whole world went with it. With a firm grip, the ranger she'd forgotten stood at her side righted her. He offered a weak smile, one she couldn't manage to return.

"Jedadiah Harte," he said, thrusting his hand toward her father. "Pleased to meet you."

The judge's eyes narrowed to slits as he slowly acknowledged the gesture. Tom's handshake bore a bit more enthusiasm, but the wariness he wore like armor could not be missed. "Tom Beaudry," he said, "and this is my father, Judge Beaudry."

Jed seemed to be doing a little sizing up of his own, and when he'd finished, he offered the Beaudry men a smile. To Grace, he offered a protective squeeze of her hand, which he quickly released.

"I believe you and I have met, Judge Beaudry," he said slowly. "Couple of years back I ran into a fellow named Collins. Bart Collins, I believe."

"Collins?" He shook his head. "Doesn't sound familiar."

Jed nodded. "I reckon you see all kinds in your line of work."

This time her father's eyes turned on Grace and rested

there for a moment. "I suppose I do," he answered, focusing once more on Jed.

"This Collins fellow, he'd done some dirty work down toward New Orleans, and he was right reluctant to go back. Once I explained it a different way, old Collins up and changed his mind. I believe you tried his case."

The judge's wrinkled face softened slightly and a look of recognition began to grow. Numb, Grace smoothed her skirt and watched in awe as her father actually began to smile. What she wouldn't have given just once during her girlhood to have him smile at her that way.

At least she'd learned her Heavenly Father had no such limits to His compassion. Reminded of Him, she quickly lifted the uncomfortable situation to the Lord in prayer.

"So you're Ranger Captain Heartless Harte," the judge said, admiration lacing his words. He cast a glance at Tom, who seemed as surprised as Grace at their father's reaction. "You know who he is, don't you, Boy?"

Tom nodded. "Anybody who reads a paper knows about Heartless Harte."

Jed grimaced but said nothing. Finally the clang of the dinner bell broke the silence.

"Perhaps you two would like to wash up before we eat," Grace said unevenly.

The ranger led the men away while Grace raced to the porch to snag Adam and his basket and escape to the kitchen. Today the comforting smells of sweet potato pie, ham, biscuits, and a mess of fresh collard greens only made her stomach hurt. The baby must have sensed her nervousness because he began to cry.

"Sounds like someone wants his dinner," Theresa commented. "You go on and feed the little mite, and I'll see t' the gentlemens."

Grace nodded and lifted the baby out of his basket. "Where are Ruth and the children?" she asked as she bundled Adam in his blankets.

"Gone t' have a picnic." She gave Grace a sideways look. "Don't you 'member? You helped those angels pack the hamper last night."

She did remember, barely.

Adam's wails calmed as he began to look for his dinner. Scarcely had she carried the baby into the bedroom and begun to nurse him before the sound of heavy footsteps thundered through her parlor. Low, deep voices spoke in even tones, preventing Grace from hearing what they said.

Having so many men in the house at once discomfited her. Even when Ben had been rangering, she'd never had to play hostess to more than a couple of extra men.

Ben.

The thought of him surged like a knife through her stomach as she looked down on his peacefully nursing son. The son he would never know this side of heaven. Tears shimmered but did not fall.

Her memories of Ben, while they could never be forgotten, had begun to fade until they seemed to fit neatly into a corner of her heart. Now she could safely revisit them without feeling the blinding ache of his loss. Now she could see that she could go on living without Ben Delaney, and while life would never again be perfect, it could still be sweet.

Especially with her three precious babies.

And with the ranger, came the errant thought.

Grace gasped. Had she really come to think of Jed in that way? She shook her head. Of course not. He was her friend, her helper, and of course, a source of constant irritation and amusement. He would never replace Ben in her life or in her heart.

Never.

"Adam, your father would have loved you so much," she whispered. "You're not going to meet him in this life, but I intend to love you enough for both of us."

While the sounds of dishes clanking and men talking drifted under the closed door, Grace shifted the baby to burp him, then settled him to finish his feeding. A short while later, he fell asleep, full and satisfied, and she placed him in the center of the feather bed with pillows on all sides to prevent him from falling.

One last look at her sleeping son and she fell to her knees to pray. "Father, I know I'm becoming a real pest, but the ranger says You don't mind if we talk to You a lot, so here I am again."

A lone tear gathered at the corner of her eye. She blinked hard, but it fell anyway. Laughter trailed the sound of scraping chairs and shook her already frazzled nerves. She swiped at her eyes with the back of her hand and swallowed her frustration.

"Lord, You know what's in my heart. I just don't know what to pray for anymore. I won't leave this place Ben and I built, and I can't give my babies to my father to raise like he raised me and Tom. I don't want Jed to leave because I will miss him something awful. I don't know what to tell You to do." She took a deep breath and let it out slowly. "Father, You are a mighty God, and You can work all of this for good. I turn over my family and the ranger and this whole mess to You and ask it in Jesus' name. Amen."

A calm descended, lifting Grace to her feet. With a newfound confidence, she opened the door and headed for the kitchen, ready to take on all three men in her life. Unfortunately, she found the kitchen empty, although just outside the door she could hear the laughter of children and the soft, deep voice of her father.

She crept closer to the window and watched in utter amazement as the stern man she knew lifted little Mary to his shoulders and carried her around the porch at a slow gallop. Bennett played the bottom of a copper pot like a drum and sang along with words that made no sense. Ruth stood in the distance holding the picnic hamper and smiling while she spoke in soft tones with Tom.

Things that had once seemed so confusing now seemed crystal clear. She knew exactly what she had to do.

He knew exactly what he had to do. After speaking to the preacher and the judge, and rereading the letter from San Antonio he'd been holding for the past month, Jed's path seemed crystal clear. He slipped the paper back into his saddlebag and placed his Bible on top of it.

The judge, he decided, was a decent sort, even if he had committed the error of cutting a perfectly wonderful lady out of his life for following her mind and not his. He and his son would take good care of Grace and her children, of that he'd assured Jed. Tom, the brother, seemed a bit more enthusiastic about staying at the landing until it could be sold, but the judge had given his word the Delaney family would receive his finest care and hospitality in New Orleans.

And if you couldn't trust a judge, whom could you trust?

With Grace Delaney safe in the arms of her family, Jed was released from his promise and free to move on. Surely the Reverend Spivey's visit had been a sign that the Lord meant for him to be on his way.

After all, he had a long way to go before he felt like he could stand before the Lord and answer for his sins.

Jed cinched the saddlebag and made one last trip to his cabin. His gift to Grace sat just inside the door, and he gave it one last long look. Unhappy with what he saw, he knelt beside the bed he'd made for Adam to make absolutely sure the rails looked straight and the finish was smooth.

The cradle had been made of the finest rosewood scraps he'd seen this side of the Mississippi. Shaw had laughed when he told him how the table had been broken, and Jed had hated that he had been the one whose clumsiness had reduced the once beautiful masterpiece into something less than furniture.

He'd planned for a month how he would take those scraps and build a proper bed for little Adam, and it had taken him the better part of another month to actually build it.

The boy needed a bed in the worst way, so all the time he spent was well worth it. It irked Jed when Grace carried the boy around in a basket that made him look like Moses hiding in the rushes. A boy deserved a proper bed.

He also deserved a man around to teach him how to grow up right. All three of those children did.

Saying good-bye to Bennett and Mary this morning had broken his heart. He'd already decided he'd have to find the time to help with the planting come spring, but another visit before then just might be in order.

After all, the Rangers had put him in charge in Galveston, and he could run the office as he saw fit. He'd just have to look up a few of his more trusted men and hire them on to help. That would free him up for more time to do his preaching and his visiting.

He began to tally a list of potential candidates as he used the back of his sleeve to polish the post to a soft luster. Two or three good men came to mind right off, and he made a note to write to them as soon as he got settled in Galveston.

This decided, he stepped back to give the finished product a critical examination, then frowned when he noticed the side rail on the left looked a bit uneven. Perhaps he should put off his trip to Galveston until tomorrow to give him time to fix it. He could write his letters tonight and send them the first chance he got.

"It would also give you another night to sit and eat pie and pretend you're not all starry-eyed and foolish over the boy's mother too," he said under his breath, as he spied his hat on the cot and made a grab for it.

"Captain Harte," the reverend called. "Are you ready?"

No, he longed to say. *I'll never be ready.*

"I'm ready," he answered, wiping a speck of dust off the carved headboard with the tail of his shirt. "Just came back for my hat."

Eight

G race stood on the porch and looked to the east, shielding her eyes from the harsh glare of the morning sun. As the ranger rode slowly toward her, she couldn't help but be reminded of the first time he'd approached her on horseback. She lifted her gaze skyward and gave thanks to the Lord who'd seen fit to bring him back from death. She stepped forward to meet him, stopping at the edge of the clearing.

"I reckon I'll be leaving," he said.

"I thought that's what you were up to." She shook her head. "You take care now and don't forget us country folk once you get to the big city."

"I'll never forget you, Grace," he said slowly, his voice as rough as pine bark and his face half hidden beneath the brim of his hat. "Would you mind if I come back for pie and a visit with the young 'uns once in awhile? At least until you pack up and move to New Orleans."

She smiled and hoped her sadness didn't show. "I'd like that a lot, and so would the children." A gust of north wind tossed her shawl and made her shiver. "But I don't intend to leave Texas. This is my home, and you're welcome here whenever the trail leads you to it, Ranger."

Jed nodded then looked away, trouble etched among the fine lines on his face. "I wish you'd just call me Jed," he said. "Ranger is what I do, not who I am." He extended a hand and caught her fingers with his. "I aim to be a lot of things besides just a ranger, Grace."

The warmth of his fingers surprised her, and so did the softness in his face when she stared up at him. "What do you aim to be, Jed?"

"I'll do whatever it takes to earn what the Lord has given me," he said with a shrug.

"We receive salvation as a gift." She paused. "It's something we can never deserve." She took his flinch to mean she'd reached a nerve. " 'For by grace are ye saved through faith; and that not of yourselves: it is the gift of God,' " she continued, the words seared on her heart and their meaning forever impressed on her mind after a night spent in seclusion pouring over God's Word.

Jed allowed his fingers to slip away from hers and wrapped them around the rein. "Have you spoken to your brother or the judge?"

She shook her head, as much to answer his question as to catch up with his abrupt change in conversation. She'd hidden herself away from her family, claiming ill health, but truthfully, she'd needed the time to face them properly. There were things she needed to discuss with her Heavenly Father before she took them up with her earthly one.

"I'll do that this morning," she said slowly.

Her answer seemed to satisfy him. He nodded and pressed back the brim of his hat to reveal the bright amber of his eyes and the inky darkness of his hair. She focused on these, the little things about Jed Harte, rather than to see the whole man, the man she would miss desperately. Although the Lord seemed to give her plenty of guidance on how to handle her father and brother, He had been virtually silent on the subject of Ranger Captain Harte. Every time she asked Him to lead her, He sent her to the Bible and the verse she'd just repeated to Jed.

It had been most frustrating.

"Would you mind if we prayed before I go?" Jed asked, gently leading her attention back to him.

"Of course," she whispered, as she watched him swing a leg over his saddle and land on the hard-packed earth in a single smooth motion.

As the horse protested with a whinny, Jed led the mare to the rail and tied the reins. Grace memorized it all, the length of his arm, the quickness of his hands, and finally, the look on his face when he turned to take both her hands in his. She drew nearer and closed her eyes, assuming he had done the same.

"Father," Jed began, "bless this fine woman and her family, and hold them in Your loving care. Keep them safe and help Grace to raise those young 'uns in Your Word."

His voice stumbled, and he paused to clear his throat. Grace's eyes remained shut tight, sealed by tears she refused to allow.

"If it pleases You, give me and the reverend a good ride and a safe passage to Galveston. Always lead me to do Your will and be sure Grace finds the surprise I left for her in the cabin. Amen."

Grace lifted her head and their eyes met. When he gave her the lopsided smile, she thought she would faint. "Surprise?"

And then he kissed her.

Right there in front of God, the Reverend Spivey, and all of His creatures, he kissed her good and proper on the lips. Well, it was good, if not proper.

"Surprise," he whispered in a ragged voice. Then, before she could recover, he rode out of her life just as abruptly as he'd ridden into it.

"He's a fine young man."

She whirled around to see her father sitting in a rocker on the porch. "Yes, he is," she answered, still a bit unsteady. Knowing he had witnessed all or part of their kiss made her feel worse.

The judge's eyes narrowed, making her feel like a child instead of a full-grown woman with three children. She shook off the emotion along with the urge to delay what she knew she had to say.

"Mr. Harte and I had quite a talk last night," he said, patting the chair next to him.

She squared her shoulders and said a prayer for strength. "I would like to apologize for my lack of hospitality."

"You felt unwell." He made a slash through the air with his hand. "Perfectly understandable. I enjoyed the time spent with your children." His face softened. "Bennett's a brilliant boy, and Mary is a delight. You've done a fine job with them, Gracie."

"Yes, they. . ." She looked up in astonishment. "You haven't called me Gracie since—"

"Since you were a child." He rose slowly. "I know. Just

one of the mistakes I made in raising you."

"Mistakes?" She shook her head. The Honorable Judge Thomas Beaudry did not make mistakes, at least none he would admit to.

He took a step toward her. "When your mother and little brother died, part of me went with them." Gripping the porch rail, he looked beyond her rather than at her. "I suppose it might seem like I didn't care for the two of you, but I can assure you nothing is farther from the truth. Believe me when I say I loved you and your brother more than life itself."

Grace tried to swallow the lump in her throat but couldn't quite manage the feat. "I never knew."

The leaves began to rustle as the north wind danced through them. "I wanted to protect you and keep you to myself, and when I realized I couldn't. . ."

His voice faded as he beckoned her to come to him. "I'm so sorry. I was a stupid, stubborn man," he said, enveloping her in his arms. "Forgive me."

It took a few minutes, but Grace finally found her voice. "Yes," she whispered. "Of course."

Too soon, the judge pulled away and motioned to the rockers. "Sit down, Grace. We've got ten years to catch up on."

They settled beside each other, Grace's heart still pounding at the feelings coursing through her. "Thank you, Lord," she whispered, her face turned so her father could not see.

"I suppose you'll be coming back with Tom and me," he said casually. "I'd be honored to have you and the children home again."

"Father, Texas is home now." She paused. "For my children and for me. Someday I hope Bennett will take over this place and love it like his daddy did."

"His father was a good man, Gracie," the judge said slowly. "Another of my regrets is that Ben didn't live to hear me say so."

Grace smiled. "Life's too short to hold any regrets."

"I suppose you're right," he said as he leaned back in the rocker and gripped the arms. For the next few minutes, he told the most amazing story of how Jed had come to him demanding certain conditions for Grace and the children. Before he finished, her father had agreed to all of them. Asking forgiveness, he added, had been the one stipulation the ranger did not demand. That, he stated, would have to come from the judge's own heart.

"So you see, after I got over the man's impertinence, I saw the point." He gave her a sideways look, then reached over to cover her hand with his. "He was right and I was wrong. I just hope someday I'll earn your forgiveness."

Grace studied the unfamiliar blue veins and dark spots decorating the back of his familiar hand, then slowly dared a look in his direction. "My forgiveness is something you don't have to earn, Father. It's always been there for you."

This truth, discovered in the wee hours of the morning, had set her free. She'd released her anger for her father to the Lord, and He'd taken it all away, replacing it with love.

❧

Unfortunately, none of the Scriptures helped her to release Jed. All through the winter, even after the judge left for New Orleans while Tom stayed behind to help Shaw run the landing, she felt the ranger's absence. The children often asked of him, but she refused to allow them the hope he would return as he'd promised. While she rocked Adam in his beautiful cradle, she waited for letters that never arrived and dreamed of a life she would never have.

Then one day, while she was turning the soil for her spring garden, a lone rider approached. Jedadiah Harte had returned. Dirty hands and all, Grace ran toward him, laughing like a child. Jed slid off the horse and met her halfway. "I missed you, Grace," he said as he wrapped her in his arms. "I'm a poor excuse for a letter writer. Thought I'd tell you in person."

He smelled of soap, sunshine, and trail dust, a glorious combination. She could only nod before the first tear fell. When he released her to hold her at arms' length, he wiped it away with his sleeve.

"How long can you stay?" she asked, unable to think of anything but silly small talk with him staring at her.

"Well, now," he said slowly. "That's a good question. The fellows I hired to work the ranger office in Galveston are good hands. Don't have to worry about that part of things. As for the preaching, it's something I can do just about anywhere. I'm a right decent carpenter and figured someday to build a church of my own." He paused and looked unsure of himself for a moment. "I had a mind to ask you if I could stay awhile."

"Oh?" Her hopes soared. Could he possibly mean what she thought he meant? "How long is 'awhile'?"

Jed smiled his lopsided smile and her heart began to

pound. Her fingers sought his, and when they entwined, she felt a deep peace settle around her. "I bothered the Lord about us all winter, Grace, and He kept sending me to the same verse you quoted the day I left. The one about the Lord's grace."

"I didn't think you were listening."

"I tried not to." Jed shook his head. "I have a mind to stay and grow old with you, Grace," he said softly. "If you'll have me to wed, that is."

Out of the corner of her eye she saw two riders approaching. "Jed, who is that?"

He smiled. "The reverend offered his services if I could convince you to say yes. And the other one's your father. He intends to give away the bride."

"Is that so?" She stifled a giggle. "Seems like you were pretty sure I'd agree to take you on."

"I don't miss," he said with a grin. A moment later, with the riders fast approaching and her still silent, his grin dissolved and worry crossed his handsome face. "Grace," he said slowly, "you didn't answer me."

"I didn't, did I?" She allowed another moment of quiet to pass between them before allowing her happiness to show. "Oh yes, I reckon I'll marry you."

Jed threw back his head and let out a yell, one she'd heard Ben imitate many times. Lifting her gaze skyward, she smiled. The little part of her heart where Ben's memory lay was full to overflowing with love, and now the rest of it would be filled as well.

KATHLEEN Y'BARBO

Kathleen is an award-winning novelist and sixth-generation Texan. After completing a degree in marketing at Texas A&M University, she spent the next decade and a half raising children (four) and living with her engineer husband in such diverse places as Lafayette, Louisiana; Port Neches, Texas; and Jakarta, Indonesia.

She now lives with her nearly grown brood near Houston, Texas, where she is active in Fellowship of The Woodlands Church as well as being a member of American Christian Romance Writers, Romance Writers of America, and the Houston Writer's League. She also writes a monthly column in the local RWA chapter newsletter and lectures on the craft of writing at the elementary and secondary levels.

A Letter to Our Readers

Dear Readers:

In order that we might better contribute to your reading enjoyment, we would appreciate you taking a few minutes to respond to the following questions. When completed, please return to the following: Fiction Editor, Barbour Publishing, Inc., PO Box 719, Uhrichsville, OH 44683.

1. Did you enjoy reading *Yellow Roses?*
   - ❏ Very much. I would like to see more books like this.
   - ❏ Moderately—I would have enjoyed it more if —————————
   _____

   _____

2. What influenced your decision to purchase this book?
   (Check those that apply.)
   - ❏ Cover
   - ❏ Back cover copy
   - ❏ Title
   - ❏ Price
   - ❏ Friends
   - ❏ Publicity
   - ❏ Other

3. Which story was your favorite?
   - ❏ *A Woman's Place*
   - ❏ *The Reluctant Fugitive*
   - ❏ *Serena's Strength*
   - ❏ *Saving Grace*

4. Please check your age range:
   - ❏ Under 18
   - ❏ 18–24
   - ❏ 25–34
   - ❏ 35–45
   - ❏ 46–55
   - ❏ Over 55

5. How many hours per week do you read? _____

Name _____

Occupation _____

Address _____

City _____ State _____ ZIP _____

If you enjoyed

Yellow Roses

then read:

Frontiers

Four Inspirational Love Stories
from America's Frontier by Colleen L. Reece

Flower of Seattle
Flower of the West
Flower of the North
Flower of Alaska

_H_EARTSONG ♥ PRESENTS

Love Stories
Are Rated G!

That's for godly, gratifying, and of course, great! If you love a thrilling love story, but don't appreciate the sordidness of some popular paperback romances, **Heartsong Presents** is for you. In fact, **Heartsong Presents** is the only inspirational romance book club, the only one featuring love stories where Christian faith is the primary ingredient in a marriage relationship.

Sign up today to receive your first set of four never-before-published Christian romances. Send no money now; you will receive a bill with the first shipment. You may cancel at any time without obligation, and if you aren't completely satisfied with any selection, you may return the books for an immediate refund!

Imagine. . .four new romances every four weeks—two historical, two contemporary—with men and women like you who long to meet the one God has chosen as the love of their lives. . .all for the low price of $9.97 postpaid.

To join, simply complete the coupon below and mail to the address provided. **Heartsong Presents** romances are rated G for another reason: They'll arrive Godspeed!

YES!   Sign me up for Hearts♥ng!

NEW MEMBERSHIPS WILL BE SHIPPED IMMEDIATELY!
Send no money now. We'll bill you only $9.97 postpaid with your first shipment of four books. Or for faster action, call toll free 1-800-847-8270.

NAME _____

ADDRESS _____

CITY _____ STATE _____ ZIP _____

MAIL TO: HEARTSONG PRESENTS, PO Box 719, Uhrichsville, Ohio 44683